MW00965676

# RED TRANCE

ALSO BY R. D. ZIMMERMAN


Blood Trance
Death Trance
Deadfall in Berlin
Mindscream
Blood Russian
The Red Encounter
The Cross and the Sickle

# RED TRANCE

## R. D. Zimmerman

WILLIAM MORROW AND COMPANY, INC.
NEW YORK

Copyright © 1994 by R. D. Zimmerman

All rights reserved. No part of this book may be reproduced or utilized in any form or by any means, electronic or mechanical, including photocopying, recording, or by any information storage or retrieval system, without permission in writing from the Publisher. Inquiries should be addressed to Permissions Department, William Morrow and Company, Inc., 1350 Avenue of the Americas, New York, N.Y. 10019.

It is the policy of William Morrow and Company, Inc., and its imprints and affiliates, recognizing the importance of preserving what has been written, to print the books we publish on acid-free paper, and we exert our best efforts to that end.

ISBN 0-688-13030-5 (alk. paper)

Printed in the United States of America

BOOK DESIGN BY M. C. DEMAIO

# SEPTEMBER 1993

# PROLOGUE

Lev had been killed only days ago. Sveta had just been innocently knifed. And it was all because of him. Because of that asshole, Pavel Konstantinovich Kamikov.

Oh, sure, I'd been angry enough at times in my life. I'd been furious enough to want to lash out at someone and strike him dead, like the bus driver who'd plowed into my sister. And I'd said it, too. Cursed: "Let me kill him." The difference this time was that right then and there, that night as Tanya and I hurried off the broad sidewalks of Nevsky Prospekt and onto Rubinshtein, one of the toniest streets in this decrepit city of St. Petersburg, I really meant it. The bastard deserved to die. Little did I know he really would.

I glanced over at Tanya, a tall woman with blond hair and my closest friend here in Russia, as we half ran toward Pavel's apartment. Her eyes were swollen and red, her full cheeks streaked with tears. She was crazed, of course, for she was the intended victim, not Sveta, and I saw her reach into the right pocket of her raincoat.

"Tanya," I demanded in Russian, my American accent barely showing through, "give me the gun."

She clutched the hidden weapon, shook her head, continued down the dark street.

"Tanya," I insisted, my breath steaming in the chilly air.

*"Nyet,* Alex."

"We have to be careful." I eyed the gas gun, wondered how

much protection it might actually provide. "What if he has a real one?"

She didn't hear me, didn't want to. I was simply afraid that her gas pistol, the likes of which had become so very popular in these rough times in Russia, might place us in deeper trouble. It was shaped like a real pistol, thick and solid, black with a wooden grip. There was no telling it from the real thing except, perhaps, for the barrel. And that was what worried me. If Tanya got close enough to corner Pavel, perhaps waved that thing right in his face and demanded the truth, he might see that that barrel was a bit too wide, just the right size for a blasting spray of debilitating gas. And who knew what he'd do in response, whether or not he might have a real gun to overpower Tanya's ersatz one.

It was late September and late evening, almost ten, and the straight, narrow Rubinshtein Street, though lined with the larger and most expensive apartments in Petersburg, looked little more than a semiorderly street of slums. The road itself was dotted with potholes, and the drab brown buildings, long in need of paint and stucco, appeared all the worse because the street lights had yet to struggle to life; I'd heard a rumor that the city was always tardy turning on the lights as a means of saving electricity. Really, the only way to tell this was a well-heeled district was by the three or four parked vehicles, imported ones like Audis and BMWs that with the depth of night would vanish into locked and guarded garages far from the vulturelike marauding thieves.

Looking at a second-floor apartment, Tanya said, "*On doma.*" He's home.

I glanced up, saw the front windows glowing. Until recently his had been a communal apartment, some five families all sharing the bathroom and kitchen, but then Pavel, with his mass of money, had bought it all and returned it to pre-Revolution splendor. Sure he was home. No one wasted light bulbs or energy in these times, not even someone like Pavel. But was he alone? His thug of a driver could be there, in which case Tanya and I would be entirely stupid to go up.

Down the street I heard tires squealing and saw a pair of headlights sweeping around a corner and toward us. Instinctively I grabbed Tanya. She stopped on the sidewalk, wouldn't budge, just stood there, staring at the ferocious vehicle charging through the night. I tightened my grasp on her arm, jerked her off the sidewalk and into the darkness of a doorway.

"Don't move!" I snapped, holding her in the shadows.

I could see that it was a big car, perhaps a Mercedes. Shit. They were looking for us, had to be. This was getting way more complicated. And way more dangerous. But then to my surprise, the car did not stop. Rather the sedan merely slowed as it passed in front of Pavel's building. I wondered if they were checking to see whose car might be out front or if perhaps they were using their satellite phone, calling Pavel to see if we were there. In any case, the vehicle moved past as slowly as a trawler, then suddenly burst off, shooting past us and down the street, turning right on Nevsky.

"*Poshlee.*" Come on, said Tanya.

She broke away, and there was no pulling her back, no matter the danger, because Lev had been her husband and Sveta her best friend. She was obsessed only with avenging those she'd loved; to her it made no difference if we met the same fate. I, on the other hand, was a bit more practical. I didn't want to go down with Pavel. I'd always been afraid of dying in Russia.

Tanya bolted across the sidewalk, across the empty street. I hurried after her. Above us the streetlights began to tremor with life, finally bursting on. I looked up, couldn't tell if one of Pavel's lights had just gone off. If it had, if he were leaving, so much the better. It would be far easier meeting him on the staircase rather than trying to force our way into his apartment.

We entered through the double door, passed by a row of clunky wooden mailboxes and down a dingy hallway with a low ceiling. Fashionable or not, the place reeked of stale urine, for as usual drunks had ducked in here and relieved themselves. As we approached the broad stone staircase, we heard voices from above. The two of us stopped, listened. One of them was a man's, deep and confident, Yes, it was Pavel. The other was lighter, softer. The voice of a woman. Naturally. He'd taken advantage of so many: a bastard from start to finish. But was she coming with him? No, they were bidding each other farewell. One of them was leaving. But who? The first steps sounded rather heavy, and I carefully peered up and saw a hand above grab onto the railing. So it was him.

I nodded to Tanya, said nothing, saw her lift the gas gun from the pocket of her long raincoat. So what, we were going to stand there and greet him? It sounded too simple. Perhaps, I thought, we should move to the side, let him descend all the way, make sure we could corner him. That might be the surest way. Yet now that Pavel was nearly at hand, now that we nearly had him, what were we going to do? I eyed Tanya, saw the hatred sharpen in her eyes. What did she actually hope to accomplish with the gas gun? Make him beg for mercy, force him to cry out in pain?

From the street out front, I heard a roaring car come to a sudden and abrupt halt. Oh, shit, I thought. And then one, perhaps two doors opening, next slamming shut. Was it the Mercedes again? Perhaps they had indeed called Pavel before, perhaps to find out if he was ready, and learning he wasn't had raced off to pick up something or someone else. Then again, maybe it wasn't them. Perhaps it was his driver, in which case this was more serious than ever.

The fear washed over Tanya as well. The realization of what might be happening struck her just as quickly, and the two of us slipped back and around, disappearing into a dark hallway with several low doors through which, if we were lucky, we might escape into the courtyard. I checked one of the doors, twisting the old, rusty knob and finding it open. Something rustled back there in the dark, and I froze, listened intently. Mice, I thought. Or maybe a cat hunting mice. Turning back to Tanya, I held a finger to my lips, and she looked at me, nodded.

The door to the street creaked open, there was a deep cough, some steps. Yes, someone was coming in. Two men, perhaps.

Also hearing the noise, Pavel called from above, "Oi, is that you? Sorry I'm late! I'm coming, I'm coming!"

At the sound of his voice Tanya started trembling. I could sense the anger rise and boil within her as Pavel rushed downward. Shit, this was far too intense. I wasn't going to be able to stop her. I knew it then, just seconds before Pavel reached the bottom of the stairs and only moments before Tanya burst out of the shadows, the gas gun aimed high.

"*Bozhe moi!*" My God, shouted Pavel.

The rest happened so quickly. Tanya first aimed at Pavel, who froze at the sight of her, but then she leapt forward, turned down the hallway, fired on the two men coming in the front door. Her pistol exploded as loudly as a regular one and ejected a brass casing as it shot a broad, sharp spray out its barrel. There was an instant of silent shock, and then the two men cried out, gagging and coughing. I hurried behind Tanya, and through the mist of gas saw them doubling over, dropping to their knees. Christ, we were going to be lucky to get out alive.

And then Tanya spun back to Pavel, blurting, "You killed him."

"Wh-what?" replied Pavel.

"Lev. And then you went after Sveta."

"*Nyet.* You don't understand, I—" Pavel looked at me, begged, "Alex, please! This is all some sort of mix-up! You must believe me!"

"Like hell," I replied. "It was your fault, wasn't it?"
"Alex, of course not! I—"
Suddenly I heard something behind me. I turned, saw a woman leaping out of one of the two low doors. In the dim light, I recognized her, the one from the restaurant. The short one. What was she doing here? This was complete chaos, complete insanity. She was charging forward with a large knife and shouting a string of hate. I jumped aside. One of the men in the lobby was swearing and cursing, and a moment later there was a shot, again from Tanya's gun, and a burst of noxious gas rose around me, scorching my eyes. I tried to breathe but it was like inhaling peppery fire. I grabbed my neck, struggled to clear my throat of the acrid fumes, and then I was falling forward, dropping to the stone floor, pawing for air, clawing at my burning eyes that were bursting with stinging, bitter tears.

And then another shot rang out, this from a real pistol. I heard someone cry out. Pavel. Crawling on my hands and knees, I turned, looked toward the stairs. Through the cloud of gas, through my watery, sizzling vision, I saw him clutching himself, holding his stomach in disbelief. He'd been shot, and he started to stumble, to fall toward the railing, to grapple for something, anything. It was useless, though, for just then a second and finally a third shot exploded in the stairwell. I rubbed my eyes, saw Pavel dance with death, and watched as he toppled forward, rolling clumsily down the stairs and landing in a big lifeless mass, his fat face staring up at me, his eyes open wide and unblinking in permanent shock.

To the right I heard running steps and then a car racing away, while next to me I heard sobbing, deep and pained. It was Tanya, leaning against the wall and crying from both the shock and the gas that swirled around and around us. I looked back at the body, saw a stream of rich, deep blood seeping toward me. So Pavel was dead, which marked the beginning of an entirely new set of problems, for I'd witnessed it all. In this land of confusion and deceit, in this place where the ironclad rule of communism had been crudely overtaken by the red of violence, I most certainly knew who had blasted Pavel Konstantinovich from this world and into the next.

# Chapter 1

"I suppose you're going to want to know everything, aren't you?"

"Yeah, probably."

"It was really a mess," I muttered.

"So I've gathered."

"For a while I didn't think they were going to let me out of Russia."

"Neither did I."

I paced slightly on the veranda of the mansion that belonged to my sister, the one and only doubly disabled, brilliant and beautiful Maddy. With that long slim face, those elegant cheekbones, and the beautiful cropped brown hair all so calmly presented, she appeared serene, even rather disinterested. But I knew better. This tall, slender woman, my older sister, who'd been confined to a wheelchair for a few years now, was a true whiz, far craftier than the Russian police and even the KGB, both of whom had interrogated me endlessly after the murder. Maddy wore black pants—always black pants because she was sightless and hence she could blindly choose any top or sweater and it wouldn't clash—and a thick wool jacket, and I reminded myself that whatever the image she was now presenting, she most definitely had a vested interest.

It was late September and Yeltsin had just dissolved the Russian parliament, a dispute that was sure to turn ugly. I was now far from all that, though, and as I stood there leaning against a pillar, my fingers drumming the wood, I turned toward the cool blue waters of Lake Michigan. My mind drifted away, eagerly so. I'd showered and changed since the long trip back—I now wore my customary blue jeans and denim shirt beneath my brown cotton jacket—and I imagined that if this sprawling Victorian mansion had not been here in the States but there in *Rossiya,* it would have been in even worse shape, probably not painted since the Revolution instead of since the early sixties, as it last was. And it probably would have been chopped up into some sort of sanitarium, a cancer ward perhaps, with bossy, bosomy babushkas in white robes and white hats pushing rags on the ends of sticks and shouting at people. Well, maybe not, I thought, looking at the mainland now streaked with autumnal reds and browns some ten miles to the east. Had this once great house been plunked down on not an American but a Russian island, say in the middle of a lake just north of St. Petersburg and only a few kilometers from Finland, it probably would have instead been some sort of psychiatric hospital for dissidents. Either that or it would have been taken over by the KGB and consequently well maintained.

"You know," I said, glancing over at my sister who, of course, sat in her wheelchair, a plaid blanket over her stilled legs, "I saw a house like this north of St. Petersburg in Repino, a little village. That house was wooden, too. Clapboard, though yellow, not white, and done in sort of a mock Russo-Finnish Empire style, not a mock Victorian-Dutch Colonial like this place. It looked like it could have been used for the set of *The Three Sisters.*" It was just at the beginning of my jet lag, and I thought, Focus. Get to the point. "It was built by a count who'd made a fortune in sugar beets."

"This house was built by a baron of sorts, too. A Chicago man who made his fortune in beer," Maddy said, brushing at her short hair and adjusting her oversized sunglasses.

I was barely back, my mind was still over there, and I all but ignored her, saying, "And during the Revolution the count was killed—I think he was hacked to death or some such gruesome thing—and then I'm not quite sure what happened to the house. But when I saw it—that was back when I was a student in Leningrad some fifteen years ago—" I cut myself off, ran my right hand through my thick, curly hair, and peered off into the blustery day. "Fifteen years. God, how could it be so long? Shit, we're getting old, Maddy." I shook my head, paused. "What was I saying?"

"The Russian house."

"Oh, yeah. Anyway, not long after I first met Lev, he drove me out to the country. We were hunting for mushrooms. That's when we came across that place, that house. We were walking through the woods, and suddenly this thing appeared. We peered through a chain-link fence, and there was this magnificent summer palace. It had been taken over by the KGB—which was the best thing that could have happened to the house in terms of repairs—and they were using it as a retreat center. Some newer guesthouses had been built, small things scattered about, but they were out there, those KGB guys and their families, living like nouveau royalty. Then an armed guard with a dog came and chased us away."

"I wonder what's happened to it since. You didn't go there this time, did you?"

"No. I asked Tanya about it and she told me the KGB was trying to turn it into a hard-currency resort for the Finns."

"Really?"

"Yeah, but then that got messed up because the count's grandson had recently come back and was trying to reclaim it. Without much luck, I might add, because there are no laws in Russia right now. Then again, if you really want something all you have to do is come up with the appropriate bribe."

"Fascinating."

Tapping the pillar again with my fingers, I supposed it was. But mostly it was horrible because now Lev, like Pavel Konstantinovich, was dead. And while I thought the latter deserved his fate, Lev most certainly had not, for there was no gentler soul on earth. What, I wondered, would Russia be without him? How would I ever be able to imagine that country without his sunny face?

"This is such an interesting time in Russia, isn't it?" asked Maddy.

"When you've got a country where the mafia's the only growth industry, I guess you could say so."

"Isn't it getting any better?"

"In some way, yes—you can now buy kiwis and bananas on the street—but in other ways, no. The average monthly income is somewhere between twenty and forty dollars."

"Oh, heavens."

"Yeah, and that's up from six months ago when it was fifteen or twenty. I pity the people on pensions, I think they might only get fifteen dollars now if they're lucky."

Maddy said, "What do you think's going to happen?"

"I don't know, but trust me, things are going to get ugly between

Yeltsin and those hard-liners holed up in the Russian White House. If everything falls apart, it could make Yugoslavia look like a kid's birthday party. We haven't really won the Cold War yet, we've just made them put down their missiles and pick up handguns. And with Russia out of control, the world's not a safe place. Don't forget, they still have a huge stockpile of nuclear weapons."

"Well, what about . . ."

I turned away, blocked out her words. Didn't hear a thing. For years she'd been a shrink, a sightless one, who saw ways into the human soul that other therapists blindly missed. She was so skilled—no, make that cunning—at getting people to open up. Only I was her brother—a few years younger, face broader, as was the body—and I knew her ways; she'd been like this forever, right from the get-go. So I knew her tact, her scheme. Get me talking about my disastrous trip to Russia. The things I did. The people I saw. What it was like. How was the food, Alex? And tell me, what's the Russian mafia like? Did you meet any of them? Was it maybe one of their hit squads who first offed Lev back in that alley and then Pavel Konstantinovich in the stairwell?

"Don't worry, Maddy," I said, cutting her off at the psychological pass.

"What do you mean?"

"You're going to hear it all and then some. The whole story."

A breeze came whooshing off the lake, up the hill, wrapping and pushing around me. The old doors into the living room rattled and I heard something squeak. Turning, I saw an empty wicker rocker tilt back and forth as if some sort of ghost had just flown in and made itself at home. Pavel, that's not the ghost of you, is it?

"Alex," gently said my sister, "just relax."

"I am relaxed."

"No, you're not. You haven't stopped fidgeting since you got here. Right now your foot's tapping the floor. I can hear it."

I tensed my body, tried to still myself, said, "Russian prisons are disgusting, trust me, and I hardly slept at all after they arrested me. But then when they let me go, I went straight to the airport, and as soon as the plane took off I popped two of these great sleeping pills and passed out." I looked over, saw that the wind had stopped but the chair continued to rock. "I suppose I should have tried to stay awake to get back on this time, but I slept almost fifteen hours on the way back. I'm just kind of wired."

"Who wouldn't be?" Maddy went on, saying, "You're home, little brother. You're safe now. There's nothing to be afraid of."

Yes, this was home now, this thirtysome-acre island just south of Mackinaw Island and just off the coast of the state of Michigan. This private island that my absurdly handicapped and absurdly wealthy sister owned and reigned over like a beer baron or sugar count. No, that wasn't right. I wasn't supposed to even think that. My older sister, blind since her early teens and paraplegic for the last few years, wasn't handicapped and she wasn't disabled, either. She was differently abled, quite truly so. Denied the joys of sight and mobility, Maddy had discovered other gifts, insights and a far broader sense of the world we inhabit, that empowered her with eerie capabilities. That had always made me nervous, for my beautiful Maddy, so slim, so regal-looking with her long neck and striking face, could grab the truth by the tail and pull it out of you bit by bit by bit.

"Maddy, I told the Russian police everything I knew. And I'll tell you, too. It's just going to take some time."

"Sure. Of course."

"Let me get used to the idea of being back in America."

"Absolutely. Whatever you want."

"I mean, I may be here physically, but my aura most certainly isn't. I think it's still strung out somewhere over Greenland." In a gruff attempt to steer the conversation elsewhere, I said, "So what did you do while I was gone?"

"I made a tape."

"What do you mean?"

"A hypnosis tape," she said, sounding rather flip. "I got this idea for a series of tapes on hypnosis and creativity, so I wrote a script and last week I hired a production crew. I already have a lawyer working on it, and someone else is drawing up a business plan. I had a long phone conference yesterday trying to decide about the marketing, you know, whether it's best to do it myself or sell it to some company. Do you want to hear the demo tape?"

"It's done?"

"Sure. The production people came last Friday and they worked on it all weekend. Then they went back and sort of jazzed it up." Referring to her manservant-bodyguard-chauffeur or whatever he was at any given moment, she said, "Alfred picked up the finished tape just before he met your plane. I haven't even listened to it yet, but they said it turned out great. They were supposed to have added some music and all these sound effects. Do you want to go up and listen to it?"

This was prime Maddy; whenever she got an idea, she went out and executed it right away. She rarely mulled anything over. I wanted to say it was all her money that empowered her, but she'd always been like that, even as a tomboyish girl.

"I supposed," I replied.

Maddy lowered a wandlike pole in front of her chair, a cane of sorts that scraped the ground and allowed her a sense of where she was going, what she was encountering. She took the chair by the wheels, turned it. But she wasn't about to shirk this chilly autumn afternoon and disappear so meekly into the house. I knew her. My eyes followed my sister as she began to roll across the broad gray boards of the veranda. She turned, felt for the corner of this vast house, and then nearly right on cue she stopped, for my big sister always had to get in the last word.

"I know you wanted to get back to Russia and see your friends and see how it all changed. That's why you were so eager to go, of course. To see Lev and Tanya," began Maddy, sounding quite official. "But I agreed to pay for your ticket and all your expenses—every single penny—if you'd do some research for me over there. Pavel was one of the preeminent hypnotherapists in Russia, his television show on hypnosis was very popular, and that's what I need to hear about. What you learned of what he was doing. You had a job to do, and I want to hear about his show and if there's anything that would be helpful to me in my practice."

"Of course you want to get your dollar's worth," I snidely said.

"And you will. But, Maddy, you're neglecting one thing."

"What's that?"

"You've got to be upset about all this because, after all, you and Pavel were friends. Very close ones, too. How often did you get an E-mail message from him on your computer?" When she didn't respond, I nudged, "Just about everyday, wasn't it?"

"Alex . . ."

"That's electronic mail every twenty-four hours, right?"

"Alex, please."

"And haven't you saved all of the printouts from every single one of his E-mails?" I wanted to ask how often she read and reread those messages, her sensitive fingers caressing the braille. "You still have them, don't you?"

"Stop it!"

But I couldn't, and I asked, "So who are you going to talk shop with about hypnosis? Who are you going to compare ideas and theories with? And what about movies and movie stars? You became fanatic about Hollywood just for him, so are you just going to give up trying to keep au courant on the very, very latest from L.A.?"

"You're being ridiculous." Her face was taut and red, her voice struggling not to snap as she said, "Just get some rest, and when you're up to it we'll talk. Or would you feel more comfortable writing it all down?"

I eyed her, wanted to continue poking and prodding until she broke down and let loose all the grief she must have been stuffing. But my sister was as tough as she was stubborn.

"We'll see," I said, backing off for now.

"Okay. Whatever." She took a moment to regain her composure, and then sounding overly professional and in control, added, "I know things got kind of wild over there. I know none of it was pleasant. We can talk about that, too, when and if you feel like it. I hope you do. It's best to get something stressful and traumatic like that off your chest. Otherwise, you know, it'll come back to haunt you." And then, "Anyway, I'm going to go up and listen to the tape. Come up if you want."

With a forceful shove, Maddy disappeared around the corner, racing down the side of the veranda and to the front door. And as she rushed off, I thought: bullshit.

Turning away, I stared down the hill, through the trees that were dashed with reds and yellows, and at the cold, tumultuous waters of Lake Michigan. Sure, Maddy wanted to hear all about Pavel and his TV show. Sure, she wanted some anecdotes of the grim Russian life. But what she really wanted was exactly what both the Russian police and the KGB had been after: Who actually killed Pavel? My only question was, how could I made my big sister understand?

And then I heard it again. I turned around, gazed down the veranda and at the old white rocker, which was still moving backward and forward.

# Chapter 2

In earlier chapters of our lives, I'd tried to convince Maddy to leave the island, to escape this gilded prison, and return to humanity, if only for a short visit. My first suggestion had been Chicago, our hometown, yet while I often stumbled nostalgically through my visits there, the very thought of that massive city brought nothing but sorrow to my sister. Those long straight streets were the last she'd seen before she'd lost her vision as a young teenager to congenital eye failure, and those same hard streets were the last she'd walked before a careening bus had clipped her, snapping her spine. So any idiot could understand why she wouldn't want to return to that city of pain. Which was why a few months ago I'd backed off that idea and instead invited her somewhere totally different. Like St. Petersburg. Not St. Pete, Florida, but St. Petersburg as in Peter-the-Great-Russia.

The big battle came up during the sad and tragic story of her former patient Loretta, as anyone who'd known us then would recall. At the climax of that messy business, Maddy had clearly understood that she'd become far too reclusive, that this island she'd bought as a retreat with her insurance settlement had instead become a place to hide from the world. She'd clearly understood that, had even taken my lead and compared herself to the agoraphobic Loretta. But what good had all that done? I still hadn't been able to get Maddy away from here. For a while I really thought I was going to succeed, that she would travel with me, that she would, in fact, venture all the way to a different world, a very distant one, a Russian one. But while she'd talked big of the Winter Palace, the Neva River, the Peter and Paul Fortress, and caviar and blini, babushkas, and borscht, it was all, in the end, a fantasy to her. She let me check out the airlines, the cost of the tickets, what hotel in St. Petersburg might easily accommodate a wheelchair, and then when I had all the facts and figures, she declined the trip. Just like that. I had suspected that she'd never leave this island, but I went along with it all, hoping that I was wrong and that she'd indeed surprise me. I should still go, though, she had insisted when she broke the news to me. After so much time, after so much political upheaval in Russia, I had to visit my friends over there. And she with her forty or fifty million bucks would only be too glad to pay for my trip because, actually, there was business I could do for her there. I could look up Pavel Konstantinovich Kamikov, the eminent hypnotist whom Maddy had met in Chicago years ago and had become, in my opinion, much too close to. Not only was I to observe and report on his practice and television show, I was to take him ten or fifteen newly released films on video. I'd been so pissed that Maddy wouldn't go, at that point so eager to get away from her and this stupid, claustrophobic island, that I'd taken the stupid movies and gone just to spite her.

Or had I, I now wondered, played right into a plan of hers? Had she been relying in fact on my stubborn spirit to spur me into actually going without her? Whatever, it had been a big mistake. That was now perfectly clear.

I was still leaning against a tall, massive pillar, one of the thirty-three that zipped along the front and side of the house outlining the veranda, and I breathed in cool, crisp air. V'koosni vozdoox. Tasty air. That's what a Russian would call it. Brisk and clean from its travels across the lake. Spiced with the oaks and maples, birches and pines that adorned this jewel of an island. I'd been eager to leave for Russia, the obsessive country of my college years that I hadn't seen in so long. Yet there'd been a time—two times, actually—when I was quite certain I'd never see this island, let alone my dear, wonderful sister, whom I'd forgotten I was angry at, again. I was back, however. Even though I could close my eyes and still see it all—Pavel's shock and horror—and hear it all—those three shots—I was here on Maddy's island. I couldn't believe it. All of what had happened seemed so vivid, as if it had only just happened instead of occurring over a week ago. How long would it be before that deathly face of Pavel's would fade from my memory? Would it ever? I honestly didn't know. My guilt, I feared, would gnaw at me, would keep that last image of Pavel active and present in my mind.

My head swooned with each gust of wind, and I ran my hand through my hair, as was my custom when I was lost, not sure what to do next. I seemed to be doing that a lot today, putting my hand in my curly hair. Finally, I started off, passing across the broad, gray boards of the veranda. There were only about a dozen pieces of the original Victorian wicker out here, all of which would be brought in before the first snow, and I wound my way past the few rockers and love seats. Next summer this porch would be resplendent with white wicker, for my sister had sent the other twenty-five pieces to the mainland to be stripped of nearly a century of paint and then re-paired. A few months ago I'd discovered an old photo album in the attic, which included a handful of pictures of the veranda in all its glory. Maddy had sat enchanted as I described in intimate detail everything I saw, and so now her master plan included purchasing a handful of oriental rugs and palms and geraniums, all to be scattered here and there. Her idea of a perfect summer day was, I think, to abandon her wheelchair and sit in one of the big wicker rockers, surround herself with flowers, and listen to the lake slap the rocky shore below. Not bad.

Summer was indeed the time to be out here, this huge mansion capping a hill and overlooking the freshwater sea of Lake Michigan. While at this particular moment I never wanted to leave again, I often wondered what the winter would be like and if in fact I'd make it all the way through. Though I was told the water wouldn't freeze all the way to the island, travel by boat would be impossible, for there would be a thick layer of ice extending from the shores of the mainland. When I'd mentioned my reticence about being stranded out here, Maddy pooh-poohed my concerns, told me how she'd retained the use of a helicopter in Petoskey and had a clearing built as a helipad behind the old chicken coop. So I could be air-lifted out, just like out of old Berlin. How comforting. But did that mean I could flee this place for something as simple as a toothbrush at the Walmart or a movie . . . or only in case of some dire event?

I headed around the side of the house and down to the front door, a huge opening on the west side of the house. Inside the entry hall, I paused, stared at an old carved couch covered with yellow silk, some framed Confederate money on the wall, and then at an old pump organ off to one side. On my immediate left was the billiard room, while the dining room sat straight ahead and the living room to my right. Chill out, Alex, I told myself. You're back. You're in your sister's house. Everything's going to be okay.

"Maddy?" I called, not eager to search the entire house for her. I assumed Maddy had already gone to her retreat to hear her tapes, wondered where Alfred and Solange could be, and then from up above I heard this swaying, throbbing sound. I stepped forward and looked up. The entire stairwell was open, a shaft some twenty feet wide and sixty feet tall, that rose through all three floors and was capped with a Tiffany dome that had been somehow dismantled by the beer baron's underlings and shipped up from the 1893 Chicago World's Fair. And that's where the sound was coming from, up there, Maddy's trance room, the huge former ballroom on the third floor. Oh, brother, I thought. Maddy and this hypnosis tape business could be a lark, but I doubted it because dear Sis never embarked on fruitless ventures. She had a nose for not simply interesting ventures, but very profitable ones, and she most certainly had the willpower—not to mention the financial wherewithal—to make it all happen. In short, she was as big a dreamer as she was a doer, a rare combination indeed. I had to be more like her.

Everything in this oversized house was itself oversized, and I headed through the billiard room, skirting the large, carved billiard table, and passed beneath a variety of mounted heads—moose, several deer, a couple of antelope. In the corner, alongside a seven-foot rattlesnake skin, was a door, which I opened and crossed through. The back hall separating the main house from the servants' wing was a breezeway of sorts, lined with junk-filled armoires, old washtubs, endless mops, a couple of refrigerators, an old oak icebox. And, at the far end, the elevator.

After my long trip back from St. Petersburg via Helsinki, Amsterdam, New York, Detroit, and finally Petoskey, the lift sounded good, so I pressed the call button and waited for the car to descend. When it arrived, I opened the wooden gates and stepped into the elevator that had been converted from a rope-pulled affair to electrical power, and then I was off, ascending to Maddy's haven. Or heaven.

All of this struck me as excessive and so American. This house. All the rooms. All the junk. Having just arrived from Russia where living space was so tight that even this large elevator probably would have been converted into a bedroom, I rose skyward in a bit of shock. And then up top, of course, there was even more stuff. A myriad of items abandoned by a wealthy family over nearly one hundred years. The servants' quarters in the rear part of the attic were packed with the jetsam of an upper-class family—old ball gowns, stacks of leather-bound albums, wicker baby carriages, dressers, boxes of dishes, a wooden barrel of soap flakes. I'd even once discovered a crate of antique Venetian wineglasses, so fragile and valuable that my sightless sister insisted that they not be drunk from, though since then I'd found her several times caressing and admiring each one.

I made my way through all that, pressed past headboards and chairs, past a pair of mounted longhorns, and wound my way to the door that opened into Maddy's trance room, where I paused. The music was loud now, growing and throbbing all the while. Very ethereal, which was to say very New Agey, which was also to say vintage Maddy, for denied the usual ways of exploring this world, my sister had developed her own ways—primarily via hypnosis—of comprehending what this was all about, life and everything, in particular her own strange fate.

I placed my hand on the doorknob, turned it as slowly as I could, and the music exploded over me like water bursting from a dam. Not only had Maddy produced a tape in my absence, but she quite obviously had had an elaborate speaker system installed. I peered in, saw my sister pushing herself in a broad circle, her head swaying with the rhythm.

As soon as I took several steps, I saw Maddy blindly turn, listen in my direction, take note of my movement.

"Come on in, Alex," she called over the music, recognizing the sound of me. "I was just replaying the lead-in of my tape. I really like it, don't you?"

"It's, well, loud."

"Oh, come on, Alex, don't be so stuffy!" she shouted as she went streaking across the room.

"I'm sorry, but I've just spent over twenty hours in a jet. My ears are a little touchy at this point."

While the back part of the attic had once been the quarters of a handful of servants—two bedrooms, a large living room, a bathroom, separate staircase—this front part was open and raw. Once a summer ballroom, it was the size of a small gymnasium and had a smooth maple floor perfect for dancing and a ceiling that arched some thirty feet. Maddy had cleared everything out of here—another bizarre list of items, including a couple of dozen mattresses, extra leaded glass windows, even parallel bars from the twenties—as if she were cleansing her own life and starting with a clear palette. This more than any other part of the house was all Maddy, for the only furniture in here was two black leather recliners we used for hypnosis. No, I was wrong. Off to one side was a new acquisition, a polished ebony grand piano, sans piano bench. So had the miraculous Maddy, empowered by hypnosis, learned how to play while I was gone? I didn't dare to venture a guess, but somehow I wouldn't have doubted it.

"Come on out into the middle of the room. Listen to the stereo part," she said rather girlishly. "Didn't they do a cool job?"

I moved toward her, looked up to some beams, and saw tiny but extraordinarily powerful speakers. First there was a gentle crashing of waves over there to the right, then the water flowed toward the middle of the room and off to the left. A soft shooting star–like sound went zooming over us, then wrapped around and split in two, then came whooshing back and forth in a quite amazing feast for the ears.

And finally the recorded voice of my sister, sounding much the goddess, beckoned: "Hello, this is Dr. Madeline Phillips, and I'd like to welcome you to Creative Paths, a special—"

Holding a remote control, Maddy raised her hand from her wheel-chair and zapped the distant stereo into silence.

"That's enough for now," she said. "I don't want to spoil the rest for you—I want you to hear it all at one time. You'll be my guinea pig, won't you?"

"Aren't I always?"

"Oh, stop," she replied with a short, nervous laugh. "Once you've rested up, I want you to put on some earphones and go under."

Yeah, I thought. Go under. Enter. Experience. I wandered across the broad room, past the two leather recliners and to the French doors that opened on to a balcony and Lake Michigan. I closed my eyes, imagined myself flying out these doors and far away just as I had done so many times in trance. Unfortunately, just as quickly, I saw myself jetting back to St. Petersburg and that ratty stairwell. I shook my head, turned away. Block all that. You're here now, I told myself.

"You see," rattled on Maddy, "my hypothesis for this tape is that hypnosis is not only a simple but a clean way to access creativity. You know how it's usually the tortured people who are the most creative?"

I understood what she was saying, and I nodded.

"Alex?" she called. "Are you listening?"

I spoke up. "Of course." I eyed the long, gleaming piano. "Nice grand, did you learn to play while I was gone?"

"Pay attention, Alex."

"I am, but tell me, who were the poor suckers who carried it up? Or did you have it sky-hooked in?"

"I'll tell you all about it and give you a show later on. What I was saying is that it's often the children of alcoholics or people who've suffered abuse or some sort of catastrophe that become the famous painters and dancers and actors."

"Sure," I replied, feigning interest; I had to feign well, too, because Maddy dear could practically detect my body temperature from the sound of my voice.

"The pain they experience cuts open some gash, some wound, and they ride that pain into a creative part of the mind that most people don't ever have access to. I'm sure that's one of the reasons why there're so many gays in the arts—they have to reach beyond this straight world to make some sense of their own." Maddy wheeled herself a few feet, then started rolling again in a large, slow circle. "I understand a person's pain often gives birth to creativity in an effort to heal that pain, but . . . but I just can't help but think there's another way to tap into that creative vein. You know, a cleaner way to get there. And something more gentle. Hypnosis, for example."

It was an interesting concept, one that actually made a lot of sense. With her training as a psychologist, she always had great insights, and, shit, who knew more about pain and trauma than Maddy? But why was she getting into this now? I eyed her, wondered where she wanted this conversation to go, for she was rarely without a goal.

"Maddy, it all sounds interesting, but you know what?" I said. "My head's spinning a bit from—"

"You see," she went on as if she hadn't heard me or perhaps didn't care. "I really want to do something for hypnosis. Broaden its understanding and acceptance, I mean. Yes, forensic hypnosis is interesting and very useful. No, I should say very important because America is drowning under a tidal wave of crime and the traditional way of solving a crime just isn't working. But I want to do something more widespread, more for the masses. I mean, Pavel and his TV show—what a wonderful thing. He was brilliant."

I could have guessed as much, and I shook my head, said, "Maddy, I don't want to get into that now."

"But he did such great things for hypnosis. He created a popular show and—"

"Maddy, I know you two swapped a lot of trade secrets, but I saw him in action. Really, he wasn't anything more than a charlatan."

"Well, if he was a charlatan, then that's what I want to be too."

I couldn't believe how blind my own sister could be, and snapped,

"Christ, Maddy, what the hell are you talking about? Don't you dare aspire to be anything even remotely like Pavel."

"But, Alex, he wrote me everything he was doing, and believe me, he was onto something. I was inspired just thinking of the two of you meeting."

"Well, you shouldn't have been. You should have forgotten all about hypnosis. You should have invited one of your old friends from Chicago up for a visit. Or do you have any friends left? Frankly, you've been spending way too much time by yourself."

"Nonsense, Alex. I just like long, quiet periods for contemplation, and that's how I got the idea to create a series of tapes. I want people to understand what a great thing hypnosis is. They say we only use ten percent of our minds, and if hypnosis can access only a tiny bit more, then that's fantastic. What if, for example, hypnosis can make great art greater?"

"Michelangelo, Ella Fitzgerald, and Mikhail Baryshnikov have done just fine without you." I sensed where my own witchly sister was goading me, however, and I curtly said, "Maddy, let's talk about this later."

"But, Alex—"

"Please, no buts, Maddy." My true feelings came blurting out. "Pavel was slime. Pure slime. And he deserved everything he got."

She gasped, "Alex!"

It wasn't easy to knock the wind out of Maddy, to leave her speechless, but I looked across the wide room, saw her motionless, mouth open and empty. She couldn't really think Pavel was all that great, could she?

Oh, my God. I stood staring at my sister, and it was all too clear. Maddy sat there not moving, hands in her lap, those sightless eyes hidden behind the big sunglasses, her face oddly pale. And I knew it. He'd gotten to her too. Just the way he'd gotten to the others. I couldn't believe it. Couldn't believe my sublimely wise sister hadn't seen through him. A clump of anger crawled up my spine, bristled up the back of my neck. Damnit all to hell, I'd never seen anyone more manipulative than Pavel.

In an instant I knew what to do, and I walked over to the recliner, the one on the right, and sat down. I looked out the French doors, out into the blustery fall day. Time to fly, I thought.

"Maddy, come over here. I'm lying down."

She turned her head in my direction, quietly said, "What?"

"Screw jet lag and getting all settled in. Screw trying to figure out the best way to tell you. You simply have to take me back. There's no other way."

"Back? Back where?"

"To St. Petersburg."

"What?"

"We have to do it now."

"Do . . . do what?"

"Hypnosis. A trance. I have to tell you everything right from the start. There's no other way you'll ever understand."

"Understand what?"

"Why Pavel got what he deserved."

"Alex, don't say that."

"Come on, it's time to do some hypnotic exploration. You wanted to hear the gory details. Well, you're going to get 'em." I added, "Just promise you won't be too mad."

"I . . . I can't promise you that, Alex," she muttered as she slowly wheeled her way toward me. "Actually, you're the one who doesn't understand."

"What are you talking about?"

"Well . . ."

I sensed this was the other shoe, and I demanded, "Well, what?"

"Pavel and I had been in contact."

"Of course you had. You two and that goddamned E-mail. I remember you rushing to your office first thing every morning to check for messages from him."

"Well, Alex, lately most of what we wrote about wasn't about hypnosis."

"What was it about then, movies? What star was in what film? What director had a project under way and how much the film was going to cost?"

"Actually, no, it wasn't."

As soon as she said it, I mumbled, "Oh, shit, Maddy."

"Mostly it was personal, and . . . and . . ."

"And what, Maddy?" I suddenly sensed the unthinkable. "Don't tell me this. Please don't tell me you were in love with him."

In a voice meeker than I'd ever heard, my sister said, "But, Alex, I was. And he felt the same for me. We were in love. The two of us. We were in love with each other."

# Chapter 3

My God, my sister felt that much for a man I was glad was dead? How could Maddy the Wise have not seen through him?

I lay on the recliner, my hands clenched into tight fists, and struggled not to feel defeated. It was true, Pavel was in the grave, so there was no way I could lose Maddy to him, not really. But I knew my sister better than any other person, perhaps even myself, and I knew she wouldn't let go of Pavel so easily. She was extremely focused, which was to say rather obsessive, and I speculated that the memory of Pavel would live on in the dark confines of her world for months, maybe even years. Maddy often slipped into self-hypnosis to relive past pleasurable experiences, to visualize the world she could no longer see, or even, I suspected, to escape into romantic fantasy. Using her power, her witchlike gift, she would plunge herself deep into a trance where she would create another world, a manufactured dream filled with color and beautiful vistas in which she could stroll or dance or, who knew, maybe even fly. It wasn't that Maddy was merely so brilliant a hypnotherapist, for she probably wasn't any greater than the best of them, not Milton nor Erickson. It was simply that when she'd had the challenges of sightlessness and paraplegic heaped on her, she'd refused to be buried alive, so to speak. Like grass struggling to burst through a horribly thick, terribly black layer of pavement, hypnosis had enabled her to break through a seemingly impenetrable barrier.

Sure, her hearing had been honed to the point she could detect things I could not. And, yes, her intellect and wit had been challenged and consequently heightened due to her prisonly lack of mobility. But hypnosis took her light-years beyond that. Which was all to say that if my wretchedly isolated Maddy had found someone not only to love but who had at least professed to love her back, she wasn't going to let go of him even though he might have died. No, I knew better. She'd play God, bringing Pavel back to life in a trancely world she created and ruled, visiting him there, loving him there. I hated even to imagine what they might do together in hypnotic fantasy.

So I had no other choice. I realized that I was going to have to give it to Maddy full strength. Not expurgated. Not softened. I'd tell her as much as I told the Russian police, which I hoped would be enough to make her see not only the terrible side of Pavel Konstantinovich Kamikov but why so many people wanted him dead. And that, I was certain, would be strong enough medicine to force Maddy's view of Pavel into perspective.

"Come on," I called. "We've got to do this now."

She wheeled herself slowly over. "Alex, now I'm the one who's not sure. Maybe you were right. Maybe you should get some rest before we do this."

"Nope. There are few things you have to know. Besides, like I said, I'm too wired. I really did sleep all the way back and now my internal clock is all messed up. St. Petersburg is either eight or nine hours ahead or behind. I can't remember which way is which. Right now I don't think I'll ever be able to sleep again, so we might as well do it. You might as well get me while I'm fresh." I glanced to the side, saw her pulling alongside her recliner, and started to get up, saying, "Here, let me help."

"No, don't!" she barked. "I'm fine. When I need help, I'll ask."

"Right."

I settled back down, and watched as Maddy unstrapped the Velcro strips that held her legs in place, set the brakes on her chair, and then leaned toward the recliner. I wanted to get up and lift her onto the recliner. I wanted to help her get comfortable, perhaps cover her legs with a light blanket. But she was determined, bitchly so, to do most everything herself. Her thin legs had atrophied, perhaps, but she was resolute not to let anything else slip. And I was sure nothing would, knowing my sister, who was nothing if not absolute.

Once she had hoisted herself on to the recliner, Maddy settled in, running her hands down her legs and straightening them on the black leather. She scooted back, then remembered something and reached to the holster on the side of her wheelchair.

Taking a cordless phone, she dialed two numbers, and in a voice that was so nice it was even sweet—a tone she never employed with me, her brother—she said, "Hi, Solange. Alex and I are upstairs, and we'd like to not be disturbed. I suppose we might be up here for a while, so if you could just put our dinner in the fridge that'd be great. We'll get it when we finish."

Yes, I thought. Best not to stop until I'd made my ugly point. Best to force Pavel Konstantinovich Kamikov out of Maddy's head as quickly as possible. Best to get right into the story and go all the way through.

I groaned and closed my eyes. Where to begin? How to begin? I took a deep breath, grasped it deep within my body, and exhaled. Trance. Think trance, I told myself. Just that command was enough, and my eyes grew heavy and drifted shut. Let go of all the tension. You've done this hundreds of times. Just open yourself. St. Petersburg really wasn't all that far, just a concept away. Do like Ma Bell. Reach out and touch someone.

It was very quiet off to my left, and I quietly called, "Maddy?"

Voice low and slow, she replied, "I'm here."

My priestess, my princess, of the trance was doing her rain dance, so to speak. Her warm-ups. Her stretching exercises. She was focusing her thoughts and energies, going into a trance herself so that she could lead me on. Maddy had used hypnosis for years in her practice down in Chicago, had employed its power to unlock the secrets of the mind so her clients could see and understand the mysteries of their lives. Now, in a very real way hypnosis gave Maddy the gift of second sight. Yes, absolutely. Not second sight in terms of future vision, but second sight in a broader, somehow more powerful sense, for in trance she saw the all of it—the past, the present, and often, it seemed, even the future. I just hoped that this time around it would do the trick.

Her breathing became louder and longer and decidedly deeper. I hitched on to the rhythms of her body, harnessed them so to speak. No, that wasn't quite right. Maddy was hypnotizing me, bringing my subconscious under her control and influence, wasn't she? Yes, she was harnessing me and my knowledge, which meant I'd have to be careful. Maddy was quite clever at cruise directing, at steering a story the way she wanted it to go.

Her voice very soft, she asked, "Are you sure you want to do this now, Alex?"

"Absolutely."

"Okay . . . then let it all go. Everything. Every last bit," she began. "Let the tension melt from your mind and your body. Let any clots of resistance disappear."

As the warm, magical waves of hypnosis began to nip at the edges of my body, I hoped I knew what I was doing, hoped that I'd be able to maintain my defenses against my prying sister. There wasn't any other way to do this, was there? No, of course not.

A light sensation began massaging the bottoms of my feet. I sensed myself more than ready to fly up, fly away. Yes, I was right there, ready to go. I'd experienced the phenomenon so many times now that hypnosis was like a magic carpet always at my beck and call.

"Are you comfortable, Alex?"

"Yes."

"And you're ready to return to St. Petersburg?"

While there might be certain things I'd keep her from seeing, there were other things she had to know, and I replied, "Yes."

"Good. You're an excellent hypnotic subject, and you know how to go deep into a trance."

Yes, I thought, lying there, I do know what I'm doing. Not long ago Maddy had given me the standard test, the one that measured your hypnotizability or some such thing. And it showed what we both knew, that I could easily plunge to the deepest level, the somnambulistic state, as simply as if I were diving to the bottom of a pool. She'd done a standard induction, administered the thirteen tests of hypnotic phenomena, and when she'd told me there was a fly in the room, I'd heard it buzzing about, then felt it land on my cheek, even though I knew somewhere, somehow that this was all pure fantasy. When she'd further suggested that there was a speaker behind my recliner telling me something, I'd heard a voice ordering me to cross my arms. And when she'd held a piece of cloth beneath my nose I had, as Maddy had commanded, smelled nothing until she snapped her fingers, at which point the ammonia-soaked rag made me cough. Simply, my mind and body responded completely to what was being suggested as though that were the only reality.

So I was good. One of the best. A star. And St. Petersburg was right there. I only had to regress a few days, really only a few hours. No, I had to start earlier. At the beginning. Two weeks to be exact. Back up my memory and play it all again, see it all again. Yes, hypnotic role-playing was extremely effective at piecing together past events. So reverse to the time when you arrived in St. Petersburg. Go back to that awful time. Poor Lev. It all happened so unexpectedly. We were right there, sitting in the car. And then my trip exploded with disaster.

"I'm counting from ten to one, Alex, which will open all the doors and take you deep into a trance." She waited a moment, then pronounced, "Ten."

The knowledge of what I was to see again made me shiver, for not only would it seem perfectly real, I knew I'd witness the whole story like a hidden observer. I'd not only be in the events, but as described by the famous hypnotist, Hilgard, I'd be outside, looking at the whole of it with a much greater and quite profound perspective.

Here I'd been talking about Pavel's death, but really it was Lev's murder that was so terrible. His death was what started it all, what sent the whole trip hurtling downward. I wasn't eager to relive it, of course, to back up the videotape of my memory and look at the events all again. When it was all happening, I had thought for sure I wouldn't survive. But I had. And I had to remember that as I now went back to those tense days, I had to remember what Maddy had taught me in earlier stories, that I was returning to the past with knowledge of the future. So as horrifying as my trip to St. Petersburg had been, I had to bear in mind that I would live through it again.

"As I count nine and then eight you find yourself more and more relaxed, and falling deeper and deeper," chanted Maddy. "Take the rhythm and tone of my voice and follow them back to that special place you know so well. Let yourself be absorbed totally and completely. Let the numbers take you back to your recent time in St. Petersburg. Allow the magic of life to mesh with the magic of hypnosis. And seven."

Yes, I thought. She was right. There was magic, for here I was on a recliner in a mansion on an island. I was with Maddy, my sightless, nonambulatory sister who was nothing if not a survivor. She had risen above all the inequities in the world, found the magic in life, and via her I had seen glimpses of it. And there was most definitely magic in hypnosis, for Maddy had found that as well. Found the magic of hypnosis and cast me with its spell over and over. Why? How did this strange phenomenon work? I never really understood, only sensed that it opened up more of the mind, allowed me to cross into my subconscious, into a broader landscape of my mind that was somewhere between sleep and a deep yet relaxed state of concentration. That's right, hypnosis allowed me to be mentally open and free, so relaxed that everything unfolded and became not only less tangled and simpler, but clear. I might not have been smarter in trance, but I was definitely wiser.

"Six. In hypnosis, all the unknowns of the world fit neatly into the structure of what can and cannot be. Five." She breathed in, made a distinctive, almost whistling sound as she exhaled. "Feel yourself going deeper and deeper. Feel yourself becoming more and more empowered. Four."

No, I wasn't really going deeper. I was getting lighter. I was floating up. While Maddy said most subjects liked to feel heavy and go deep, I liked to fly; had I ever told her this, or was this my little rebellion? If I hadn't told her, then I shouldn't. That should be my secret. So in my mind's eye I saw my body levitating, rising off that black leather recliner. First just an inch. Then six inches. A foot. Yes, I was light. So unbearably light. And soon I would be catapulted right through those French doors, right out into air, and then sucked back there. Back to poor, poor Russia.

"Three. Continuing to move toward the state of hypnosis . . . letting yourself go back to that time in Russia with great clarity and with the insight of both the past and the present," preached Maddy. "And you know, Alex, that in trance things can happen very quickly— relationships, events—or they can happen very slowly. You have the power to speed things up or slow them down, just as you see fit. And two . . ."

Oh, take me. Let the trance fill me entirely. I felt myself shiver with excitement. I was a trance junkie. Loved letting go. Going far away. I was floating in a black sea now. Or black space. I was up and beyond Maddy. Ready at a moment's command to whoosh off. And why was I going? Where was I going?

Oh, yes. Russia. St. Petersburg. What for? Not to search for the truth. Not to find it as I had in the tales of Toni and Loretta. No. I was going back to tell Maddy about someone. That horrible Pavel. The lecherous one. I was going back to expose him and explain why, if anyone, he deserved his fate. And while I was there, of course, I was going to remeet the four people whom the Russian police had questioned so seriously; it had been my testimony that had enabled them to identify the killer among that small group of suspects. I just had to make sure—

"And one."

# Chapter 4

The trip didn't get bumpy, really, until I landed in St. Petersburg. Or I should say, we landed. Even though I felt as if I were flying in a dream, tearing through a trance, I was flying in a plane, and the flight from Amsterdam via Helsinki was all quite smooth until we descended out of the broad, gray skies above Russia, until we flew over the endless flat green forests, and finally touched onto the concrete runway. And then everything started bouncing and banging like hell. I grabbed the side of my seat as the slick jet from the West careened down the neglected landing strip and pulled to a quick, almost desperate stop. Glancing out and into the late September day, I saw my first vision of the new Russia: a dozen parked passenger jets, all seemingly abandoned with their engines covered, and I wondered if these planes weren't in use because they couldn't get spare parts or because of lack of fuel. It was something like that, I was sure, for it was readily apparent that this tragic place was more pot-holed and crumbling than ever, a vast superpower defeated by the Cold War and that now lay in ruins even though not a single bomb had been dropped.

I shook my head, for now that I was here I was scared. Maybe I shouldn't have come.

*"Why?"*

I anxiously ran my hand through my dark hair, looked around the bright interior of the jet, searched the half-filled craft, and then I realized that that hadn't been another passenger talking and it hadn't been the pilot either.

*"No, it's me."*

Yes, Maddy. My sister cum ghostly flight attendant. No, it was my Maddy cum trance attendant—coffee, tea, or ?—for she was talking into this imaginal re-creation of my trip as if she were reaching into one of my dreams. Even though I couldn't see her, she was there, a godly spirit who was present to facilitate and direct this mesmerized trip into the recent past.

*"Yes, I'm here to listen and help as you reveal who—"*

No, this wasn't cheap entertainment. I hadn't agreed to this re-flying, this retelling, this reliving, of my trip to St. Petersburg simply to finger which one of those four had been the killer. I only wished to make perfectly clear why Pavel aggravated so many, why I was glad for his death and would never mourn it. Was that clear, did my sublime Frau Doktor understand that?

A long moment passed before she beckoned. *"Agreed."* And next she added, *"This is your trance, of course. You are in control. I'd just like to understand as much as possible."*

And then some, I was sure.

*"So tell me why you were afraid even as the plane landed?"*

Because it started shortly after I arrived at the airport. Lev and Tanya were waiting for me, all full of joy at seeing me again. I thought everything would be wonderful, but then Lev went to change money. After that there wasn't a moment of peace, not really, and in the ensuing days I relearned all over again that Russia was, as Churchill said, "a riddle wrapped in a mystery inside an enigma."

*"Go on."*

Well . . . the jet started rolling. We passed the national terminal, a hulking, rusting building with these five huge spoutlike skylights on top. There was, to my surprise, a jet emblazoned with the words Air Ukraine. And then looking at the Aeroflot planes, I saw how the Soviet flag had been painted over with the new Russian one of white, blue, and red stripes. Farther on sat an abandoned truck, all rusty, and various equipment strewn about the weeds. As we slowly taxied along, there was no activity of any kind, no other aircraft either landing or taking off; a handful of idle workers stared as we passed, marveling, I was sure, at this gleaming jet from the West.

The runway was so decrepit that it took forever to reach the other side of the airport and the international terminal, a small building that had been under construction for so many years that it actually looked like it was being torn down. The jet stopped, some stairs were rolled up, and we passengers boarded a bus and were carted through more abandoned equipment and up to the terminal. I was maybe in a bit of shock, couldn't believe that I was back, but then I walked into a dark room and my nose was hit with a rolling cloud, something that smelled heavy and thick and just a tiny bit sweet. It startled me, this coarse smell of *papirosi,* Russian cigarettes, mingled with the sweet undeniable odor of Red Moscow perfume, which meant that there were not only soldiers stationed here but babushkas sweeping and mopping.

I showed my passport to a boy soldier in a glass passport box, and I stood there like an idiot as he thumbed through my documents. He puffed up his chest, stared at me, again checked my passport photo, then raised his eyes to study me one more time. I gazed down at the counter between us until finally with a nod he allowed me entry into Mother Russia, and I entered the luggage claim area, a space that looked like an abandoned Amtrak station in Gary, Indiana. Yes, an Amtrak station because it was all beat up and decrepit and there weren't any red banners proclaiming the wisdom of Lenin and the 25th Congress of the Communist Party. None of that stuff. Only billboards that shouted capitalism: Camel cigarettes, a German restaurant down on Nevsky, Wrigley gum. Well, then, I mused as I studied the bright, colorful advertisements, maybe things had really changed.

As I waited for my suitcase, which seemed as if it might never come, I turned and looked past the tables where customs officers were haphazardly inspecting luggage. My heart tightened with excitement. There they were, Lev and Tanya, my tall, blondish friends from my college days. I'd met them on the street when I'd been a student here fifteen years ago. They'd noticed my jeans and my running shoes, and they'd come over on some pretense and after a few moments invited me home. Next we were best friends and they were plying me with borscht and blini and vodka. And now all these years later they were just a few feet away, right there and mashed in a doorway with dozens of other excited greeters. I raised my hand in a slow wave, and they were stilled, falling as calm as if at a funeral, which in the end made them appear so very sad, so very Russian.

It all happened in a blur. My black nylon bag came clunking out on an old luggage carousel, I ignored a Russian porter who wanted to change dollars, then the customs inspector looked at my suitcase, shrugged, waved me through, and I was passing out the door, into the cool fall day, and into their arms.

"Oi!" was all Tanya moaned as she came running forward, eyes teary, arms wide. "Oi, oi, oi!"

Crashing into me, she overwhelmed me like a huge ocean wave. It was as if I'd just come back from the moon, which I supposed I had. All the way from America. There I was. Back in the Soviet Union—no, it was Russia now—after all these years, suddenly enfolded in the embrace of Tanya. Suddenly assaulted and pelted with kiss after kiss. And then Lev rammed into us. Embracing me. Kissing me on the cheek. Hugging Tanya and me tightly in his long arms and laughing and laughing. Yes, this was Russia to me, this near-smothering group hug. Russians were so staid on the street. Then they popped the cork and all this emotion came flowing out without any attempt to restrain it. Right at that moment I though of the film *Dr. Zhivago*. I'd seen it with a couple of Russian immigrants back when I'd lived in Minneapolis, and they'd laughed hysterically at the scene where the rich young woman gets off the train with all her luggage and is so politely greeted by her well-to-do parents. All wrong, my friends had said. For Russians it was impossible to hold back. On the emotional front it was either all or nothing.

"*Stolko let, stolko zeem.*" So many summers, so many winters, proclaimed Lev.

We spoke in Russian because neither of them spoke English, and their language came flowing out of me, and yes, it had been so long since we'd seen each other. We'd written each other at least once a year, and I pulled back, my own eyes teary because who would've thought we'd ever see each other again. Not me, and certainly not in a post–Soviet Russia. I was sure I'd never see the end of that monolithic institution in my lifetime. And now here were my two best Russian friends, married for eight years already, and the Soviet system was washed away. I studied them, wondered why I couldn't have known this, that we'd actually meet again. When I'd left Leningrad as a student, boarding a train for Moscow and then flying out from there, Tanya and Lev had been too afraid to come right onto the platform, fearful that KGB might be watching, and so we'd met in a dingy corner of the station. Certain that our friendship would be forever stained and tainted by politics, our farewell had been laced with tears and vodka.

"My God, you two look great," I exclaimed.

And they did. Tanya had short blond hair that was quite fashionably cropped, blue eyes, full cheekbones. A beautiful face with only the lightest makeup. She'd put on some weight, not much, which was to say she hadn't followed the typical Soviet path where a woman peaks at age twenty-four and then rapidly descends to a dour, matronly fate by age thirty. No, Tanya had always been different, always sought more for herself. She'd dared to dream, and she wore a blue blouse and beige pants, both of fine quality. The shoes were black leather, sleek and sophisticated. And the pleated tan raincoat looked the latest. All very Western, in fact. Very cosmopolitan. Nothing at all Russian except the teeth, which were a tad too crooked and a shade too discolored.

"A bit older," replied Lev, lighting up a cigarette.

He was tall, slender, and he was pulling on his blondish beard that was streaked with gray around his chin. His face was very narrow, nose wide, eyes deeply set with crow's feet shooting off. Shoulders broad. Yes, he was older—we were all in our late thirties now—and his hair was no longer bright blond but duller, melting into gray, and receding into bays. But the eager smile was the same, I thought, as I studied him there in his short nylon jacket and jeans. Always the smile that rose like a shield at the first sign of stress and distress.

Abruptly my heart tensed and twisted. A horrible vision of the future was overtaking our reunion. I stepped back in horror, stared at Lev as if I were watching a movie that I'd seen once before and . . . and I knew what was going to happen to this man, didn't I?

Tanya pulled me against her, pulled me back to that moment, squeezed me, kissed me on the neck over and over again, "It's so good you're here. I can't believe it." She started to cry. *"Bozhe moi."* My God. "I can't believe it."

Yes, I was certain of it now. This was perhaps the greatest thing about coming to Russia. The appreciation. The adoration. Just the all-out dumping of affection. I'd never felt so cared for nor so popular as I did in this strange land. Just by being a Westerner, particularly an American, I was an instant celebrity.

Lev leaned over and kissed me on the cheek again, then scooped up my suitcase, took me by the arm and hurried us along. It was all so strange. I turned around, scanned the area, searched for someone, some official, to check out with. I saw a couple of guys inspecting a gleaming pale gold Mercedes, someone lingering at the end of the building, an older man holding a child. But nothing else. No officials, no soldiers, ready to chase after us and demand what we were doing, an American and two Russians so freely cavorting.

I stopped, looked at them with a big grin, remembered how as students we used to carry on like world-class spies, and said, "Wait, you mean, I can just go?"

They nodded, laughed, and Tanya said, "It's a free country now, can you believe it?"

I hooted in disbelief. When I'd last been here, there was no way I could have been met by Lev and Tanya; the KGB would have questioned them, and they might have been booted out of the university as a result. And there was certainly no way a foreigner could have just driven off with a Russian; it was the duty of the travel agencies Sputnik or Intourist to make sure every foreigner was accounted for. But here we were, climbing into a car, blasting off for who knew where without anyone's permission. Such normalcy, such freedom I'd never thought possible here.

Tanya steered me into the rear seat of a small red car, a Lada that had seen too many miles, and then she climbed into not the front seat but the back, cozying up beside me. She leaned over, took me by the arm, kissed me on the neck. I kissed her back, quickly so, then looked up front, saw Lev's smiling reflection in the rearview mirror. All this outpouring was merely so very Russian, I reminded myself. Or was it? Lev and Tanya had already been dating when I was a student, but then one night after a troika—the three of us killing a bottle of vodka—Tanya had taken me aside, confessed her love for me. Lev had passed out, I remembered, and Tanya and I had kissed with great lust and passion until the alcohol swept over us and we'd blacked out as well. She'd never spoken of it again, and though I wondered if she even remembered her words or our lengthy embrace, I could see the truth in her eyes as well as feel it in my heart. There was always Lev, though, just as there was always my lingering question, how important was I to Tanya just because I was an American? Was I merely the ultimate status symbol, way beyond *jeanzi* and Adidas? As her husband now started up the car, Tanya squeezed my hand, stared into my eyes, and my heart tremored all over again. I doubted if I'd ever know, nor right then was I sure if it really mattered.

Eager to chart safer waters, I leaned forward, asked, "When did you get your driver's license, Lev?"

"Last year. Tanya got hers too." He proudly added, "We bought this car just six months ago. It's a few years old, but it still runs."

"Aren't we modern?" laughed Tanya. "We're getting so civilized. But there're still such problems. The price of gas keeps doubling and tripling, can you imagine? So now we know how to drive, we have a car, but who knows how we'll be able to afford all this."

Again she raised my hand to her lips and kissed it, all the time muttering how wonderful it was to see me, how this was so incredible.

And, yes, it was. Amazing. I felt her moist lips on the back of my hand, wondered, We're not already headed for trouble, are we? I glanced up, saw Lev looking at me in his rearview mirror, which this time reflected neither his smile nor jealousy but a great sadness. What was going on here?

*"But you do know, don't you?"* called a faraway voice. *"That's your trance sense. You've regressed from the present to an earlier time, so as you retell this, you already know what's going to occur, don't you?"*

Yes, and none of it was good, so much of it painful. I looked out the window, stared at the flat fields, the sparse trees. Would it be better if I hadn't come back? Would any of this have happened if I hadn't returned? No, of course not.

*"Keep perspective, Alex. You can't change the past. You can only understand it with the wisdom of hindsight."*

So I pushed back those fears, that knowledge of what was going to happen within a few short minutes, and I let myself feel the warmth of Tanya seduce me into Russia and into the story. Lev jerked the wheel to the right, drove sharply around a huge hole in the road, we all laughed. Yes, this huge country was nothing but one big pothole. Everything was falling apart. We raced from the international terminal, down the narrow, straight road that led to the main highway, and then roared past greenhouses and big, filthy trucks and buses crammed and listing with people, and into the city. Circling the War Memorial, the spot that marked the advance of the Nazis, we zoomed on, Tanya holding my hand as tightly as if she were trying to keep me from falling off a cliff, which in the end saddened me. Her desperation. Soon there were large buildings lining either side of the street, gray structures with stores below and five or six floors of apartments above. I stared out the window, saw people filtering in and out of decrepit stores, but saw no sign of the endless queues I'd seen on television.

"Where are all the lines?" I asked. "That's all we hear about— the food shortages over here."

"Russia," laughed Lev, "is a new country every three months. And in this quarter of the year we have no lines for food because no one can afford to eat."

"Everything's horribly expensive," added Tanya. "People on pensions have it the worst—what they receive for retirement doesn't buy more than a kilo of sausage each month. On the other hand, we really have everything now—coffee, meat, potatoes, bread. Lev, what did we see the other day? What do you call it?"

"Lettuce."

"Yes, we even have Western lettuce now. Really, the only problem is sugar, and that's because all the bootleggers have bought it up. Vodka in the stores has gotten so expensive that everyone's making home brew. So this month there's virtually no sugar in all of St. Petersburg."

"See these kiosks?" said Lev, pointing to twenty or so temporary buildings all lined up. "They sell Marlboros, whiskey, Mars bars. Even orange juice."

"They're not private, are they?" I asked, because before virtually every store had been operated by the government.

"Of course they're private." He grinned and added, "As long as they pay off the mafia, they can sell whatever they want for whatever they want."

I shook my head, muttered a shocked, "Oh."

As we raced along, I stared at the buildings, mid-rise structures that went on and on. Everything was falling apart. I could literally see balconies falling off buildings. Huge cracks cutting through apartments. Everything was filthy. As at the airport, gone were the huge red banners proclaiming "Glory to the Communist Party!" and "Long Live Lenin!" and on and on. They'd been ripped off as if they were Band-Aids. And what was underneath were vast, festering wounds.

"You looked shocked," said Tanya.

"It's worse than I thought it would be."

"Everything's awful," she laughed. "Everything. Nothing works anymore."

"It was like that before, too, but now at least we don't pretend that all is wonderful," said Lev, looking at me in the rearview mirror. "And it's a madhouse. But the business opportunities are fantastic. It's a real Klondike, Alex. A real Klondike, you'll see."

Tanya proudly said, "We're opening a store in the beauty shop where I used to cut hair. We're going to be real *biznizmeni*."

"Really? That's great," I said.

"It's going to be a clothing store," added Lev. "We have a fabulous location, right across from the Moscow station. Right by the subway stop there."

"And I'm going to be the buyer." Tanya proudly smoothed her raincoat, then opened it and displayed her blouse. "We're going to carry clothes like these. Pretty nice, don't you think?"

"They're not Soviet, are they?"

"Oh, come on, Alex," she laughed. "Don't be ridiculous. They're from Stockholm."

Lev was still staring in the rearview mirror. But he was no longer looking at Tanya and me. No, he was studying the road behind us. Reflexively, I turned. There were a handful of cars behind us—a tiny Moskvich, a green taxi, a couple of Zhiguli—though one vehicle in particular stood out among the pack. It was light gold and clean and all shiny. The very same Mercedes I'd seen in the parking lot of the airport. Were they following us or were they simply taking the same route from the airport?

Lev swerved around a huge hold in the road, and we pressed on and into the city. We—.

*"Slow it down, Alex. What about that Mercedes? Let yourself briefly scan the next week. What do you notice?"*

Yes, I thought. That trancely sense of mine was telling me, reminding me, that, yes, I would see that car and the two men inside it again.

*"And what are your feelings on an emotional level?"*

It made me worried. A nervous tremor rippled through me. The men in that car were the new men of Russia. The new controllers, the ones who'd replaced the KGB, and who were now the new princes and counts who controlled and profited from all the little people of the country.

*"Alex, what do you mean? Who were these people?"*

They were the mafia, of course. And they hadn't been meeting anyone at the airport. No. They'd been there observing us. Watching, noting. And now they were following us. Right from the start. But I didn't know any of that. Not then. If only I had. If I'd even suspected, then I wouldn't have asked that stupid question. The one that started it all.

Quite innocently, I asked, "Lev, how many rubles are there to the dollar?"

# Chapter 5

Lev replied, "That's a really good question."

"*Bozhe moi.*" My God, said Tanya. "It's been flying every-where. In the last six months it's been as low as five hundred rubles to the dollar and as high as twelve hundred. Who knows what's going to happen to us. Next year it could be up to two thousand to one."

"You're kidding?" I shook my head. "Do you realize that when I was a student here one ruble cost a dollar sixty-five?"

"Right," said Tanya, always quick with numbers, "and now there are about eleven of our rubles to your one American penny."

"When I started as an electrical engineer," began Lev, smirking as if he were telling some kind of sick joke, "I earned one hundred and eighty rubles per month. Now, just to keep pace with inflation, I make almost thirty thousand per month."

"Holy shit, Lev, that's still only a little over thirty bucks."

He shrugged, for it was all beyond his control. "We're like Germany after the first war, don't you think? Inflation is eating every-thing. There's no sense even saving a kopeck. God only knows how we're getting by."

I shook my head, not able to comprehend, not able to believe that Lev's salary, particularly with his education, could be so low. Quite obviously this was a ruined country, one that was still struggling to rise from the ashes of the Cold War. But could it? Was it even possible? I couldn't really see how, which was a depressing thought, for the only tradition Russia had was tyranny. Even at this first glance, I surmised the situation was now as dangerous as during the height of U.S.-Soviet tensions, for with so much economic instability the country was ripe for some type of militaristic or fascist takeover. And yet the U.S. was doing so little, a gross oversight that might in the end be horrendously expensive, both financially and in terms of human life.

I said, "It'll be interesting to see what rate I get at the hotel exchange."

"Oh no," insisted Tanya. "You mustn't change money there. On the street you can get ten, maybe twenty percent more."

"On the street? You can change openly now?"

From the front seat, Lev said, "Pretty much so. In fact, we can stop and change some for you. I know a place where the rates are the best."

I shrugged, replied sure, that would be okay. I should have told him, no, don't bother, just take me to the hotel. But back then I was curious and I couldn't have seen, of course, what was to happen. How dangerous it really was. So instead we went shooting through the city I'd always known as Leningrad but was now St. Petersburg, a metropolis of the tsars and commissars that was dreary and gray and poverty-stricken. Speaking more and more quickly in Russian, Tanya went on about the astronomical prices of food and other goods—a jar of decent instant coffee was a quarter of a month's income, two bananas a day's wage—and how her mother would have starved to death if they weren't taking care of her. Shaking my head, I stared out the window, already understanding why the brutal authority of the Communists could be yearned for. The car slammed into a deep hole, Tanya screamed. And I thought, these were the bomb craters of the Cold War.

We came to the Moscow train station, then turned left and onto Nevsky Prospekt, their great avenue and the real heart of the city. Throngs of people, clutching everything from toilet paper to obviously priceless roses, pushed up and down the broad avenue. On both sides of the street, a seemingly endless mass of people pressed along, a surprising number in jeans and bright nylon jackets.

Tanya pointed to the circular metro station, exclaimed, "That's where our store is going to be. Right down that street. See? See the store called Springtime Beauty Salon? That's where I worked, doing hair for five years, and that's our spot. It's a fabulous location. So many people! Everyone's going to come and we're going to be as rich as you Americans!"

Then Tanya started in on clothing, how there was a huge discount warehouse in Stockholm with all these great clothes. She hadn't been there yet. But she'd heard about it, seen many samples of their clothes because one of their reps had been here and flashed all these dazzling dresses before her. He'd even left her with some samples too. Like her raincoat, she bragged. Soon she'd get a visa, be able to fly there too, and then she'd visit the warehouse herself. Stockholm was only an hour away, she said, lifting one finger. Just a measly one-hour trip. And then she'd go and buy everything for their store, bring it back, and sell it just like that.

"Half of the things will be for sale for rubles, the other half for *valuta*," hard currency, she said. "With the *valuta* we'll buy more clothes in Sweden, and with the rubles we'll start another business here. Maybe apartment remodeling or something like that."

"Or maybe we'll start manufacturing one of those watering things you have in the West," ventured Lev. "I saw a picture of one once. You put it out in the garden and it shoots water over all the vegetables. It would be fabulous at the dacha—everyone would buy one."

I rolled my eyes. From weapons to sprinklers. Actually, it wasn't a bad idea.

Tanya started talking about how they needed a foreign partner, the need for foreign capital, how much they could do and would do, and so on. I knew what that meant, of course, and I was sure I'd hear a great deal more about it. I'd have to brace myself, though, because Tanya had always been terribly convincing as well as persistent. Which made her just like every other Russian I'd ever met. Investing in a Russian venture, however, might prove lucrative.

Nevsky had much more traffic, and I glanced out the back, saw no sign of the gold Mercedes, only a great mass of cars and buses and filthy trucks. As we drove on, I was entranced at how utterly familiar the city seemed. In many ways it seemed as if it hadn't changed. Or as if I hadn't left. The drab faces of the stone buildings and once-grand palaces went by one after the other, and it just felt so utterly familiar. So many of my old memories leapt into view— the bridge with the horses over the Fontanka, the dome atop the bookstore, Dom Knigi, and the spire of the Admiralty—that I was overwhelmed with a kind of morose melancholy. If I'd pursued a career using my Russian, where would I be now? At the embassy in Moscow, here at the consulate in St. Petersburg, perhaps at Radio Liberty in Munich? Working for my sister and exploring the world of forensic hypnosis was certainly different, but I feared that rather than expanding my horizons, my world was shrinking to the size of her island.

If only we'd kept on cruising around this glorious city that could be, might be glorious again if a series of miracles came to pass. If only we'd continued on down Nevsky, past the Winter Palace, across the Neva River. But when we passed Gostini Dvor—the ancient and decrepit department store now closed for a total make-over—Lev took a sharp left. As I peered at the crumbling yellow structure on our left, Lev began to slow on the side street. And then all at once, fifteen or twenty men on foot appeared out of nowhere, surrounding us and zeroing in on our car.

"What's going on?" I asked nervously.

"Don't worry," replied Tanya, her voice hushed. "They're just money changers. We often get our dollars here."

One of the men reached for the passenger door, opened it. This was the ultimate in drive-in service—your own personal banker climbing in your car—but just then the blue light of a police Jeep came flashing down the street and toward us.

"*Gospodi.*" Dear Lord, gasped Lev.

He quickly leaned over, pulled the door shut, then slammed down on the gas. We took off with a jolt and the gathering of men rapidly dispersed as the *militsiya* approached.

As we sped down the street, with a grin Lev said, "Changing money's not as illegal as it used to be, but it's still not entirely legal either."

"You mean everybody's doing it, right?"

"*Da, da.*"

"Listen, I can just cash a traveler's check at the hotel."

But he wouldn't hear of it. To him it was as much a matter of principle. He wanted to show me how things had really changed, and so we circled around, continued on down Nevsky, passing Kazanski Cathedral, the apple-green Stroganov Palace, the Griboyedov Canal. When we were within a short distance of the Admiralty, Lev took another left. Punching the gas, he cut down a small street, went speeding down a narrow passage, took another left. I glanced down a side street, saw the main cathedral, St. Isaac's, a huge granite structure with its massive gold dome. Yes, I realized. We had to have been within a block or two of the Astoria Hotel, which I'd heard had been fully restored.

Lev braked and pulled over, parking his small Lada at an angle. A handful of other cars were parked nearby, but otherwise the street was quiet, which was odd considering the proximity to Nevsky. What were these drab, lifeless buildings here, offices or apartments? Tucked almost secretively between the busy heart of the city and the Astoria with its wealthy Western guests, it was no surprise there was a lot of dollar trading going on here.

Turning in his seat, Lev said, "How much money do you want to change? There won't be any problems, but you should let me do it. They'll see by your clothes that you're not Russian and they won't give you as good a rate."

I shrugged, reached into my coat. "I don't know. I guess three or four hundred dollars."

Tanya started laughing. "Don't be silly, Alex. That's way too much. First of all, that's a lot of money—a year's salary for most people. Second of all, you'd have a hard time spending all that. There's nothing to buy, remember? And third, if you did find something to buy, you'd get a better price with dollars."

"Not to mention," added Lev, "that if I get eleven hundred to one, you'd be carrying over three or four hundred thousand rubles. Maybe the traders will have big notes, but if they only have small bills you're talking about a whole sackful of rubles to carry around."

Now I laughed, for none of this made any real sense. "Okay, I'm convinced, but let me at least do a hundred."

"That's more than plenty," said Tanya. "If you need more, we'll give it to you."

"Make sure they're fresh bills," advised Lev. "The cleaner the money, the better the rate."

I'd heard that one before—that it was best to bring new bills as well as small ones—and I rummaged through my wallet, found five twenty-dollar bills, all clean and crisp. As I pulled out the money, I couldn't help but be a little hesitant, a little concerned. When I'd been a student here I'd been cornered by the KGB, who'd seen me merely pulling out a single American dollar and showing it to some students. They'd thought I'd been trading money, which I definitely hadn't, and yet they'd cornered me, demanded to know what I was doing.

"You're sure this is all right?" I asked.

*"Da, da, da,"* assured Lev.

Paranoia in Russia was for me, at least, a hard thing to shake, and I turned and scanned the street. I thought I saw someone lingering, a woman, but she disappeared into a building. There were no other pedestrians, yet wondering about that Mercedes, all clean and shiny, I looked around but saw only Soviet-built vehicles. Still, I had this odd sensation that we were indeed being observed. In fact, I don't know why, but I was quite sure we were.

As Lev climbed out, I called, "Be careful."

"Don't worry, I'll be fine," he replied.

Again taking my hand as the two of us sat in the backseat, Tanya said, "Not to worry, Alex. Lev trades all the time. Everyone does now. It's the only way to stay alive."

I shrugged, and my eyes stuck to Lev as he made his way along the sidewalk, then about thirty feet down turned right and passed into an archway. I pictured an interior courtyard, dark and dank, a place filled with garbage and rarely touched by sunlight. I didn't like this. Even then. But what did I know, really? Why shouldn't I have followed their advice?

*"Just stick with the story."*

I stayed with Tanya, and the two of us gossiped on. We talked about our plans for the week—I told her how I had to see Pavel—and then she jumped in and talked about recent changes—Yeltsin this, Yeltsin that—and where the country was trying to go, what could happen versus what probably would. How the old Communists were using their connections to suck money out of the country. The rampant corruption. As I was assaulted with information and opinions, I nodded, ran my hand through my hair, for I understood the words at least. What it all meant, however, was something entirely different.

Nearly ten minutes later, Tanya checked her watch, looked up at me, and said, "What could be taking him so long?"

I pulled myself forward, the worry gnawing at my sense of peace, and said, "Want me to go see?"

"No, I'll go. Knowing Lev, he's probably found a friend and they're having a smoke."

Tanya got out, opening the right rear door, stepping onto the street, smoothing her clothes and her long tan raincoat. She walked around the front of the car, and I kept my eyes on her. I hoped there were no problems, and I studied the street again, saw no yellow police Jeeps or any other official-looking cars.

Then suddenly, just as Tanya was passing in front of her own car, someone started shouting in the distance, No, someone was screaming. Her face shot with panic, Tanya glanced once at me in the car, then started running, for she'd recognized that voice. It was Lev, and she took off, tearing toward the archway.

I threw open the car door, leapt out, and just as I was reaching the sidewalk, Tanya cut into the courtyard. And then the next moment I heard a gunshot, loud and shrill. Fear swelled my heart as I tore onward. Somewhere up there in that courtyard I heard car doors slamming, next tires spinning and squealing. I rounded the corner, entered the short passage and raced into the heart of the building, and I saw her there, sprawled out on the granite cobblestones and looking quite lifeless.

"Tanya!" I shouted.

She was on her back, head twisted to the side. Oh, dear Lord, had she been shot? Knifed? I searched her for a mortal wound, then turned and saw Lev, another twenty feet ahead, his body also splayed out on the ground.

I dropped to my knees by Tanya's side, scanned her for any large wounds, saw none, and then I carefully reached down to her unconscious body. The right side of her face was bloodied and her eyes closed. When I touched her, she moaned, started to move. My panic didn't subside, however, for this was it, everything that I feared about the old and the new Russia now playing out before me.

"Tanya!" I nervously called as I tried to make her comfortable. "Are you all right?"

"Oi . . ." she moaned, voice very faint. "Lev? Where's Lev?"

She rolled over on her back, brushed awkwardly at the grime on her face. As she struggled to wake up, she groped at the wound on her cheek and winced in pain. Desperate to sit up, she mumbled something about a man, a dark figure who'd jumped out of nowhere.

"I . . . I didn't see him," she moaned.

I wrapped my arm around her back. "Just take it slow."

Again she asked, "Where's . . . where's Lev?"

"Over there," I replied, motioning with my hand.

Once I was sure she was able to sit up without falling, I charged over to Lev's all-too-still body. My heart was bursting with fear—had he been robbed?—and I stopped a few feet away from him. Lying in the middle of the dark courtyard, he was chest down, his head twisted sharply and much too oddly to the side. I saw a thick pool of blood rapidly seeping from him and winding through the cobblestones, and I knew to expect the very worst.

"Oh, God," I gasped.

I rushed around him, dropped to the ground, and placed my hand hesitantly on his back. At first there was nothing, no movement. Then there was a faint, sharp squeak. Shit, I thought, he was alive, barely so, and struggling to breathe. He couldn't die.

"Lev, we're here!" I desperately shouted.

He flinched at my words, and carefully and slowly I took hold and rolled him over. His ash-blond hair was streaked with grime and blood, his face drained of all color, and his eyes fluttered but did not open. I looked down, saw that his clothes and jacket were a sodden, red mess. As far as I could tell, he'd been shot once in his chest. As he struggled for air, I heard that high-pitched noise again and a bubble of blood rose and burst from the wound. With horror, I realized one of his lungs had been punctured.

Tanya's voice rose in a terrified scream, calling, "Lev! Lev!"

She struggled to her feet, started stumbling toward us, her face streaked with mascara and terror. She tripped, nearly fell, gathered herself, then rushed over and dropped to my side. With trembling hands, she reached out, touched him, and screamed. Next she pushed me out of the way and reached out, took her husband's head in her lap.

"Lev! Please, no! No! Oh, God, no!" she sobbed.

Tanya's voice rose in another high shrill, and moments later a door opened and an old man hesitantly peered out. When he saw us huddled over Lev, he opened the door more fully, then stood there shaking his head.

I shouted, "Call the *militsiya*! Get an ambulance!"

Crying, Tanya clung to her husband, tried to keep him here with her, in this life, on this planet. She brushed his hair back, kissed him on the forehead, pleaded over and over again.

She caught her breath, then turned toward me, and shouted, "Go! Get out of here!"

I stared at her in shock. "What?"

"You have to leave before the *militsiya* come. Go on, leave us!"

"But—"

"Go!" she angrily screamed. "This is Russian business. It's too dangerous, Alex. Leave! You don't want to get involved!"

I started to rise to my feet, hesitated. How could I abandon them? I had to stay, make sure Lev got to the hospital, make sure they did everything and anything to save his life.

"Get out of here!" she coarsely shouted.

"You—"

"*Nyet!* Just go!"

As I started moving away, I called, "I'll be at my hotel. Call me. I'll be waiting!"

She nodded, wrapped her arms around Lev, pulling him into her lap. I took one last look at them, that dark, bloody mess huddled together, and then I trotted out of the courtyard. My head was light. I rushed onto the sidewalk, stopped, caught my breath. A lady with a big black purse stopped, stared at me strangely. And then somehow I pushed on. Lev's keys were still in the ignition. I opened the trunk, got my suitcase, and then as the police sirens started wailing, I hurried off to Nevsky.

# Chapter 6

Everything was a blur after that. My head was spinning and swirling, my heart beating wildly. I didn't know what time it was, nor even what day. I'd crossed continents and oceans, landed in the strangest of times in the strangest of countries, and then one of my oldest friends had been killed. Killed? Yes, I knew Lev wouldn't survive, for the wound had been far too deep and far too brilliant. I cringed at the volcanolike image of his chest that continued to erupt in my memory. Not only was the wound fatal, I sensed, but Lev was dead already. Absolutely. By the time I reached Nevsky Prospekt, I felt it deep within me. Lev had passed from this world and into the next.

Lugging my suitcase, my brow blistering with frantic sweat, I darted to the far side of Nevsky, then stood on the curb and started flagging a taxi. Despite my desperate appearance, I must have looked terribly Western—the shoes too clean, the jeans too new, perhaps even the teeth too white—because one of the light green cabs pulled over immediately.

*"Dollari?"* demanded the driver through the open window. *"Rublei—nyet. Dollari—da. Yasna?"*

Of course it was clear he wouldn't accept rubles, that he only wanted dollars. And of course I didn't care.

*"Da, da,"* I replied.

The driver, a hefty man with a big, babyish face and light brown hair, leaned over and pushed open the back door. I threw in my suitcase, hurling it to the far side of the seat, and clambered after it. My hands trembling, I touched my brow. God, I was dripping wet.

My voice shaking, I said, "Hotel Pribaltiskaya."

*"Da, da, da."* He turned around in his seat and held up all ten fingers. *"Dyesat dollarov, ladna?"*

I was sure ten dollars was an exorbitant amount—twice, I later learned, the usual cost—but so what. I motioned him on, he nodded and smiled with great pleasure, and in a flash we were off. I glanced down a side street, saw the flashing blue light of a police Jeep. Leaving was the right thing to do, wasn't it? I hated to run away like this, but I had to trust Tanya. I had to trust her that it would be less complicated without the presence of a Westerner, particularly an American. After all, this was still Russia.

The taxi swerved around a crammed electric trolley bus and past a couple of hulking palaces as it charged toward the beginning of Nevsky. I thought of Lev lying back there, of the grieving Tanya, and I turned around again. Something was gnawing at me, and I looked out the back of the speeding taxi. My heart was pounding. I didn't know why, but I was certain that I needed to be more careful than ever. Staring out the rear of the taxi, not quite sure what I was looking for, I searched the street, the sidewalks, but could note nothing of concern.

As we shot off the end of Nevsky Prospekt, the taxi careened to the right. I looked to the right, saw the vast Palace Square that was spiked in the middle with the towering victory column. Behind it, like one huge wall in an open-air room, stood the Winter Palace, the thousand-room, apple-green palace of the tsars that formed the bulk of the Hermitage. At the closest corner of the building I eyed a handful of tourist buses and a gaggle of Westerners being shepherded along.

In an instant the small taxi burst onto the Palace Bridge and across the broad Neva River. My eyes skimmed the flat waters, hitting upon the distant golden spires of the St. Peter and Paul Fortress, the resting place of so many tsars and tsarinas. Automatically I looked to the left, saw the familiar brown building, the very one that had been my dormitory and which was reputed to have been a whorehouse during tsarist times. I'd lived there, and now nothing seemed to have changed and no time seemed to have passed. I rubbed my head, tried to convince myself that I was within this scene, within this picture, and actually back here. Yet it was no wonder that I was perplexed, for St. Petersburg itself was a city confused by its own history.

It was far too much to absorb, and I closed my eyes. I just sat there, bouncing in the backseat as the driver sped onto Vasilevski Island, then turned left and toward the Bay of Finland. The vehicle leapt and bounded as it clambered over streetcar rails bursting from the streets, swerved to avoid the endless potholes, next slammed to a halt as an old man, one of the few who'd survived the Revolution and two world wars, slowly made his way across the middle of the street.

Nearly ten minutes later, the taxi raced down a broad street, one that was lined with high rises, new ones already falling apart. There at the end, right on the edge of the bay, rose this huge thing, a modern, monolithic structure. It was the Hotel Pribaltiskaya—the Pribalt—a modern building soaring some twenty stories tall.

My arrival happened in a daze. The driver roared up to the bottom of a huge granite staircase, I threw ten dollars at him. And then I was making my way up to the hotel. A couple of guys started waving fur hats and flashing cans of caviar, soon followed by another handful of hawkers. What was this? Such brazen *spekulatsiya* had been strictly forbidden by the Soviets. But now?

In my best Russian slang I told them, *"Otdixhai."* Buzz off.

"Where are you from, the Baltics?" one of them asked, upon hearing my accent, which was quite similar to a Lithuanian or Latvian one.

"America."

Another laughed, pleaded, "Change dollars?"

I shook my head.

"Come on. I'll give you the best rate in all of Russia."

As always, Russia and Russians were unrelenting, for to them no only meant the beginning of negotiations. They buzzed around me like bothersome mosquitoes, and these men with their tourist wares pursued me up the steps, nearly right to the front door. None of which was important. Nothing was, really. Not my entry into the dimly lit granite lobby of the Pribalt, the whores leaning from the second-floor balcony of the bar, the surly desk clerk, my paying in dollars and ascending to my room. Nor my entering my chamber, a fine room that looked like a very nice room at the Y, with red carpeting, red bedspreads, and dark wooden furniture. I put my suitcase down by the large television. There was only one thing that mattered right then.

*"And what is that?"*

There was something that was important, I sensed, but at the time I didn't even know it, wasn't even aware.

*"In this hypnotic retelling of the story, Alex, you have the ability*

*to see beyond that time. You have the ability to verbalize what you'll later learn."*

I looked around the room, and it was perfectly clear to me. Whether by hidden camera or hidden microphone, I didn't know, but I was most definitely being spied upon.

# Chapter 7

*"Alex, I want you to slow the story down a bit. Take a nice, deep breath,"* she coached. *"There's something important here that you need to explore further."*

There were large windows all along the front of the room, and I stared out at the broad, still waters of the Bay of Finland. The view was nothing but a steely plank that at some unseen point hit the horizon and turned into a plane of gray clouds. I breathed in, held it. Next released and let the air trickle over my pursed lips. That's right, I told myself. Go for the bigger picture.

*"How do you know you're being watched?"*

I never learned for sure, not then.

*"So you're only aware of it now?"*

Exactly. I didn't realize it when it was all happening. I only became aware of it in this retelling of the story, which in its own weird way made sense. Maybe this would explain all the rest of it, why I was chased and who was next killed.

*"Tell me how someone could be watching you, Alex. Why do you think this now, at this time?"*

As if on command, the phone in my room started ringing. I turned, stared at the cheap, plastic telephone, a little red thing with a flimsy plastic dial. How could this be happening? I stood there horrified, because when all this had really taken place, no one had called me. My phone hadn't rung just after I'd entered my room.

*"But someone's calling you in this mesmerized version of the story."*

That was impossible, wasn't it?

*"No, it's not. You're seeing things with a different perspective now, Alex. You're using the very unique power of hypnosis to re-create this story."* My coach called, *"Do you remember how in the tale of Loretta—"*

That bloody trance. So much death. It had been so horrible. I'd seen Loretta's stepmother, Helen, lying in a pool of blood, just as I'd seen Lev lying in that courtyard.

*"Yes, and do you remember how your imaginal unconscious took over, per se?"*

Of course I did. That story had taken a twist, pulled me into some fantasy or rather some nightmarish corner. There'd been a phone then, as well, and it had started ringing. I'd charged into a mysterious room, where'd I'd answered the phone and where a monster had emerged out of nowhere. Some sort of horrible, rank creature all cloaked in mealy gauze. I'd been locked in a room with this thing and it had come charging after me, ready to rip me to death.

*"Yes, your fear took shape and form and a kind of life. That was how your subconscious visualized what you were up against."*

The telephone continued screaming and shrieking. I stood at the end of the narrow bed, stared at the phone as it nearly tremored with each shrill ring. I didn't know what to do because how was any of this possible when really it had all been different?

*"It's possible because of the way you're utilizing hypnosis, Alex. You're allowing yourself to combine all of your knowledge and intuitive powers, and sometimes these two crystallize in metaphor or fantasy. Just let things unfold. We'll sort them out later."* My other-worldly master suggested, *"Go ahead, Alex. In this hypnotic version of your St. Petersburg voyage, the phone is ringing as well. You may answer it and you may listen to what your subconscious wants to tell you. There's something to be learned here."*

Moving toward the phone, I stepped into a dreamier version of the story, one that might not have actually happened, but that might hold great truths.

*"Exactly. You know more, both then and now, than you actually realize."*

Oh, Christ, What was all this about? Who could be calling me? As the phone rang and rang, I slowly moved over to it, then lowered my hand. On about the tenth ring I picked up the receiver. Biting my lower lip, I put the phone to my ear.

I hesitated, finally said, "Hello?"

In response came deep, heavy breathing, and finally a hoarse voice that warned, "A word to the wise, my friend, someone's . . . someone's watching your every move."

My body tensed, and I asked, "Who?"

The labored breathing continued before the voice replied, "Just watch out for—"

With that the line went totally dead. I shouted into the receiver, but there was nothing, only flat silence as if the line itself had been cut.

Shit, I thought. Not again. In the bloody trance of Loretta, this same goddamn thing had happened. I'd been lured into a trap by a shrill telephone, answered that phone, and then I'd turned around and there had been that ungodly creature determined to rip out my guts. I closed my eyes, now turned around in my room at the Pribalt, certain that that thing had followed me from one trance to another as if from one book to the next.

Instead, there was nothing. Except for myself, the room was empty, and I sighed with relief. But what did this mean?

*"You know, don't you?"* she suggested.

Now that I thought about it, yes, of course I did. But I couldn't imagine why the KGB would be spying on me, why I might be of interest to them, particularly in this day and age. I was no scientist, no government diplomat. I thought back nostalgically to the days of the Party, when everything was much clearer, when you knew exactly what to be afraid of. Then again, they might not be interested in my actions per se, but in whom I was associating with. That in turn caused me to wonder what Tanya and Lev could be involved in. Or Pavel. Maybe the KGB knew I was going to be seeing him, and perhaps he was of interest for his hypnotic exploits, not to mention his television program.

My attention was drawn to the far wall. Just to the right of the television, just over the dresser, there was a mirror, which I quickly went to. I wrapped my hands around the frame, half sure that I wouldn't be able to budge it. But the looking glass moved easily. That was to say, it wasn't attached and there was no camera behind it. Next I went to a standing lamp in the corner, ran my fingers around the rim of the shade. I detected no bug of a microphone. Nor did I find one when I unscrewed the light bulb. I checked the lamp by the bed as well. Then I again reached for the red phone which sat on the stand between the two twin beds. Turning it over, my fingers pushed and probed for any hidden device that could be monitoring my life here. There was nothing. I examined the built-in radio that was also between the two beds, but there was no way I could disassemble it and probe its innards.

This was useless. I knew for a fact that in Soviet days all hotel rooms for Westerners had been equipped with listening devices. They might not have all been used, but they were there in each room just in case. Or was I just being paranoid? I didn't know, couldn't help but remember that infamous story. Rumor had it that during Soviet times a member of an American hockey team had been determined, as I now was, to find the microphone in his hotel room. He searched everything, and finally, pulling back the carpet, he found a large bolt in the floorboards. Certain that this would reveal a listening device, he proceeded to unscrew it, which proved no easy feat. He was a strapping guy, though, and within seconds of removing the bolt, there was an enormous crash from the floor below as a chandelier in the downstairs dining room went crashing to the ground. So I could look and look, and all I'd probably do was create havoc, like break a light bulb in a country where light bulbs were as dear as crystal goblets though infinitely more scarce.

Putting my hand to my chin, I stood there in silence. Within moments my eyes fell on the door. When I'd been in Moscow as a student I'd searched my hotel room and found the door wired with monitoring equipment. They'd wanted to keep track of when I'd come and gone, and there'd been a tiny device, which was triggered every time the door was opened and which I'd detached every night and which in turn they'd reattached every day when I was out. Compulsively, I now went to the door, opened it, studied the hinges, ran my fingers over the screws. Either this was far superior technology or again there was nothing.

Standing in the open door, I heard low voices down the long corridor. I peered out and way down saw the matronly *dezhurnaya,* the key lady—one of whom sat on every floor—perched behind the desk. The older woman was talking to someone, a tall, thin figure, clothing dark, whose back was toward me. I stared at them through a fog of disbelief. What kind of dream or nightmare was this?

*"It is your subconscious trying to show you something."* The voice suggested, *"Would you like to pursue it?"*

Absolutely, for there was a great truth to be learned here, something that was connected to us all, Lev, Tanya, Pavel, and me.

I stepped back into my room only long enough to grab my plastic room key, and then headed out. Closing the door behind me, I started down the corridor. At the sound of my steps, both the *dezhurnaya* and the figure glanced in my direction. They looked surprised, as if they'd been caught, and I knew, of course, that they'd been talking about me.

I stared at them, but my vision became oddly weak and the figures melted into a blur. I couldn't make out the person, that spy, who was interrogating the key lady. I couldn't even tell if it was a man or a woman, but it didn't matter, for the spy said something quickly to the key lady and then turned and darted off. I quickened my step and broke into a run.

Rushing up to the *dezhurnaya*, I demanded, "Who was that? What's going on?"

"What are you talking about, *molodoi chelovek?*" young man, she asked with an altogether pleasant smile. "There wasn't anyone here."

"Of course there was. I just saw you talking to someone."

*"Nyet, nyet, nyet.* I've just been sitting here knitting and minding my own business."

That was bullshit, of course. The old Soviet kind. I stared at this sweet-looking, older woman with the rusty tinted hair and three or four gold teeth and the intricately lined face, and thought how nothing had changed. Russians were just a bunch of sheep; if their masters told them that a cow had five legs, that's what they'd say too, even though they damn well knew the truth. It was a survival technique, one that had in many ways served them well, dating way back to Ivan the Terrible. So I knew I'd get no further with this woman.

I took off, running down another hallway, this one leading to the bank of lifts. But when I reached the glass-enclosed elevator lobby, it was empty. I pushed on. Just a few feet beyond was one of the tiny *boofyeti*, the little cafés on every other floor that sold tea, fatty salami sandwiches, champagne by the gram, hard-boiled eggs, cookies, and other hard-to-find delicacies. The door was open, I heard a forest of voices and went in. There were only twenty or so seats and it was packed with a bunch of Russians glommed up at the counter, for not only was it a treat to be in such a nice hotel that was so well supplied, they were buying extra food to take home. Hotels for foreigners, obviously, were still among the best stocked.

I pushed past a couple of women, scanned the place. There was no sign of the spy until I turned, glanced into the kitchen. I spotted the familiar figure ducking between several racks. Pushing through the line, I tore around the counter and across the linoleum.

The saleswoman, the only one working there, waved a serving spoon at me and shouted, *"Molodoi chelovek—nyet, nyet, nyet!"*

I paid her no attention, lunging past a refrigerator, into the back room, past the racks. No one was there, but the rear door was open, which I bolted through. Immediately I found myself in another corridor lined with more rooms. Checking to my right, there was no one, only a long empty hallway that seemed to stretch forever. Turning the other way I saw the spy ducking through another doorway. As quickly as I could, I ran down the hall, entering a service room that was painted all red and filled with large cloth bags of soiled sheets. The doors to one of the service elevators were just shutting, and I lunged forward, threw out my right hand, thereby triggering the sensors. Automatically, the closing doors reversed themselves and started easing back.

And just as quickly, a fist came flying out. That's all I saw. This hand. It came hurling at me, catching me square on the chin. A black bolt of pain zapped through my head, I stumbled back, and then I fell unconscious to the ground, my head, I think, landing on one of those bags of laundry.

# Chapter 8

I quit that mesmerized dream and woke up because my head was throbbing as hard as if I'd actually been punched. Moaning, I opened my eyes and found that my face was still somehow nestled in the dirty linens.

What?

No, none of that was right. I blinked, wondered for a moment if I were back on Maddy's island, stretched out on the recliner next to my hypnotically controlling sister. It wasn't all that far away, not at all. Just like Dorothy, I could click my heels and be back there in a second, couldn't I?

*"Of course you can, Alex. This is your trance."* As if she were a goddess sucking in a sky full of clouds, I heard my sister inhaling and inhaling . . . and then letting it all go, spewing it out in a near-whistle of tranquil exaltation. *"Where would you like to be?"*

I blinked, realized I had to be back in Russia because I had been and probably always would be obsessed with that mysterious land. No matter how repulsed or frustrated I became by the inequities, the stifling bureaucracy, and now the crime and decrepitness, I would always be drawn to that misanthropic land. Perhaps it was really true. Perhaps I had been a Russian in a previous life, which, of course, would then explain this . . . this morbid nostalgia.

*"Yes. Remember my childhood vision—you as a tsar?"*

No, impossible. This was not the time for that, there was a story to be told, something to be learned, and so I turned around, so to speak, ventured no further down the path of past lives, instead forced my eyes open, concentrated on this life, and saw that my face was indeed buried in some sheets. Rather, a downy pillow. I moved my head, lifted my hand, ran it over the nubby red bedspread. Oh. I was in my room at the Pribalt and my head was on a pillow, not on a bag of laundry. And, yes, I was still in Russia.

A very familiar voice from there whispered, "Alex?"

I rolled half over. Tanya was seated next to me on the bed, her eyes so red, so swollen, that it looked as if she'd been struck. Actually, she had been hit, for the left side of her face was scratched and puffy. She reached out and touched me on the leg, her fingers hesitant at first, next sinking desperately into my thigh.

"I knocked and knocked, but you didn't answer," she said, running her other hand into her tangled blond hair.

Quite right, I thought. It hadn't really been my pounding head, but her banging on the door that I'd sensed. Tanya. That was who and what had rallied me back to that time and place. And I had trouble waking because I was so utterly exhausted it was more like I passed out than fell asleep.

Her voice very faint, she said, "I . . . I was worried about you, so I got the *dezhurnaya* to let me in."

"Oh." I rubbed my face, felt as if I had slipped into some unknown world. "What time is it?"

"Eleven o'clock."

I glanced toward the large windows. It was dark, which meant it was night, not morning. What had happened? I'd traveled all this way, hadn't slept in two days. Then I'd been met by Lev and Tanya, he'd been attacked. And I was sent to the hotel. Yes, I remembered pacing and waiting and fretting here in my room, desperate for news, feeling as if I'd been banished to Siberia. I'd been so worried about them. At some point I must have lain down. And zap. I'd fallen into a black hole of sleep where I'd had some nightmare about the KGB spying on me. Too strange to be true, yet too real to be dismissed.

I propped myself up, fearing what I knew, hoping it had all been part of that nasty dream, yet knowing that it wasn't, and asked, "Where's Lev?"

She bit her lip, couldn't talk, turned away. As she shook her head, a deep sob bubbled out of her and burst.

I said, "Oh, no."

Through her tears, she muttered, "He . . . he was dead before the

ambulance arrived. He died in my arms, right while I was holding him.
I'm . . . I'm not sure he knew I was there . . . right there with him.''
   I sat up, swung my legs around, wrapped my arms around her. It
was then that I noticed all the blood. While it had been wiped from
Tanya's raincoat, everything else she wore, from her blouse to her
pants, was stained with Lev.
   "It can't be!" As she cried, she stroked the right leg of her pants,
which was encrusted with a huge blood-black stain that was now all dry.
   I clutched Tanya, felt the pain rise from my stomach, next grab
my throat and choke me, and finally come spilling out my eyes. How
many years had I known Lev? Fifteen. All this time—*stolko let, stolko
zeem*—had gone by since I'd last seen him, and then I'd returned to the
embrace of his friendship. And now he was gone. Forever. Jesus
Christ, I wanted to back all this up. It had been such an arbitrary
decision to pull down that side street, change a few dollars. Why
hadn't I insisted that I was tired, that after my twenty hours of travel
that I wanted to go to the hotel and shower first? Why hadn't Tanya
said something like, Later, Lev, can we stop for tea and do all that
later? Instead, we'd driven directly toward his death as if we'd had no
control, as if it were as inevitable as a sunset.
   I stroked her back as we both cried, held her, said, "Dear God,
I'm so sorry."
   Tanya broke down completely, wailing so loudly with her pain
that within a few moments there was again pounding on my door. I was
about to get up when the door was opened and the *dezhurnaya,* the
very same one from that very same dreamish KGB encounter, bustled
in. What was this all about? She stood there, hair tinted that odd rusty
color, hand to her mouth, and her mouth half opened and exposing that
handful of gold teeth.
   "What's the matter?" she asked with great concern as she peered
in. "The girl's not hurt, is she? You haven't been drinking vodka and
hurt her, have you?"
   I bluntly replied, "Her husband was killed this afternoon."
   "*Bozhe!*" God, she gasped, eyes bursting with fright. "How? A
car accident?"
   I shook my head, didn't know what to say, how to put it other
than, "Changing money."
   "*Kakoi koshmar.*" What a nightmare. "Was it the mafia? They're
everywhere." She shook her head. "What's happening with this country? So much disorder. It used to be so safe and there used to always
be bread in the store. Where's Lenin when we need him?" And then

she said, "You're an *Amerikanets,* aren't you? Do you have this kind of democracy in *Amerika*?"

Oh, Christ. I stared at her in disbelief. Lev was dead, didn't she understand? There was no way I was going to get into politics and the questions of disorder right now.

She took note of my blank expression and said, *"Oi, byedniki."* Oh, you poor ones. "I'll go get you some tea."

Departing, she left the door ajar, and I sat by Tanya, held her tight as she sobbed and cried and melted in her pain. I kissed her forehead, rubbed her back, tried to think of something, anything to say, but of course there was nothing that could bring him back nor anything to soothe the pain. Why had I ever returned? What had I ever expected to find here?

Minutes later the *dezhurnaya* returned, bearing two glasses of steaming tea, all the while muttering, *"Byedniki, byediniki."* She set the tea by the bed, came over to Tanya, a near stranger, stroked her head, and said, "You're hurt, too. Look at your pretty face all red and scratched. Have you seen a doctor?"

Tanya nodded.

"Good. Now, do you have family here?"

She silently shook her head.

"Not even a babushka?"

Tanya grimaced, bowed her head in sharper pain, managed to reply a sorrowful, *"Nyet.* My mother lives in Murmansk."

The *dezhurnaya* turned to me and ordered, "Then you must take care of her. Do you understand, *molodoi chelovek?* She needs to see someone about that nasty scrape. It's your job to make sure she's all right."

"Yes, of course."

"Now, get her to drink this tea. It's nice and hot and has lots of sugar—I put in all I have, all I've been saving. She needs it. She's been crying so much and had such a horrible shock. Imagine, someone hitting such a pretty woman and then killing her husband. *Bozhe moi."* My God. *"Molodoi chelovek,* you take her home and get her cleaned up and into some clean clothes. *Bozhe,* she's filthy. You take her home and stay there with her. Get her into clean clothes and make sure she's not alone. You must take care of her."

"Of course."

"If you want more tea, just let me know. I might be able to find a couple more spoonfuls of sugar." She shook her head. *"Byedniki, byedniki. Kakoi kashmar."*

*"Spacibo bolshoiye."* Thank you very much, I said.

The warm, domineering, and opinionated *dezhurnaya* was well on her way to becoming everyone's grandmother, that was to say a typical babushka, and she slipped out, muttering about chaos and food prices and so much crime, oi, oi, oi. When the door clicked shut, I reached for one of the thin, clear glasses, held it near the top, just by the rim as I'd long ago been taught, and passed it to Tanya.

"Drink some," I said.

She carefully took the steaming glass, and her tears were literally dropping into the tea as she sipped. Going into the bathroom, I unwound a good amount of toilet paper, blew my own nose and wiped my eyes, then uncoiled a whole wad of it and brought it back to Tanya. She set down the glass, then began blotting her face. She started to say something but it came out all garbled, didn't make any sense. Reaching for the tea, she took another long sip.

"First they made me see the doctor, and she thought I'd probably been hit with the same gun that was used to kill Lev," she finally said. "And then I was at the police station for hours. It was awful. Just awful. They didn't want me to leave, but they were sick of my demanding that they do something."

"What did say?"

She shrugged. "Just like the *dezhurnaya,* that it was mafia. At first they weren't very nice. There was this police captain. He said it had to have been mafia business, that Lev had to have been one of them." She wiped her nose. "They asked me all sorts of questions, pressed me on all sorts of things like money changing. They didn't believe I didn't know anything about the mafia, they just kept pushing and saying that Lev was one of them and that it was just all a fight."

Tanya started crying again. There was nothing I could do but sit close by and hold her and rub her back.

"Finally," she continued, "I convinced them that Lev wasn't a mafia man, that he didn't belong to some gang or whatever. I said, yes, he was changing some money, a few dollars, but that was all. Nothing else. No big stuff, as they claimed."

"So what are they going to do?"

"I don't think anything."

"What?"

"The police—they're afraid of the mafia. They might look around a little and ask a few questions, but why should they get themselves killed? The mafia's everywhere. They run this city now." She shook her head. "Besides, if someone is killed doing something illegal, then they really don't care. They'd just as soon see all the criminals kill each other. It makes their job easier.''

"But Lev's not a criminal. Besides, you said everyone was changing money.'' I shook my head, muttered, "This whole country's a mess.''

Then again, as Tanya suggested, the police were probably first and foremost looking for an excuse not to pursue this, for I could only imagine how underpaid they could be, particularly in comparison to a bunch of crooks. I doubted if the *militsiya* were making as much as fifty thousand rubles a month—not even fifty bucks—so why should they risk their necks against a bunch of thugs who were making millions? Thinking about it, though, I was sure the police could be bribed. During the Communist regime, they'd do extra favors for such "gifts" as crystal glasses or maybe even something so extravagant as a color television. Now they'd certainly jump through hoops for extra money, particularly dollars. Wouldn't anyone in a country where inflation roared at more than 2,000 percent per year?

"Tanya, if you want, I could pay them,'' I suggested. "The police, I mean. I could pay them dollars to pursue an investigation. That would get them moving, wouldn't it?''

She shrugged, leaned over, kissed me on the cheek. "Maybe they'd do something. Maybe they wouldn't.'' She looked away, seemingly lost in thought. "I . . . I . . . .''

"What?''

"They really don't have much to go on—no weapon or anything. I mean, if there was something really to pursue, then it might be worth it.'' Tanya shook her head. "Alex, I don't know. All they have is what I saw, and that certainly isn't much.''

Her words plucked a familiar tune and all of a sudden I knew how this might play out, and I asked, "What are you talking about?''

"Lev was falling to the ground just as I came around the corner.'' She disappeared back into that moment, that horrible scene. "He'd already been shot.''

Trying to picture what had happened, I asked, "What else did you see? Was there anyone else? There had to be someone, probably the person who killed him.'' I slowed down. "Think back to that time, did you see anyone or hear anything?''

"Not really.''

"What do you mean?'' I pressed.

"Well, I kind of saw someone.''

"What did he look like?"

"Just black. Just a large black mass." She bent forward, touched her cheek. "There was this big dark shape that came lunging out of nowhere. He struck me."

"But his face? Surely you must have seen something."

"I . . . I don't know. I don't remember."

I backed off, gently coaxed, "Tell me what you do remember, Tanya."

"Falling to the ground. Looking across the courtyard. Seeing . . . seeing Lev there, dropped in a heap."

"What else?"

"A roar."

"Their car?"

"*Da.*"

"They must have sped out the other side of the courtyard." I thought of Maddy, how she could midwife information into the conscious world, and I tried to mimic her soft, coaxing tact, her suggestive tone of voice. "What did the car look like?"

Tanya turned to me, her face blank. "The police asked the same thing. I don't know, Alex. If I saw something, I can't remember."

Frustrated, she started to cry again. I wrapped my arm around her, pulled her gently toward me. That information was hidden away inside her. I sensed it. Knew it. The only clue as to the identity of Lev's killer was stuck somewhere in her subconscious. It was just a matter of loosening things, bringing that image back up. And I, of all people and after all this time and these odd tales, knew how that could be accomplished. I'd been there before, of course.

"Tanya, my sister uses hypnosis in a very special way," I began. "She uses it to reexamine things that people have witnessed. Like a crime. It's very common for a victim to block out a traumatic incident. It's just too painful to recall. So Maddy puts people into a trance, makes sure they feel safe, then regresses them to that time, to that incident, and then they can look at what happened. It works too. Most of the time you pick up on new things. It's sort of a controlled recreation, and it helps you remember what you actually saw."

She sat back, pondered the idea, looked at me a tad oddly, asked, "You want to hypnotize me?"

"No," I replied. "I mean, I could, but I think there's someone better right here in St. Petersburg. He's a specialist in hypnosis. I was supposed to see him anyway. He's the man Maddy wants me to meet with. He's a friend of hers." Not even suspecting how wrong this could be, what trouble this would lead to, I said, "His name's Pavel Konstantinovich Kamikov."

"The one you told me about." She nodded. "The one with the TV show."

"Yes, and I'm sure he'd do it. I'm sure he'd put you under and help you remember what you saw."

As if she was catching a glimmer of all the trouble that lay ahead, Tanya didn't answer for a long time. She just sat there, looking out the large glass window and into the darkness outside and beyond that lay so thickly over the Bay of Finland.

"Lev was so different," said Tanya. "Even when we were students, he wanted a different world, something quite different from the Leninist one that had always been dictated to us. Maybe it was because of people like you—young Americans that came in with jeans and backpacks and smiles on their faces and all those nice white teeth. Maybe it was because of the BBC and the Voice of America. I don't know. But Lev understood there was another world out there, one where you not only could be rewarded for taking responsibility, but one where you could also question things. I mean, openly question things. And he really changed both me and my life because of that. He helped me lift up my head and see the world around me."

"Of course."

"Did you know his great dream? He just wanted to travel, did you know that? He didn't want to move away from Russia. He just wanted to go out for a while, to be let out of this enormous cage. You know, to be like you when you were a student and go from country to country. He just wanted to see the world." She bit her lip. "But now he never will."

No, I thought. Now he was seeing the universe.

Tanya sat back a bit, looked at me, and said, *"Da, da, da.* Let's do it, this hypnosis stuff. If I don't, I'll always be looking at a black screen, wondering what I really saw and who could have done this to Lev. I'll always wonder why he was killed by the change he wanted so much."

# Chapter 9

Just as I'd been commanded by the key lady at the Pribalt, I took care of Tanya. Before leaving the hotel, I stopped at one of the dollar bars and bought a carton of orange juice and some mineral water. And then we exited the hotel and were accosted by a bunch of taxi drivers, one of whom whisked us back to Tanya's apartment near Peace Square, which, since the USSR had reverted to being called Russia, had reverted to its pre-Revolutionary name of Hay Market Square, and which wasn't all that far, really, from where Lev had been slain.

After climbing the narrow staircase around and around all the way to the top floor, I unlocked her door with a huge, old steel key, then clicked on the single overhead bulb. It was a tiny flat, a garret really, one that Lev's great-aunt had lived in since the 1920s, and which, upon her death, Lev had inherited the right to rent. Lined from floor to ceiling with books, it was just a single room, with a windowless closet-turned-kitchen on the left, and on the right a bathroom so minuscule and cramped that there wasn't even room to hang a towel. But it wasn't a communal apartment—they had to share neither the kitchen nor bathroom with anyone else—and it was comfortable.

Tanya tumbled into a sort of numb daze, so much so that the sight of Lev's boots by the door and a T-shirt on the back of a chair didn't even faze her. She simply did as I commanded. I removed her raincoat, then ushered her into the bathroom, where I told her to undress and slip into a hot bath; she needed to soak away the grime of Lev's death. I sat on the couch, waiting, listening. She tossed her clothes out and onto the floor, descended into the hot water one leg at a time. I could tell Tanya barely moved, that she was just sitting still, for there was no swirling of water, no vigorous washing. After fifteen minutes I called to her, told her it was time to get out, which she slowly did, the water sprinkling off her body as she rose from the tub.

I unfolded the couch, a clunky dark brown thing, and converted it into its nightly form. Tucking Tanya under the sheets and a comforter, I lay down on top of all that bedding and next to her. Outside the single window a streetlight glowed, and I saw the ridge of Tanya, her back and side, for she had rolled away from me. I feebly reached out, awkwardly touched her on the shoulder, wondering what might be rekindled between us. There was no response, however, because there was of course nothing but our grief to consummate, and so I simply kissed her on the shoulder as if to say you're not alone. Lifting my watch to within inches of my face, I peered at the dim light of the dial. It was well after two in the morning in some time zone, just which I wasn't sure, and I felt a numbing jet lag crawl up my legs, my arms, like some hallucinatory drug.

I blinked once, remembered closing my eyes but nothing else until the following morning when there was again pounding. My eyes half opening, I realized that neither one of us had moved all night.

Her voice deep, Tanya mumbled, "Someone's here."

Lying there in my wrinkled clothes, I stared at one of the towering bookcases, then rose and opened the door. A woman was standing before me, brown hair, about the same height as Tanya, and her eyes a throbbing red. It was Tanya's closest friend, Svetlana, whom Tanya has apparently called at some point yesterday afternoon.

Sveta paid me no attention, went rushing past, heading right to the bed, and clung to Tanya. "You didn't call back like you said you would, so I went to the police station this morning!"

They hugged each other, cried, and went on and on about Lev and the police and what had happened. It was clear, of course, that Sveta would take over, that to be with Tanya was her job now, for there was certainly a myriad of things to be done. Friends and family to call. Funeral arrangements to make. The two women barely noticed me, and so I disappeared into the bathroom, its ceiling perhaps only an inch above my head, and splashed my face with cold water. Coming back into the small main room, I clearly saw that this wasn't my place, and so I told Tanya I'd be at the hotel, that perhaps we could see each other that evening, and left.

Still wearing my traveling clothes, I hadn't changed in almost two days and I looked like hell. My curly hair was flat, almost matted, my beard dark and stubbly with a couple of day's growth, and my clothes soiled and wrinkled as if I were homeless, which in a way I was. What I needed was a long, hot shower, some clean clothes, and breakfast, after which I had to call Pavel Konstantinovich Kamikov and deliver his parcel of videos. Was he expecting to see me today or not until tomorrow? I couldn't remember what Maddy had arranged, but then again, I realized, I had no idea what day it actually was anyway.

The day was bursting with sunshine and September crispness, and the random golden spires and onion domes of the city throbbed with brightness. This was an extraordinary city, an imperial capital gone to hell, but at least not ruined, for the Soviets had not done any major demolition of the historic center as they had done in Moscow; indeed, after the nine-hundred-day siege of Leningrad in World War II everything had been carefully rebuilt according to Peter the Great's plan. Feeling as if I were suffering from a severe hangover, I sat silent in the taxi that took me across narrow canals and past endless palaces and kilometers of iron grillwork. Nor, I thought, noticing the drab buildings, had the city been destroyed by Western commercialism, though I wondered how much longer it could hold out on that account.

Bursting out of a narrow street, the taxi raced on to a large square, past the Astoria itself, past St. Isaac's Cathedral and the Bronze Horseman—Catherine the Great's statue to Peter the Great—then across the Neva and back to the Pribalt. At the most distant end of the vast island, the driver dropped me near the base of those broad granite steps in front of the hotel, and in quite a daze I made my way up and toward the front doors. This morning instead of accosting me with their souvenirs and tins of caviar, the eager hawkers waved a friendly greeting.

Right in front of the large hotel there was another road, a curving drop-off lane not for taxis, not for regular cars, but reserved only for the most special of guests. I wondered what the pecking order was, who was allowed to drive right up to the building, and I glanced to the left, saw a pale gold Mercedes. Was this, could this be, the same vehicle I'd seen at the airport and then on the road back into town? It was quite possible. Then again, foreign cars were less and less rare. There might actually be two such Mercedes here in St. Petersburg. And leaning against the trunk was the driver, a huge guy, bald and wearing a gray suit with an open white shirt. I stopped, stared at him. He was picking at the fingernails on his right hand, and I saw from the year tattooed on his knuckles—a peculiar Soviet custom—that he was born in the forties. Looking up at me, he wiped his nose on the back of his hand, then went around, opened up the driver's door, and climbed in.

I passed through the dim lobby, rode the elevator with two extraordinarily tall prostitutes who were obviously extraordinarily eager to do anything for the sake of a dollar. I ignored their smarmy smiles, their feigned laughter, and pondered again if my room was bugged or if in fact I was being followed. It was possible, I supposed, but I just couldn't imagine why someone would be interested in my doings. What would be the point?

*"You tell me."*

I didn't know, couldn't imagine why I would be so important to anyone here, or what they could learn from me. It just didn't make sense. After all, I wasn't an employee for the U.S. government, or anything like the CIA.

*"No, but this paranoia is something you keep coming back to. Why?"*

Russia was a strange place, many layered, darkly secretive.

*"But did something happen to you when you were studying there, Alex?"*

No, it couldn't be connected to that.

*"To what?"*

To the two men in the dark suits. The ones who'd come and visited me after my college trip to the Soviet Union.

*"Go ahead, Alex. Explain that. Everything's fine. In this hypnotic version of your trip, you are completely safe."*

I thought back to my student days. After Leningrad I'd been in Moscow for nearly a week. While there I'd met a refusenik, a would-be Soviet Jewish emigrant who'd been denied an exit visa, and he'd given me an envelope, a thick one, to take back to America, which I'd dutifully smuggled out.

*"And?"*

And back home I'd mailed it off, just as I'd been asked. Two weeks later these two guys had appeared on my doorway, waving official badges of some sort, and it was only then that I realized that the envelope hadn't contained a collection of short stories as I'd been told, but scientific data.

The elevator chimed at my floor, and I stepped out of the lift and then exited the glass-enclosed elevator lobby. Yes, I needed to consider that which had happened so long ago. I hadn't realized how stupid and dangerous it had been to transport those papers across the

Soviet frontier; thank God I'd been wise enough to not be further involved, for the two suited men had desperately wanted me to begin a correspondence with the refusenik.

As I passed around the corner, all that quickly slipped from my mind. I stopped still, for down the lengthy corridor I eyed the *dezhurnaya*—though definitely from the same mold, there'd been a shift change and this was a different lady—and a dark figure standing next to her. I studied them without moving, at first certain that the second person, the one standing there, was one and the same, the very spy I'd chased in my hypnotic dream. But then I realized I was all wrong, that this was the real thing, that these were actual people, not some fantasy figures, which in turn made me wonder if that tall, bulky figure down there was a real spy.

I didn't really much care, for I was way too tired, and as I started forward I could now see that the person talking to the *dezhurnaya* was in fact a man. And as I approached them, there was no funny stuff. The man did not suddenly dart off nor did the key lady, her hair gray, face broad and etched with lines, pretend that she knew nothing. Instead, the two of them heard me coming, looked my way. The woman slipped on her glasses, studied me. Perhaps it was the shoes that told her.

She asked, "Are you the *Amerikanets* who arrived yesterday afternoon?"

I nodded, replied, *"Da."*

"Well, there," she said to the man standing next to her. "The mystery's solved. Here's your missing man."

The man, tall and balding with a scruffy gray beard, quickly demanded, "Are you Alex Phillips, brother of Dr. Phillips?"

I nodded, wondering what this was all about.

*"Slava boga."* Thank God, he said with a hearty laugh. "I was afraid something had happened to you. I'm Dr. Pavel Kamikov. I called and called, but you weren't in your room. So I came this morning and the maid said your bed wasn't slept in. Where have you been all this time, my friend? I was so worried that something happened to you. Nothing did, did it? You're all right, aren't you? I promised your sister I would keep a very close eye on you."

He took my hand in both of his and pulled me forward, wrapping himself around me and embracing me as if I were a long-lost brother who'd returned from somewhere terribly distant like the moon or California. I flinched, wasn't sure why I felt so uncomfortable. It wasn't merely that I automatically knew he was as overbearing as most Russians tended to be, reaching into your life and wanting total influence and control at the expense of all other friends. No, there was something more, something very disturbing about this man. He pressed me against his large stomach like a lover, kissed me on my cheek in a most un-Westernly greeting, and I sensed it, felt a deep, resonating hum emerging from his body, slipping out of his chest. Yes, I knew, that was where he would be shot. In the lower part of his chest, right above this big gut. It wouldn't kill him at once. Rather, he'd suffer a wound, stagger a bit, wonder why and what and then moan and collapse quite dead.

*"You can flash forward if you like, Alex. You can move to that scene, that time,"* suggested a faraway voice that was actually very close. *"Who would want to shoot this man?"*

Many people would. With reason, too. But I couldn't move forward to that time because there was too much that needed to be explained. Too much yet to tell.

*"Of course,"* uttered the oddly impatient one. *"So this man embraced you, and then?"*

I pulled away from him, said, "A friend had trouble last night."

A great look of concern washed over his face, and he took me by the arm, started walking me down the corridor to my room. He was a savvy Russian, of course. Not that all Russians wouldn't understand what I meant by that, but he could tell this was serious. If you said a friend had trouble, you usually whispered it, for historically that meant big trouble, something connected with the authorities, usually the KGB, and too often incarceration.

He glanced back to make sure the *dezhurnaya* couldn't hear and asked, "What happened?"

The words fell numbly from my mouth as I said, "One of my friends was killed."

Pavel's big, jowly face paled. *"Shto?"* What?

Stopping in front of my room, I told him what had happened. How we'd gone to change money and Lev had been shot to death. How Tanya had gone with the police. How she'd come to me later on.

*"Ewzhas."* How terrible, he muttered, shaking his head in despair. "My country is lost right now. St. Petersburg is somewhere between your Wild West and your gangster Chicago in the thirties. Everyone's killing everyone. Lord help us."

Then a diatribe of mother language came flowing out of his mouth, a long string of crude swearing that came so rapidly I understood only a few things. I caught the word *mother* a couple of times. Four *fuck*'s. And a lot of *hell*'s. Pavel further went on to say a lot more about the disorder that had descended upon all of Russia, and how the Communists were sure to come back just because people were tired of being hungry and scared. He went on and on, shaking his head as he buttonholed me against the door of my room.

"You can't believe how dangerous the streets are now," he ranted. "Six months ago we had a bomb threat at the television studio. It was some gang trying to force me to accept their 'protection.' Fortunately, I have a cousin in the business—a very good man—and now I'm under his *kreesha.*" His roof. "But that's just the way it is now. You can't do normal business without being under someone's *kreesha.*"

I took my plastic key card but didn't open my door. If I let him in, I sensed, I'd get only an ongoing lecture on the political dangers facing the country as well as his own personal plan to fix things. And there was nothing I hated more than being talked at.

So I cut him off, saying, "Pavel, I have to take a shower and change. I've been wearing the same clothes for two days now."

"What? Oh, sure," he said as if he hadn't noticed.

"I'll meet you downstairs in half an hour," I told him. "How about getting something to eat? We can talk more then."

"Sure, sure. I didn't have much breakfast either."

I escaped into my room, where I peeled off my old clothes as if I were shedding a dreaded skin. And then I just stood beneath the hot spray of the shower, letting the water pound and beat some sort of reality back into me. I was jet-lagged, there was no doubt about it, and I just kept repeating it was morning and this was Russia. And Lev was dead. Yes, I thought. There would be more violence too. A dark cloud was lingering on the edge of my mind.

Glad to not only be getting rid of them, but to be accomplishing something, I unpacked the fifteen videos my sister had sent, then dropped them into a Marshall Field's shopping bag I'd brought along just for this. Once again, my sister's generosity amazed me, for they were all just-released movies, from *A Few Good Men* to *A River Runs Through It* and *Unforgiven*. At some ridiculous cost she'd even managed somehow to get her hands on a copy of *Alladin,* which wasn't due to be released until next month. Sure, Maddy was loaded, but this package of videos had to have cost a bundle, well over a thousand bucks. What, I wondered, was she getting out of this, besides a devoutly loyal friend?

I found Pavel downstairs in the glitzy store, the Russian Star, a new and, to my amazement, private store that accepted only *valuta,* hard currency. I stopped, took note of the new Russia. This was all decidedly different from before, when hard-currency stores were not only government-operated but restricted to Westerners only. Now apparently anyone with *valuta* could shop here, and Pavel was wandering about as if this were the way things had always been, a plastic shopping basket casually filled with a carton of cigarettes, a fifth of Johnnie Walker, and a handful of precious chocolate bars. Noticeably absent were the typical lacquer boxes, the rows of nesting dolls, the racks of dangling amber necklaces, and I watched Pavel as he zeroed in on a gleaming display of German washing machines.

Carrying the shopping bag of videos, I passed a full wall of blue jeans, came up behind him, and said, "Things have changed a lot since I was last here. They never sold anything like Western clothing or refrigerators."

He shrugged his shoulders, made a low grunt as if to intimate things had changed and then some a billion times over, next nodded toward the fridge, and said, "This isn't a bad price."

I only saw that the cost was marked in dollars, which meant real things still cost real money. Still there was progress. He, a Russian, was allowed in here, after all. I remembered how as a student I'd dressed Tanya up as an American—complete with a backpack, running shoes, and yellow slicker—and snuck her into a Beriozka, one of the Soviet souvenir stores, showing her what was available to foreigners but not Russians.

"Here," I said, handing him the bag full of movies. "This is from Maddy. Enjoy." And then I added, "Let's eat."

He peered into the bag, taking a quick, eager look, and his eyes opened wide in excitement, as he exclaimed, *"Gospodi,* how wonderful!" As furtively as a spy, he quickly closed the bag lest someone notice all this loot, recovered, and said, "Yes, you must be starved. I must feed you."

Like a giddy kid, Pavel hurried to the cash register by the door, where he paid for his cigarettes and chocolate. Standing behind him, I studied a rack of postcards, noted that not only were they interesting photographs of the Winter Palace, the Peter and Paul Fortress, and the countless other treasures of this city, but they were beautifully printed on good paper stock. None of the typical shabby stuff that had littered the Soviet Union. Impressive. Looking around at this beautiful, clean store, I felt like I was looking at this country through stereo glasses, one eye seeing the present Russia, the other still seeing the old one, and both eyes together trying to form a new vision of this tortured land.

Another surprise: the wad of U.S. dollars in Pavel's wallet. I peered over his shoulder as he went to pay for his goods, and I saw that his wallet was stuffed with more dollars than I would ever carry at any one time. I was amazed. He had to have been toting around nearly a thousand bucks—well over a year's wage and a veritable fortune by Russian standards—and I wondered not only where it came from but where he changed his money, if he dashed into dark courtyards as poor Lev had done. Or did he have a bodyguard do all his street work? In any case, he was an exceedingly rich man, which definitely made me more nervous than it did impressed. Sure, he was a big guy. A *sheeshka* of sorts. But that didn't really explain—

*"Sheeshka?"*

A pinecone.

*"A what?"*

A big cheese. He had a television show, so maybe that's where he obtained all that cash. It made me uncomfortable, however, just the sight of a Russian with so much *valuta,* for in earlier days only the biggest black marketers and racketeers dared to carry funds like this, an offense that landed many in jail for the horrendous state crime of speculation. Perhaps such thinking was all just a bit too Soviet of me, but I knew it wasn't. This was a clue. Yet another piece of a complicated puzzle.

*"And what does the larger picture show?"*

That Pavel was exceedingly well connected, which would come out later, all in due time, for we moved on, passing through the broad lobby and to the other side of the hotel, where we ate at the Scandinavian Table. It was a breakfast buffet, a smorgasbord of the morning, and a woman sat in the doorway collecting not rubles, but again dollars, marks, krona, francs, or anything. Any kind of *valuta.* Just not rubles.

Pavel insisted on paying with his dollars, which made me feel uncomfortable; did he want me to feel indebted to him? It only cost five bucks, but that was an absurd sum by Russian standards—some five thousand rubles or nearly the average monthly pension of a retired person. Still, he wouldn't have any other way, and I shrugged and moved on, enticed by what lay ahead because I hadn't eaten anything since the last of many meals on the flight over. My stomach growled. This was a good spread of food, from hot cereals to stewed fruits, fried eggs, chopped cabbage and beets, to meat and cheese and blini.

When I came to a tray of thick, sweltering sausages and eyed them, however, Pavel leaned over and whispered, "I'd advise against taking one of those, my friend. I had a German visitor not long ago, and he ate such a piece of meat. We nearly lost him.''

Appreciating the advice, I nodded, moved on, next stopped at a large block of yellow cheese, took a few slices, and moved on to the blini. A cute young woman dressed in kitchen whites from toe right to the top of her tall chef's hat was just delivering a hot batch of the raised pancakes. She had china-pale skin, blue eyes, light brown hair, a broad face, and she smiled sweetly at me.

"They look very fresh," I said. "Are they good today?"

She nodded, looked quite proud, but said nothing as she gently put three on my plate. I squinted to see the name that was sewn on the upper left of her robe, and saw instead the Russian letters: PECTO-PAH. How terribly Soviet and original: restaurant.

"Oi, blini," said Pavel, next to me. "My favorite. They're quite excellent here. Almost as good as my babushka used to make. And this hotel is known to have good sour cream too."

He lifted his plate toward the tray, and the young woman started to offer Pavel several of them. Then, however, their eyes met. No, rather their eyes struck in a moment of shocked recognition. All at once the woman's face flushed red. She flinched and quickly dropped the blini back on the tray, tried to say something, but nothing emerged from her trembling lips. She tried again to speak but the words again stuck not in her throat but in her mouth.

Pavel nudged me, said, "Just move on, Alex."

I did, and we slipped on down the line of food and toward the sliced black bread. Taking a piece, I glanced back, saw the young woman standing there, staring after Pavel, her eyes beading with tears.

In a deep, almost stern voice, Pavel said, "Don't pay any attention, Alex."

I couldn't help myself, not to mention that I didn't care for the way Pavel was nudging me along, and so I checked her way again. The young woman in the kitchen whites now stood flat and solemn against the wall, her eyes aimed at Pavel as intently as an assassin's rifle.

*"Wait, Alex. Think of what you're saying. What do you mean by that?"*

There was no missing either her anger or her hostility. She wanted to harm him as much as . . . as . . .

*"As?"*

It popped into my mind: As much as he had harmed her. I took note of her silky brown hair, that shapely figure with the large breasts and trim waist, and wondered how and where she and Pavel had met.

*"But why would she want to harm him?"*

It would only become clear later. Later in the stairwell of Pavel's building. Only then would it all fall into place.

Next to me, Pavel grinned and said, "I see you like our bread."

"What? Oh yeah, it's great."

I'd been missing the taste of true black bread for years—so moist, so sour—and I'd loaded my plate with more than I could probably eat. Next I poured myself tea from a huge samovar, then made my way to a table. The room was nearly filled, and all around I heard German and French, some Italian, a little bit of British English, but no Russian. Pavel and I sat down at a far table.

Immediately he peered again into the Marshall Field's bag of treasures, which he'd placed on the chair next to him, and said, "You have the most wonderful sister." He flipped through the videos, grinned, and looked up. "She even sent *Universal Soldier*. How very, very generous of her." He glanced again in the bag and a puzzled expression washed over his face. "I don't know this one, though. *Home Alone 2*. Can you recommend it, Alex?"

"It was very popular," I mustered, though I didn't much care to see a little kid clobbering others with irons, etc.

Unfolding his napkin, a glowing Pavel pronounced, "She's so beautiful, so smart. I was in Chicago four years ago, as I'm sure you know. There were three others in my delegation, and all of us fell in love with your Maddy. But I've been the only lucky one to keep in touch with her. Perhaps it's not only our interest in hypnosis, but our love of movies. You know we've been communicating via electronic mail, don't you?"

"Of course." Reluctantly, no begrudgingly, I added, "Practically the first thing she does every morning is check her computer for E-mail."

"Well, we have a lot in common, lots to talk about. And for me it has been great. You have no idea how fabulous it's been to communicate with a colleague in the West. We've been discussing theories, cases, and it's all so easy. I just type her a note on my computer and zap it off to her."

I saw the glimmer in his eye and knew that my sister had done it again. She, who was so differently abled, seemed so able to leapfrog past people's defenses and touch them, almost by surprise. Yet despite or perhaps because of the affectionate way he spoke of Maddy, I couldn't help but eye Pavel distrustfully.

"I enjoy your sister so very, very much." He slathered a piece of bread with butter, spreading it like a master painter. "And, frankly, I've never known of a blind person to cope as well as she. Or maybe that's simply the difference between Russia and America. Maybe it's just easier there."

"Well," I said, not quite sure how to reply, "Maddy has always been very determined."

After applying the requisite butter, though not as much as Pavel, I took a bite of the bread. Relished it. No, my memory hadn't deceived me. This put American bread to shame.

"Tell me, is she still jogging?" he asked. "Frankly, I couldn't believe it until I saw her. Hardly anyone runs for their health here, let alone a blind woman. She's just so amazing."

I stared at him. Oh, shit. Oh, crap. Of course he knew she was sightless because Maddy had lost her vision so long ago. But did he not know one little thing, namely that event that had taken place since his Chicago visit? Was he not aware of that big bus, that one that had struck down my sister? I stared at him. No, of course not.

"So is she still so active?" he repeated.

I didn't know what to say. I only knew I'd give Maddy hell about this when I got home. But why this deceit? What game were the two of them playing?

For now I only managed, "Absolutely."

"You must tell her when you return how disappointed I am that she didn't come over with you," continued Pavel. "I really wanted to show her all that I'm doing here. The television program, I mean. She would be most impressed. We've even just completed my first television commercial, which will air this week—you have to see it, it's wonderful—and do you know I recently sold the foreign rights to both Mexico and Thailand? I'll have to show you everything so you can tell her. Actually, I'll have some videotapes of my program and the new commercial transferred to your system of machine. And I want to send her some of our Russian movies that have been dubbed in English. We've produced some really good films, even in the Soviet times. She'll love them."

"I'm sure."

More than that I couldn't muster because I was incensed by her. My sister. What a geek. That Pavel didn't know of her confinement to a wheelchair was proof again that her island estate was nothing more than a grand place for her to hide, a gilded prison in which she had freely imprisoned herself.

He peeled a hard-boiled egg, stuffed the entire white orb in his mouth. "Of course, I'm eager for her to learn about what we're doing here with hypnosis. Since all the changes in my country, it's become very popular."

I didn't quite get what was going on between these two, Pavel and my sister, but in any case right now there was something far more pressing, and I said, "About my friend who was killed. Tanya, his wife, was there when it happened. Or rathei she walked in on it. She saw something but she's not sure what. I think she needs some help."

"Such as hypnosis, perhaps?"

"That's what I was thinking."

"So you'd like some help from me?"

"If that would be possible, yes. Tanya's very upset, needless to say, and she's at a loss. And apparently the police have nothing to go on. So I was thinking perhaps you could put her in a trance and try to help her recall what she witnessed."

"Sure, I could do that." Pavel placed his hands over his chest. "I'd be only too happy to help the brother of my dear Maddy. I'd—"

Pavel cut himself off, his attention apparently caught by someone behind me. I turned around, saw the young woman from the serving line carrying something and storming directly toward us. I glanced back at Pavel who didn't move, didn't flinch as she came right up to the edge of our table.

"*Radi boga,*" for God's sake, Pavel snapped at her, "when are you going to leave me alone?"

Standing there in her kitchen whites, her chef's hat blooming on top of her head, and clutching a large steaming bowl of some breakfast food, the woman volunteered nothing. I could see the fury bubbling within her, however, as her pale skin flushed a violent red.

"What's the matter?" taunted the perturbed Pavel. "Still can't quite say anything?"

With that the young woman screamed, her voice deep and full of frustration, and in one quick, vindictive motion she hurled the entire bowl right at Pavel's face, dumping hot, creamy cereal all over him.

# Chapter 10

It was a *skandal*. Pavel burst to his feet and spit out another long string of mother language, then leapt toward the young woman, and I think he would have struck her had not the manager, a huge woman bound tightly in an apron, come running over and wedged herself between the two of them. Standing behind the formidable human shield of her boss, the young girl said nothing, her lips pinched tight, face a hot red, fists clenched hard. She seemed quite pleased with herself, and I detected a defiant smirk on her face, which only made me wonder all the more what Pavel had done to enrage her.

Dripping with hot kasha, a porridge that closely resembled oatmeal, Pavel excused himself, said he had to go home and change. Quite right, for he was a mess, all this goo dripping from the bottom of his beard and streaking down his tie and shirt. It was a relief to be rid of him, I realized, for I wasn't ready to jump into this friendship. Not yet. He wanted to get together that night for dinner, but I declined, said I had to see my friend Tanya. So we left it that I would call tomorrow morning. He hastily departed with his cigarettes, chocolate, and Marshall Field's bag, and then I continued my breakfast, which I was quite intent on eating and which I devoured with nervous relish.

Returning to my room, I called Tanya, only to speak to her friend Sveta and learn that Tanya had been summoned again to the *militsiya*. I left word that I'd stop by the apartment later that afternoon, sat on my bed for a moment, realized that if I remained in the hotel I'd either fall asleep again or, if I did manage to stay awake, go stir crazy. Glancing out the large windows and at the bay, I saw the sun shimmering in a cool fog. No, I couldn't stay here.

Grabbing a few things, I headed out. As I emerged downstairs from the hotel, I paused, zipped up my jacket, and glanced to my right, half expecting to see the gold Mercedes. There were a couple of Ford Tauruses—after Cherokees, they were, I later learned, the most popular vehicles in Russia—but the gold vehicle wasn't there. Then all at once, a handful of men rushed me. I flinched, not understanding at first that they were taxi drivers, all of whom were soliciting my business in dollars. Or, was I German, one of them asked, for he'd gladly accept deutsche marks. Not trusting such brazen business dealings, not knowing what you could or could not do here in these times, I brushed them off, moved on. And quickly learned that the farther I got from the front door of the hotel, the cheaper the cost of a taxi, so much so that the price for a ride into the center of town plummeted from twenty to five dollars.

Russian cities hadn't been decimated by suburbanization as in America, and when I had the driver drop me off near the Aeroflot office at the start of Nevsky Prospekt, the sidewalks were swarming with activity, for the center of the city was still a thriving heart. I didn't know what to make of any of this—Lev, my visit, this new Russia— and I spent the afternoon strolling along and trying to absorb these new times in this strange place. Everything was the same but different. There were no new buildings, of course, but there was a small handful of new stores with display windows boasting Western clothes, foreign beers, and cosmetics from different, distant lands. The people on the street, however, all seemed to be carrying only the precious basics— scrounged treasures from toilet paper to soap—and yet I was amazed again at how much better so many were clothed. It was obvious that in the last decade there'd been a veritable tidal wave of jeans and colorful jackets, running shoes and sunglasses, each article undoubtedly having been carried in one at a time by student, businessman, or truck driver and then resold on the black market.

In many other ways, as well, the city was coming alive, waking from its somber seventy years and bursting with new life. On almost every corner were young men peddling bananas from crates stamped "Product of Tunisia," and from then on I saw banana peels everywhere, mountains of them overflowing from wastebaskets on the street and swept into foot-high piles against buildings. I immediately understood that it was the rare person who could afford an entire bunch of bananas, yet it was perfectly obvious everyone had to try at least one of the heretofore unavailable treats. It was amazing. No, shocking, for on my previous trip the only fruit openly for sale were golf-ball-size green apples. A bright, clean bus passed me, the side of it painted not with "Long Live the Decision of the Communist Party!" or "Lenin Is Always with Us" but with the words "Smirnoff Vodka." And in English too. Farther on, there was an antique troika, a three-horse carriage, complete with a costumed driver, for hire. What was this, private business so brazenly taking place? Yes. And I noticed that the Museum of Anti-religion and Atheism had closed and that the Kazanski Cathedral was again a real, official church.

Dom Knigi, the House of Books, was still lodged in the old Singer Sewing Machine building and still carried the same bland assortment of wares. I ducked in, saw people milling about, looking but no one buying because even though the memoirs of Brezhnev and Lenin were gone, there really wasn't anything of interest. On the next block there were artists everywhere, their watercolors tacked to buildings along Nevsky. And on the block after that finally appeared countless tables of lacquer boxes, hand-painted eggs, and amber jewelry. So this was competition. The free market. And they knew their market, for most of the salespeople seemed to speak English or French or German and all of them were eager to sell their wares for dollars. Of course.

I walked on in shock. Any such blatant activity in earlier times would have resulted in a charge of speculation, one of the foulest of Soviet accusations, and a certain prison sentence. No, none of this had been possible before, and I stopped and just stared in amazement. In front of the crumbling department store, Gostini Dvor, hungry babushkas were selling roses, random political and religious groups were handing out leaflets and preaching their views, and any amount of money changing was taking place; guys were standing around wearing signs that read BUYING DOLLARS, DEUTSCHE MARKS, FINN MARKS, FRANCS, VOUCHERS. My head whirled. People had taken commerce literally onto the streets. In a pedestrian passageway beneath Nevsky a handful of American Christians were proselytizing, trying to convert the heathen Commies. On the steps that led back up to the street several dozen people stood cuddling puppies and kittens inside their coats; I walked past, saw all these little fury heads peeking out, heard people haggling over prices. And on a side street close by, there was an entire block of men lined up selling spare auto parts from the nearly impossible to find windshield wipers to entire fenders.

Despite this radical shift in a country that now called itself *Rossiya,* Russia, and not the *Soyuz,* the Union, despite this boom of activity that was really a desperate struggle to stay alive, it was odd how comfortable it all felt, how familiar this place seemed at every step. I must have been living here in my dreams for it to seem so fresh. I think I would have even been happy had it not been for Lev's death, which shadowed me everywhere. I would have been happy to be back here, to see how much had changed in a place, a fortress, of non-change. But that just wasn't the case. My friend was dead, and . . . and . . .

"*And?*"

Yes, there was another spirit, per se, with me. Not the spirit of Lev, but a different, trancely one. One that endowed me with a broader knowledge, a deeper wisdom. Just past the infamous Five-Step-Down Meat Store, as it was popularly known, I slowed. Among all that there was to see and take in, there was something I should have noticed back then but didn't.

"*Good. Slow it down even more, Alex. Take a deep, deep breath, and open up your mind. You have plenty of time to pause and take a good, long look.*"

I stopped by a pile of banana peels swept carefully against a lamppost, and the hurried pace of Nevsky slowed for an extended moment. I closed my eyes, tried to see beyond myself and beyond that time. I imagined myself leaning against a building, right against one of the stone bases, and taking a long, relaxing gulp of air.

"*That's right, use the special awareness that hypnosis facilitates in you.*"

I did, but no sooner was I stuck with a mesmerizing rush than that other sense wormed into my mind. That same paranoid feeling as if someone were spying upon me and noting my every move. But how did I know this, for it hadn't really happened this way, I hadn't stopped in fear as I walked down Nevsky, had I? No, of course not, so was all this merely a figment of hypnotic paranoia or was I under some form of real observation?

"*In this retelling of the story, it makes no difference. It doesn't matter whether you're only noticing now in trance that you were followed, or whether your mind at this time is simply choosing to give form to your fears. All that matters is what your mind is revealing. Don't worry whether it's truth and insight or metaphor or even pure fantasy.*"

I opened my eyes, glanced back down Nevsky.

*"And what do you see in this trance?"*

A dark figure. The very same one I'd chased through the hotel corridors. That person was now down the sidewalk. Oh, Christ. Was I just being paranoid or what? I was so lost in this that I didn't really know, couldn't distinguish. Shaking my head, I moved on, came to a store still called by its Soviet name, "Porcelain," and ducked inside. About thirty white vases sat on one shelf, twenty bowls on another. That was it, no other merchandise. The two salesclerks glanced only briefly at me before disappearing again into their conversation, something about nail polish. Stepping over to the window, I peered out, saw someone hurry by. The one who'd been following me? I didn't like this, wondered how I might have been followed all the way from the Pribalt and down Nevsky without my knowing it. Then again, there could have been two or three people in two or three cars, all rotating and confusing me. There could have been a whole team of professionals tailing me. Why in the hell had I ever taken those papers from that refusenik?

Darting outside, I turned left toward the Fontanka River, came to a tea store, and headed in. There was one counter, about forty people lined up to buy a glass of hot tea, and one disgruntled woman behind the counter filling about one glass every ten minutes. The display case that should have been resplendent with cream puffs and Napoleons, cheese sandwiches, and maybe even some salami, was virtually empty except for three plain cookies. I noted all this as I hurried for the door at the far end of the room, and dashed back outside.

This was just like old times, I thought, when the KGB lurked around every corner and on the edge of everyone's fears. About a half block later I pressed myself into a doorway, stood there. Waited. No one came. No dark figure appeared. Like one of Dostoyevski's deluded characters, I scurried on, not sure what I was running from and not sure where I was running to, but fearful, even certain that something quite awful was to soon take place. I checked behind me three or four more times, saw no one, nothing. There didn't seem to be any familiar cars either. Nothing slowly circling by, hovering like a determined vulture waiting to strike. I was tempted to jump on a bus, let myself be whisked off, but when an electric trolley bus hummed up to a stop, it was so utterly and totally packed there was no way I could get on. The doors opened, two men fell out, and four young kids pried their way in. The doors then struggled but could not close, people started hollering, and two of the kids were ejected. Tilting to one side, the bus which looked every bit a refugee transport finally hummed off to a troubled fate.

Pulling up the collar of my jacket, I hurried on down Nevsky, for it seemed that for now at least I was safe, that somehow I'd lost my tail. I didn't know where I was going, really, what I was doing. Or when I'd next encounter the spy and perhaps learn what all this was about.

*"This truth will be clear to you when you're ready to see it,"* mystically called a voice.

Oh, brother, I thought, rolling my eyes.

Crossing the waters of the Fontanka, I stopped yet again, stared behind me and past the four statues of the horses. I could discern nothing in the throng of people. Once again nothing in the least suspicious. All that was left to do, I supposed, was to push back into the story. I had to wander for a few more hours and hope that Tanya would soon return from the police station. So I just kept going, heading up Nevsky toward the Moscow train station. I passed a theater, a closed art gallery, a women's clothing store cleverly called Dom Moda, House of Fashion.

Disappearing into reflection, I was carried onward with thoughts of Russia, of Tanya, of Lev, and suddenly I looked up. Right before me was the circular subway stop that sat kitty-corner from the train station, the one we'd passed on the way in from the airport. I paused on the corner in front of a gift shop, The Heritage, and watched as this constant mass of humanity swarmed into and out of the subway station. I thought of going in, buying a token—the price had risen 300 percent from five kopeks to fifteen rubles—then climbing on the ridiculously long escalator and letting myself be carried down and down and down as if into a very deep hypnotic state. But my eye was caught by the market behind the station. Crossing the street, I headed over there, circled the metro building, and passed between makeshift stands selling yet more bananas from Tunisia, tomatoes, potatoes, and assortments of exotic mushrooms, the likes of which probably could not be found in the States. On the other side, lined against one wall, stood a row of temporary kiosks, hawking everything from plastic sandals from Vietnam to Snickers to West cigarettes.

I noticed something down the side street. It was the store Tanya had pointed out, the one called Springtime Beauty Salon. That was where Tanya and Lev's store was supposed to go. Right in that space. Curiosity pulled me out of the small marketplace and down the sidewalk so I could get a better look. The large glass windows were papered over, but, yes, it was obvious this was a great location. People from the subway would surely spill this way, would surely be attracted to visions of bright new clothes from the West. How could a store in this location not succeed in a country as hungry for jeans as it was for meat?

But what now? Tanya and Lev's dreams had been shot, their hopes for the future spilled all over the cobblestones of that courtyard. Yes, Tanya could carry on. Rather, she probably would, knowing her and her determination. She'd more than likely push harder than ever to make sure the store became a reality. Really, my only question was whether Lev's death might interfere in the difficult process of opening it.

Out of the corner of my eye, I noticed something swooping my way, and I flinched, stepped back around the corner. No, it wasn't my feared tail, the phantom spy. Rather it was a car. A gold Mercedes, gleaming as if it were cleaned and polished twice a day. I knew it then. Of course this was the same vehicle that had followed us from the airport. And of course it was the same one that I'd seen outside the Pribalt. I didn't like this, didn't care to be in the same orbit with such a dark star.

Having myself become the spy, I stayed deep in the shadows, my attention totally focused on the Mercedes. This was no coincidence, this car turning down the very street of Tanya's proposed store. That meant all this was more tangled than I could have imagined, and I watched as the vehicle slowed to a gentle stop in front of the defunct beauty shop. The driver climbed out, and it was him, that bald thug I'd seen leaning against the trunk of the car in front of the hotel. He bounded up a couple of steps and disappeared into the store. Seconds later he emerged, followed by a short, gray-haired man in a blue suit, one that was as expensive-looking as it was undoubtedly Western.

*"Alex, are these the men from the stairwell of Pavel's building?"*

I couldn't move, couldn't say a thing, for these two guys were steering a third person, a woman, out of the store and toward the car. I should have gone chasing after her, but I was just so stunned. I simply stood there in the shadows of St. Petersburg as Tanya was stuffed into the back of that gold Mercedes and hustled off.

# Chapter 11

I panicked. Only the mafia had such princely cars in such a godfor-saken country. Rushing into the street, I caught a last glimpse of the Mercedes, spotting Tanya wedged in the backseat next to the guy with the gray hair. Sick with fear, I stood in the middle of the pavement, one hand in my hair, not knowing what had just happened and not knowing what to do next, as the car disappeared around the corner.

It had to be organized crime. It could be nothing less. So could this possibly mean those two men were somehow connected to Lev's murder, possibly even responsible for it, and were they now swooping down upon Tanya for the final kill? Or was Tanya not to be harmed right away, had she just been simply, horribly kidnapped?

I spun around, scanned the empty street. No one else had seen what had happened. I had to call the *militsiya,* I thought, but what would I tell them, that I'd just seen a friend of mine pushed into a fancy car and driven off? They'd certainly ask if she'd been hurt, which I didn't think she had, or if I had any evidence of illegal conduct, which I didn't. So while I was certain something quite devious was at hand, that this was probably related to Lev's murder, I doubted the police would take an immediate interest. Shit, I thought. And I hadn't even gotten a license plate number.

My next thought was to rush off to the American consulate, but of course the fate of a Russian citizen would be of no interest to them. So instead I turned around, started running down the middle of the street toward Nevsky. I could catch a taxi, I thought, and hurry to Tanya's apartment. Yes, absolutely. Hopefully Sveta or some other friend would be there and they'd know whether it was best to contact the police or perhaps hire a thug of our own to go after her. Yes, it couldn't be that hard to figure out who was who. After all, there just weren't that many big gold Mercedeses buzzing around this city of five million people.

Reaching the broad Nevsky Prospekt, I immediately started searching for a cab. There were cars everywhere, a mess of trucks and buses as well. A little green taxi suddenly shot by like a speeding gnat. I nearly leapt in front of it, but the driver only swerved and didn't stop. Why? He'd had no passenger. Did I with my frantic look, my disheveled clothing, my desperate eyes, no longer look that foreign? Had he mistaken me for one of his own? Another taxi whooshed by, that one full. Then another, that one also loaded with passengers. A minute later two empty taxis shot right past. Crap. The drivers might have been headed home for dinner, they might have been off for the night, but I should have been waving dollar bills. That would have stopped them. I pulled out my wallet, grabbed a couple of bills, readied myself to flash green American gold.

And then there was nothing, an abrupt dearth of cabs as if they'd just all been plucked off the face of the earth. I eyed the light blue Moscow Station way over on the other side of the square. It was swarming with activity. Clearly a series of trains had just pulled in and the arriving mass of people was sucking up all the transport.

I spotted a nearby bus stop, saw an electric trolley loaded above and beyond capacity, the beat-up old thing sagging and barely limping along. That was useless as well, so I turned, started jogging back up Nevsky. I darted and swerved in and out of the crowd, and immediately, hundreds of eyes were upon me, because I was a most unusual spectacle, undoubtedly a dreaded *xhooligun,* running along, darting in and out of crowds. What had I stolen? Who had I hurt? Why weren't the *militsiya* chasing after me?

I paid no attention, pushed on, unzipping my jacket as my brow blistered with sweat. I spotted an old red-and-gray phone booth, realized I could call Tanya's apartment, find out who was there. Slipping into the beat-up booth, I reached for the receiver but found only a heavy, frayed wire dangling into nothingness. This was stupid anyway. The phones used to take two kopecks—the tiny coins that were always in shortage—and I had no idea what they took now. Certainly a great deal more, for if there were a hundred kopecks in a ruble and

now a thousand rubles to the dollar, that meant . . . that meant . . .
Shit, it didn't make any difference. I didn't, I realized, have any rubles
anyway.

I burst out of the booth and continued running down Nevsky,
across the Fontanka, through the crowds. Everyone stared at me as I
pushed my way along. Who was I, quizzed their stern stares, a foreigner who'd been robbed or a *farsovchik,* a black marketer, who'd
just been roughed up?

*"And then you reached Tanya's apartment?"*

Yes, it was all the way down there at the other end of Nevsky and
off to the left near Hay Market Square, which was all torn up with construction of a metro station, work that looked as if it had been going on
for twenty years. I was totally wet by the time I reached her building,
my chest heaving for air as I pushed up and up the circular stairs. And
when I reached her apartment at the top, I saw a band of light seeping
from beneath her door. I went to knock, then hesitated when I heard
voices. Could the mafia have dragged Tanya here? Possibly. They could
be searching her apartment. But I hadn't seen the car downstairs, and
besides that was Sveta's voice I now heard in there. I detected no panic
either, nothing unusual in the tone of her words, and I started banging
on the door. Immediately all was quiet inside, as if they were shocked
by the intrusion. I heard shuffling, and a moment later the door was
cracked open. Sveta hesitantly peered out, looked me up and down.

She gasped at the sight of my sweaty image, demanded, "Alex,
what is it?"

"Tanya . . . Tanya . . ." I couldn't finish because I was so out
of breath. "Something happened to her."

"What are you talking about?"

"I was down near the store, and I saw—"

"Wait. Just calm down. Don't worry."

"You don't understand. I saw her."

"But, Alex," interrupted Sveta, "she's fine. Nothing's wrong."

"What?"

"She's all right. Tanya's right here."

Svetlana pushed back the door. I blinked. Tanya was calmly
sitting on the couch, a glass of steaming tea in her hand. Next to her
was an older man, heavyset and bald. No, he wasn't one of the guys
I'd seen her with. A younger, thin man stepped out of the kitchen, face
pale, his beard scraggly, the wire-rim glasses awkwardly bent. Sport-
ing black leather boots, he was tall and imposing, but, no, he hadn't
been in the Mercedes either.

Upon seeing me, Tanya's eyes opened wide and she said, "Alex, where have you been? You look terrible."

I stared back. "How did you get here so quickly?"

"What?" she said, looking at me as if I were nuts. "Alex, this is Lev's father, Vladimir Sergeivich. He just arrived from Novgorod." The old man nodded his head, made no pretense of rising. Nor would he, for he was clearly lost in his grief and I was little more than a fly that had buzzed in for a moment or two.

"I was just down at the store," I began.

Tanya's eyes widened in alarm, and before I could say anything more, she was on her feet, hurrying toward me. Taking me by the arm, she forcibly steered me around and led me out into the dim hallway.

Closing the door behind us, in a low, whispered voice, she said, "Alex, this isn't a good time."

"What do you mean? Are you all right?"

"Of course I am."

"But I was down there. I mean, I went walking down Nevsky, and then I came to that street. I saw the store."

"What in the world are you talking about?"

"I saw you there. I saw those guys bringing you out. They had you by the arms." I felt a sudden sense of both urgency and relief, and I wanted to reach out, hold her tightly in my arms. "I thought maybe they were kidnapping you or something."

Her face was blank, no reaction. Tanya was staring into my eyes as if she were wondering what to say. My God, I thought, what was going on here? She had to know what I meant.

Tanya hesitated, finally said, "Alex, there must be some mistake. I don't understand."

Oh, fuck. Don't do this to me, I thought, just standing there. I was sure it had been her. It couldn't have been anyone else.

"Tanya, I was just down the street. I saw the Mercedes." I insisted, "They put you in the backseat and drove off."

"*Nyet,*" she said, shaking her head. "You must be confused. That must have been someone else. I haven't been at the store for days."

"What?" Dumbfounded, I stared at her. "Tanya, I just saw you. I was across the street and I saw you and those other guys."

"Alex, please. Not now. Can we talk about this later?" She motioned to her apartment. "Lev's father just arrived. He's very upset."

"But, Tanya, I recognized that gold car too," I continued, not so easily derailed. "You've been out, haven't you?"

"Sure. I was at the *militsiya.*"

"And then?"

"Then I went to the train station to pick up Lev's father."

"So you were down that way? And you were in a gold-colored car?"

"*Nyet,* Alex! Stop this . . . this interrogation! You're being like the police," she snapped back. "Lev's father just came in on the train. And . . . and Sveta's boyfriend, Igor—that's him in there—he drove us in his Zhiguli."

I bent my head forward, pressed my hand to my forehead. Had I flipped? Was I crazed with exhaustion and stress? But if that hadn't been Tanya, who had it been? On the other hand, why had she led me out of the apartment?

"Tanya, why are we talking out here in the hall?"

Tanya gently took me by the wrist, said, "Because Lev's father is a mess . . . and he's an old-time Communist. He didn't know we were trying to open a store. He hates what's happening to the country and he certainly wouldn't approve. And I don't want him to know either. Not now, not after what's happened. I don't want him to think that his dead son was a degenerate speculator. Listen, *dorogoi moi,*" my dear, "I have to get back in there. Lev's father needs me now. Can we talk later?"

I was so confused I felt nauseous. I just nodded. She kissed me on the cheek, embraced me tightly, and told me to wait there, then disappeared back into the apartment. Slumping against the wall, I shook my head. I'd been so sure that Tanya had been kidnapped, so afraid that she'd been hurt. Yet here she was, obviously fine. And saying that hadn't been her. It just didn't make any sense.

A moment later Igor emerged, a cigarette perched between his skinny lips, the heels of his black boots clicking the floor. He studied me, pushed his bent glasses up his nose, then led me downstairs, outside, and to that car of his, a beige Zhiguli. He drove me through the dank city and back to Pribalt, but we didn't talk. I was too exhausted, too confused. I hated Russia right then. I hated it for all its lies, the layers and layers of them that were piled one on top of the other. And I hated every Russian too, because they knew how to use every last one of those lies, how to pick them up and wrap themselves all snugly-secure with them.

"*Alex, be more specific,*" called that voice. "*When you look at the broader scope of this story, when you take into respect what you later learned, is Tanya telling the truth?*"

No, she wasn't, I thought as the car bumped and swerved on the way back to the hotel. I slumped down in my seat, closed my eyes. No way in hell. I closed my eyes, visualized that empty street, the defunct Springtime Beauty Salon, the blond woman being hustled out. Of course that had been her at the store in the hands of those mafia men.

So if I couldn't trust Tanya, who could I trust in all of the Russias?

# Chapter 12

I couldn't have had a stranger night. I didn't see Tanya again. No word from her. And I was too upset to call. So I stayed in the hotel. Dinner was for dollars, so the food was pretty good, though the prices absurdly, astronomically ridiculous. Something like eight dollars for a bowl of soup. Needless to say, I was the only one in the restaurant, the only one stupid enough to pay so much for the same soup that cost twenty-five cents in one of the very lively, overly crowded, and obnoxiously noisy ruble restaurants. But I was seated right away, the service was prompt, and it was as quiet as a funeral home. That was to say, I paid for my peace.

I later avoided the buzzing ruble bar on the second floor that was full of up-and-coming *biznizmeni* and *prostotootki,* and the ever-active black marketers, the *farsovchiki.* Instead I played the snotty rich American, sulking in the dollar bar on the ground floor that was empty except for the bartender and his girlfriend, who were smooching and drinking imported brandy and watching some ridiculous game show that was blaring from a color TV in the corner. Shit, a game show? Uncle Lenin must have been spinning in his tomb.

I really didn't know this country anymore, and when I returned to my room much later, my head swooning from too many gin and tonics, the phone was ringing. It was Pavel, who again berated me with his worries and concerns for my well-being. I just sat there, holding the receiver an inch or two from my ear. He'd been looking for me all day, fretting, worrying, and was everything okay? *Da, da,* I told him. And then he invited me the following morning for a taping of his television show. Only it wasn't so much an invitation as an order. A required expedition. How Soviet of him.

"You must see my program. It's wonderful, the most popular in all of St. Petersburg," he boasted. "We only do one a month, and we tape tomorrow. You must be there because I want to do a television show like this in America with your sister."

Yeah, right, I thought. Like it was that easy to get on TV in the States.

Anyway, we arranged a time, and at eleven the following morning I emerged from the hotel and found Pavel's sparkling car, a cream-colored Volvo 740 Turbo, waiting for me. The driver, a husky, silent man, opened the rear door for me, then whisked me off to a television studio on the edge of the city. It was a long, low building of glass and white stone with a huge modernistic antenna thrusting upward into the sky. Though the sprawling structure probably wasn't more than ten or fifteen years old, it was already in severe disrepair, as evidenced by streaks of rust and a boarded-up window or two.

When I tried to enter the building, I was stopped by a huge guy with broad shoulders, thick brown hair, and a gun strapped to his side. Instantly I recognized this as one of the men supplied by Pavel's cousin, placed here for protection against further bomb threats or whatever. I supposed it was necessary to be under someone's *kreesha,* someone's roof, but it was a disturbing reality of the new, free Russia.

The hulking fellow bluntly stated, "The building is closed."

Before I could say anything, a hip-looking woman with a clipboard and spiky auburn hair came darting out of a side door, shouting, "Don't be silly, he's all right. He's our American guest." She grabbed me by the arm, pulled me along, mumbling, "These security people are idiots! Now, *beestro, beestro!*" Quickly, quickly! "The show's about to start."

She dragged me along, through a door and into a vast darkened room packed with an audience. Instantly I was amazed at the similarity to an American studio, for the audience sat in a bank of chairs and all around were large cameras with cables snaking out of them. The set was simple but pleasant, a half-dozen chairs in a broad semicircle in front of some draping white curtains. I sat down, noted that most of the audience seemed to be women in their thirties and forties; really there were only about a dozen men among this group of a hundred or so. The group was all quite attractive too. Sharply dressed as well, in pleasant dresses, trendy blazers, silk blouses. Had this audience been chosen, I wondered, for its tony appearance? If so, the ugly head of marketing had wormed its way here awfully quickly.

The room was abuzz with quick, high voices, and I felt as if I were at a rock concert, as if I'd just been hurled into a bunch of groupies who were eagerly awaiting the appearance of their esteemed one. Moments later the lights went down, a tense, eager hush rolled over the audience like a thick fog, a director started counting and then: Dr. Pavel Konstantinovich Kamikov.

Dressed in a blue suit, white shirt, red tie, and with his graying hair perfectly coiffed, he magically burst through the curtains, bounding energetically into the center of the stage. A cry arose from the spectators and a great burst of applause exploded. Bowing his head in appreciation, Pavel sucked it all up, all that adoration that actually did appear spontaneous and heartfelt. He did nothing to quiet them, merely stood there as the clapping licked his ego. Finally, he reached to the side and took a microphone from a nearby stand.

"Good afternoon, Ladies and Gentlemen, and welcome to *Mesmerizing Moments,*" he said, flashing a smooth, charming smile, and stroking his gray beard. "I'm Dr. Pavel Konstantinovich Kamikov, and I'm here today to introduce you to the wonderful marvels and strange truths of the mysterious world of hypnosis."

Another crescendo of applause rose in the studio. I sat there clapping in awe and shock. This was bizarre. Not just the enthusiastic audience. Nor simply that Pavel had addressed everyone as "Ladies and Gentlemen" instead of the lugubrious but standard "Comrades." Simply, it was all so utterly Western.

"In today's show, I want to explore the unknown world of creativity," he began, turning to one of the cameras. "All of us has within us an artistic force, a creative, energetic spirit that is imprisoned deep within our souls and that is yearning, no, actually desperate to explode into life and beauty. Some of you may dream of becoming a famous actress or actor, but lack just a slight spark. Others of you may sing in the shower, believing if only given the chance to show your talents you would make records that would be incredibly popular throughout Russia. And still others wish to escape from the hustle of the city, go to your dacha, and paint beautiful landscapes that would rival the masters of the world. Well, today, my *droozya,*" my friends, he said, "I want to demonstrate how the amazing power of hypnosis can unlock that creativity, enabling all of you to enjoy the rich and beautiful fruits of your dreams."

I closed my eyes and my head whirled and twirled as I separated momentarily from that scene at the television studio. This didn't make any sense, not with what I knew beyond this place and time. I was struck with a deep premonition. Make that suspicion. Perhaps my sister and I had become telepathically linked, but I sensed that at that very moment back in the States she was exploring a similar avenue. Yes, most certainly, she had become fascinated, even obsessed with the idea of hypnotically enhancing creativity. Only she was doing something connected with tapes and such, wasn't she?

*"Yes, exactly."* My ever-elusive sister confessed, *"Pavel and I had been communicating not just about creativity, but specifically about this show. He asked me for some ideas, and then later he sent me E-mail letting me know that you'd be at the taping that day. That's what inspired me, thinking of you there on the set, seeing what I wanted to. So while you were in the studio, I was at home developing the first of the tapes on creativity."*

When I opened my eyes, Pavel's six guests were seated on the stage. Two men, four women, all very simply dressed in dresses or pants, nothing fancy. They appeared nervous, genuinely so. He introduced them—one pianist, one actress, two singers, and two painters—and the audience applauded.

Then almost on cue, everyone fell silent, for this was the much anticipated moment: the mass induction. Like an Orthodox priest bestowing a blessing, Pavel began slowly waving both hands over the group of six. I could see him close his eyes and hear him as he began to chant and moan.

Then as if speaking from a deep, mysterious dream, his voice softly but firmly commanded, "The day fades away and darkness falls, bringing night upon us all. As the sun slips away, you feel yourselves becoming relaxed and falling from this world and into a *glubokoi son.*" A deep sleep. He raised his right hand as high as he could, snapped his finger, boasted, "I hold the sun in my hand, right here. Focus on my hand. Look! Look at this point and see nothing else. This is the sun, and as it goes down, you feel yourselves incredibly and utterly relaxed." He lowered his voice, sternly ordered, "Listen to my words, hear nothing and no one else as I lead you into a deeply mesmerizing world. Follow my words as I, Dr. Kamikov, lead you into a world I control."

A woman in the audience not far from me moaned, and I glanced down the row of seats, saw her head drop forward. Checking around, I saw other members of the audience nodding off as they also tumbled into apparent trances. What was this, a collection of lost souls who regularly returned to watch his show and drop under his influence? Undoubtedly, and I understood then why this was all going so smoothly. These were Pavel's groupies, all of them, and they knew the whole routine, when to applaud, when to go into trance. They were performing as much as Pavel was.

"*Tyezhalayet . . . tyezhalayet . . .*" You're getting heavy . . . heavy . . .

His words ebbing and flowing in rhythmic, poetic chant, Pavel pushed on, lowering his hand bit by bit, chanting and calling one moment, admonishing the next. It was all terribly familiar, I thought, yet terribly foreign. Maddy was equally as powerful as this man, and perhaps in her own way every bit as manipulative. Yet as I sat transfixed by Pavel's Rasputin-like magnetism—his domineering presence, his powerful voice—I kept thinking Maddy wouldn't do it like this. Not so harshly. Not so insistent. No, my sister had a much more inviting technique, a coaxing that pulled me into a trance, gladly and eagerly, and that made me want hypnotic insight and vision and peace over and over again. Pavel's technique was more totalitarian, rather like opening a door and shoving someone down an empty elevator shaft. But then again, did it make any difference if that's what it took to get the subject to the desired state?

As his outstretched right hand came slowly down and down, he demanded, "Follow my voice! Follow the sun!"

This was all so Russian, and the further he pushed, the more I pulled away, separating and watching and analyzing. And just like a Russian Orthodox priest, he started going to each of the subjects and placing his cupped left hand upon their foreheads.

To one after the other, Pavel commanded, "You are slipping into darkness! Into another world!"

He did this to the pianist, the painters, the singers, the actress. And each of them bowed their head forward, sucking something out of Pavel as if he were administering some anesthesia or holy blessing to ward off these painful times.

When his right hand was about waist high, he snapped his fingers and ordered, "Close your eyes, fall into the deepest of trances! Come under my power!"

All but one of the subjects, a woman, the pianist, did as ordered. She sat there, eyes open in a zombiesque gaze as she stared off into nothingness, and Pavel went up to her, bent over, placing his fingers on her eyes and physically forcing her lids shut.

And directly into her ear he shouted, *"Spat!"* Sleep!

Of course she did as ordered. Her eyes dropped shut. Her head fell slightly forward. Again as if he were administering a prayer, Pavel waved his hands some more, first over the wayward pianist, next moving down the line and waving over all of them.

Finally satisfied with his sorcery, he backed away, turned to the camera, and in a low voice said, "Now all of these people have fallen into the hypnotic world. Now they are free from the worries and stresses of their lives and have fallen deep into a mesmerized trance. Here, let me show you."

With the camera trailing close behind, Pavel went up to one of the two men, a painter. The man's head was slightly tilted forward, and Pavel lifted it back, then reached to the man's closed eyes and carefully pressed back the eyelids. There was nothing but white, for the painter's eyeballs had rolled totally upward. Several in the audience expressed their amazement in murmured awes.

"Do you see?" exclaimed Pavel. "Look, nothing but the whites. The eyes have disappeared into the head. This man is exhibiting signs of a deep, deep trance." He quickly moved to the next, a woman, pried open her eyelids, and said, "And this one too. You see nothing, I repeat nothing, but the whites."

With the rolling camera right behind him, Dr. Pavel Konstantinovich Kamikov went down the line of six, peeling back the eyelids of each of his subjects and exposing nothing but the supposed proof of trance. I was as transfixed as I was horrified, shocked that he would touch them like that, so crudely, and shout how this one and this one, too, was deeply hypnotized. There were strict ethical codes about this in America that outlined the physical boundaries between patient and therapist. On the other hand, what was culturally appropriate in America was obviously different here, fundamentally so. In any case, it would be the rare American, hypnotized or not, who would let someone paw him like Kamikov was doing. Yet these subjects here in Russia didn't even flinch. Nor did anyone in the audience seem to take issue with Pavel's aggressive manner.

Pavel then turned to the audience and said, "Now that I have successfully placed these six artistic people into a hypnotic trance, I want to show you how truly creative they can be. In hypnosis they are free from the demands and concerns of their lives, the very things that prevent them from achieving their full artistic possibilities. One by one, I will show you how great a painter, how fantastic a musician, how wonderful an actress each of them truly is." Full of energy, Pavel turned to the first person in the row of chairs, a man whose head was nodding to the right, and knelt by his chair and said, "What is your name?"

The groggy man hesitated, then replied, "Ivan."

"And tell me, Ivan, what do you do?"

"I am . . . I am a painter."

"Watercolor or oil?"

"Oil."

"Ivan, you are a great painter. You have a great vision of the world. You have a brilliant sense of clarity. In fact, everyone knows that you are a greater painter than Kandinsky himself." Pavel took the man's hand between both of his, squeezed it tightly, and said, "Ivan, will you paint a wonderful painting for me?"

"*Da.*"

"Good. One of my assistants will now take you to another room. We have an easel and some paints. You will go there and paint me a wonderful painting."

"*Da.*"

The woman with the spiky hair, the one who had greeted me, stepped onto the stage, then carefully led the groggy Ivan away. Pavel next went to the other painter, a woman named Olga, who preferred watercolors, and he gave her similar suggestions of greatness. Then she, too, was led away to produce some great work of art.

"We will allow our two painter friends to do their work," continued Pavel, turning again to the audience, "and once they have completed a quick painting, we will compare that to some of their other recent work. Meanwhile, let's hear some music." He stepped over to a young woman with short dark hair. "Tell me, what is your name?"

Only her lips moved in reply.

Pavel said, "You can speak, *dorogaya.*" My dear. "What is your name?"

Her voice faint, she said, "Rita."

"And are you a musician?"

"*Da.*"

"What instrument do you play?"

"Pi . . . piano."

"I've heard you're an excellent pianist, Rita," said Pavel, bending close to her. "You are one of the best in all of Russia, certainly as good if not better than Rachmaninoff. In fact, people come from all over Europe to hear you play. Would you play something for me?"

She nodded, and instantly a grand piano was wheeled out by two men. Pavel took Rita by the hand, slowly and carefully led her over to the piano, and sat her down. With her eyes closed and her head bent forward, it appeared that Rita was lost in a deep sleep.

"Place your fingers on the keyboard, Rita," instructed Pavel.

Rita, of course, raised her hands, placed them flatly on the keys.

"You are a great musician," sternly said Pavel. "One of the greatest of our times."

The audience sat in nervous anticipation as Rita's eager but anxious fingers rose high above the ivory keyboard.

Pavel stood behind her, put his hands on her shoulders, boomed, *"Da, da, da, dorogaya,"* yes, yes, yes, my dear, "you have so much beautiful talent. Fill us with your music!"

Her eyes still closed, Rita's hands seemed stuck in the air. Then all at once, they came striking down, hitting the keyboard in a perfect chord, then taking off at lightning speed. It was obviously a Tchaikovsky piece, full of sizzle and showiness, and Rita played it with such skill and technique, not to mention confidence, that I was sure she had to be either with the St. Petersburg Philharmonic Orchestra or a full-time soloist who indeed toured Europe. The booming music that would have filled any great orchestral hall with joy and beauty, overwhelmed the comparatively small television studio with its bravado, its grandeur, as Rita, her body swaying, her eyes closed, played on effortlessly.

Several minutes later, Pavel, his hands still on her shoulders, said, "On the count of three, Rita, you will stop playing."

As Rita continued her virtuoso performance—her fingers tearing up and down the keyboard in one particularly showy movement—Pavel started counting. And when he counted three, her hands immediately froze and the music died.

"Very good, very nice, *dorogaya*," he said, stroking her neck. "Now sit back, relax. You are indeed a great pianist and that was a wonderful performance. Once again, I will count to three. When I do, I will snap my fingers and you will wake from this wonderful trance. You will feel confident and relaxed and refreshed."

Then with a few words and a single snap, Pavel roused Rita from hypnosis. As she sat on the piano bench, her eyes popped open, and she peered around as if she'd just been shaken from a nap and forgotten she was on television.

Pavel motioned the television camera in closer, then held the microphone up to the young woman and asked, "Rita, can you tell me what you do for work?"

Rita started to talk, hesitated, then replied, "I teach piano."

"To whom, concert pianists?"

She laughed and blushed. *"Nyet.* I teach piano to children. Most of my students are ten years old."

"You don't play in an orchestra?"

"I'd like to, but . . ." Rita shrugged, touched the keyboard with one hand. "I . . . I just don't play well enough."

Pavel spun around to the camera, then to the audience, laughed, and gave a huge shrug, as if to say, How totally ridiculous. He then told Rita how incredibly beautifully she'd just played—"I believe it was a Tchaikovsky piece," he commented—and the audience burst into an explosion of applause. Rita smiled, turned as pink as a bowl of borscht.

"Do you see how much hypnosis did for this young woman?" exclaimed Pavel, pressing his point. "Hypnosis freed her from all her inhibitions, her deep-seated fears of inferiority, so that she could express truly and openly her great, great talent." He bent over, kissed her on the cheek, and said, "Thank you so much, Rita."

The woman with the spiky hair came running back out, took Rita by the elbow and escorted her away as the audience showered her again with applause. Not wasting an instant, Pavel moved back to the three people—the two singers and the actress—who still sat slumped on the stage. And one by one, he brought them forward and they displayed their amazing, hypnotically enhanced talents. While under hypnosis, the opera singer sang an aria of extraordinary beauty, a performance that certainly rivaled any given at the Marinsky here in St. Petersburg. The actress, gesticulating with her entire body in the traditional Russian style, recited one of Pushkin's poems so movingly that many in the audience were brought to tears. The other singer, a man, played a guitar and sang a song that was better than most of what was heard on any radio station. And afterward, after they were brought back to this self-conscious world, each one of these people professed little success in the arts.

It went on and on, of course. Finally Pavel dragged out the painters, first showing their former work—a dark oil painting of a samovar, a simplistic watercolor of a vase of flowers—and then with great drama unveiling their freshly done paintings. Which were undeniably better, in fact even great. Again, an audible awe wafted from the amazed audience.

Everyone was swayed, for Pavel's demonstration was nothing less than a performance of miracles. Or was it? What did it prove, this

snake oil show? Yes, all of these people were great performers, especially under hypnosis. They all possessed truly inspiring talents. But it
could have all been rigged. They could have all been coaxed or coerced
prior to the show. They could all have been paid in rubles or even
dollars for their fine performances. Really, they could easily have all
been pretending to be hypnotized. So really this proved to be nothing
but terribly good entertainment, didn't it?

I doubted Maddy would want to join Pavel on such a show, either
in America or anywhere else. In fact, I knew she wouldn't. Not only
was this simply not her style, she abhorred stage hypnosis, resented the
superficial reputation such practice gave to so little understood a sci-
ence. And I agreed with her, now more than ever. What particularly
bothered me about Pavel's show was that it did nothing to advance a
true understanding of the hypnotic phenomenon. What I'd just witnessed was instead nothing more than a bag of tricks and magic de-
signed merely to awe. So when the show concluded, when the audience
drifted out into the hallway, I left feeling not simply disappointed but
angry. What in the hell was I going to say to Pavel himself? That I
didn't care for his showy showmanship?

More animated and talkative than most Russian crowds, the audience spilled out of the studio and into the hallway. I made my way
over to a window, trying to think of what words I could pass on to
Pavel. Gazing outside, I saw the chauffeur and car that had brought me
here, wondered if I couldn't make a quick escape. The driver was right
there, talking with someone, a woman with an infant in her arms.
Perhaps I should just go out, jump in the car, and tell him to drive off.

But . . . wait. I knew that woman, the one the driver was talking
with. No, they weren't talking, they were arguing. And, yes, it was
her, the woman from the Scandinavian Table, the very one who'd
launched the attack on Pavel the other morning. She started waving the
baby at the driver as if to say, Look at this poor thing, look at all my
troubles!

It hit me, slapped me with ice-cold clarity. I knew right then that
this woman had most definitely been one of Pavel's clients. He'd seen
her, tried to help her in some way. And dear God, now she had a child.
Could that swaddled baby in the woman's arms be the offspring of
Pavel Konstantinovich Kamikov?

A voice out of nowhere snapped, *"What?"*

I studied the young woman out there, saw the way she was holding the baby, the manner in which she was pleading. It just all made
sense.

*"Did she tell you that?"* demanded my psychic coach, grilling me in an unusually aggressive tone. *"Did you ever speak to this woman and find out for sure?"*

It just fit. I'd seen so much anger in her at the restaurant, witnessed her assault on Pavel. You know, the flying bowl of hot cereal. Studying her clothing, knowing where she worked, it was obvious she was in dire financial shape. How could she not be? So quite probably she'd come that afternoon to demand money from Pavel because she had a new child and that child was Pavel's. That had to be what this was all about.

*"So you never learned for sure?"*

I stood there, watching her and the chauffeur argue, and then Pavel emerged from the studio, beaming with pride at the success of today's television show. He noticed me staring out the window, looked at what I was looking at, and when he saw this woman and her bundle, he exploded with rage. Another string of mother language came shooting out of his mouth, and then he glared at me, searched to see if I understood what this was all about, and when he saw that I suspected—our eyes held for a telling moment too long—he shouted down the hall to his security guy.

"Slava, get rid of her!"

That, of course, was confirmation enough, and that big guy with the broad shoulders and gun went hustling out of the building after her. The child could have been fathered by someone like Pavel's driver or someone else on his staff. It was possible, of course. I just didn't think so. This young woman had to have been a former client of Pavel. And undoubtedly there had been intimate moments that quite probably became too intimate. Unfortunately, things like that happened in the States and *Rossiya* as well.

*"But did you—"*

Pavel's assistant, the woman with the spiky hair, came out just then and fetched me. She led me back to his dressing room, where Pavel and I exchanged a few terse pleasantries. He asked if I liked the show, that kind of stuff, but he wouldn't look me in the eye. He was avoiding the subject of his former client because he was quite rightly afraid of the information I would ferret back to my sister. And then his assistant loaded me in the Volvo and took me out, as requested by Pavel, for a late lunch in some expensive ruble restaurant where the average monthly wage bought a pleasant, even tasty meal for two. And after that I . . .

*"Alex, answer me,"* demanded my controller. *"Did you ever*

*learn this for sure? Did anyone ever specifically tell you that the child
was Pavel's?''*

I would only learn the truth in the stairwell of Pavel's building,
just before he was shot. That was when it would all be clear.

In reply, a haunting, defeated voice uttered an echoing, *"Oh."*

# Chapter 13

As if I were operating a videotape, I sped things up to the next day. Lev's funeral. Fast-forwarding to that time, Sveta and her boyfriend, Igor, picked me up at the Pribalt, and we drove through town, all the way up Nevsky and to the Alexander Nevsky Monastery. That was what happened next. We parked outside the buttery-yellow walls of the eighteenth-century cemetery, walked down a narrow, cobbled alley between the old burial grounds that held the most famous of Russia, from Peter the Great's sister and Lenin's family to Tchaikovsky and Dostoyevski. Pressing on, we crossed a small bridge and proceeded toward the tomato-red monastery buildings and the old Holy Trinity Cathedral.

It was a beautiful, early-fall afternoon. Puffy white clouds. A blue, blue sky. The onion domes towering over the small cathedral glimmered with gold as if they were holy beacons meant to signal to God to strike here, this place, this instant, with his blessings. All around the leaves of the cottonwood trees rattled with autumnal dryness. We entered the vast central courtyard of the monastery, a rectangular space the size of a city block that was bordered by the cathedral on one side and on the other three by long, low buildings with glassed-in arches. Long ago this tranquil courtyard had been plowed with more graves, and there were markers everywhere among the trees. Actually, I realized, it wasn't so long ago. Peering around, I saw that these graves were all of Soviet times. A red star here, a hammer and sickle there. Most of them were heroes from the Great Fatherland War.

As we approached the steps of the cathedral, I paused. Everything and all time seemed to stop. As if I were looking into a dream lingering on the edge of reality, I noticed a figure, dark and slim, strolling among the graves. Latching on and focusing totally on this individual, I understood that I was looking into my hypnotically realized fears. Yes, and the person who'd been spying on me at the Pribalt, the one I'd chased through the halls, was here, now floating on the edge of Lev's funeral.

The figure turned sideways. And that's when I saw.

*"Saw what?"*

The outline. The shape. While I hadn't been sure at the hotel, I was now.

*"Sure of what?"*

That it was a woman. That much was clear.

*"Look at a feature, Alex. Focus on the nose or maybe the eyes. Take the time to look carefully and notice something. Pick out a feature on this woman and build an image from it."*

I saw dark brown hair. Squinting, I could discern that it was straight, silken, and smooth. Not a curl in it. My eyes freeze-framed that image, that bit of hair, then studied the locks, magnified the side of the head, as I next tried to make out a cheekbone, the general shape of the face. It was a pretty face, I could tell that much, and—

A hand caught me by the arm, shattering the mesmerized image. All at once I was jerked back into the real story, faced with what had really happened.

"Come on, Alex," urged Sveta. "The service is about to begin. Tanya's inside."

"What? Oh. Oh . . . sure."

As I climbed the wide steps behind Sveta and Igor, I looked back into the courtyard cemetery. I saw a face of a general engraved on a headstone. Next an airplane propeller mounted over the grave of an aviation hero. But she was gone. The woman who was lurking in my imaginal subconscious had vanished.

With paranoia biting at my heels, I hurried after Sveta, and we stepped through the large double doors of the cathedral, passing a line of beggars as we moved from the bright day and into the dark structure. All at once a cloud of incense billowed over me with its thick, sweet smell. The door creaked shut behind us, and I blinked as my eyes adjusted to the lack of light. In front of me I saw a golden face mystically staring out of an icon. And then a deep voice from up front started singing the evening service and an unaccompanied choir chanted back in reply.

As with all Russian Orthodox churches, there were no pews, and the congregation, which primarily consisted of the most ancient and bent babushkas, flowed freely in the vast space. There were icons everywhere, plastered all over the walls, all over the treelike columns, and of course, all across the altar. Beeswax candles sputtered on huge brass stands scattered everywhere. I stared up at the dark ceiling, saw frescoes of angels and saints beaming downward, and felt that I had just stepped back several centuries into old Russia.

A late-afternoon service was just concluding in the front, and the congregation was pushing toward a fat, bearded priest and kissing the cross he held. At the same time, the choir, a group of maybe a dozen or so men and women, ceased singing up near the altar, and then started moving along the side of the cathedral and toward the back. Quite a large group of people was gathered in the rear corner of the cathedral, and I looked over, saw Tanya, her head covered by a black scarf, standing next to Lev's distraught father.

Lev's funeral service was about to begin, and I moved over, saw that in this dark, smoky cathedral some seventy-five people were gathered around one thing, an open casket. I gasped, but my lip. It was a shallow casket, constructed of simple pine, the sides splayed out slightly and rising only eight inches. And lying there, his hands folded over his chest was my longtime friend Lev, his face pale as the moon and just as tranquil.

The choir regathered and started some Gregorian chant, with the women's voices rising high and shrill and the men's voices dropping deep and dark. The priest, his gold brocade robe dragging across the floor, approached, swinging a brass incense burner and sending a thick, smoky cloud rolling over Lev as if to capture his spirit and carry it heavenward. I moved closer, pressed myself among the multitude of Lev's friends, and we all stood silent as the priest started praying and chanting in Old Church Slavonic, the liturgical language of the church.

The choir started begging for godly mercy with a rolling, repetitive chant of, *"Gospodi Pomiloi."*

I looked across the casket, saw Tanya, her face fallen and streaked with tears. Lev and she had met and fallen in love when they were in college, and they'd been married for years. She gave over to her grief, sobbing as the priest chanted and prayed, as the choir sang higher and higher, then dropped to tragic depths. She leaned against Lev's stoic father, who stood there nearly unblinking. I knew that Lev had no

brothers or sisters, that his mother had died a few years ago, so here
was a widower father bidding farewell to his only child. No wonder the
shock.

I had the sense that someone was behind me, that there were eyes
upon me, shooting me in the back. I wanted to turn around, but did I
dare?

*"Go ahead. In this mesmerized version of the story, you can do
as you please."*

Yes, I had to, so I slowly looked back. And she was there, the
spy, that woman in black clothing. Trim and athletic-looking, she
brusquely turned away, then stood before an icon, lighting a long
yellow taper, bowing her head, saying a prayer.

What was this? I shook my head, turned back to the body of Lev.
When this story had really taken place, there hadn't been such a spy,
had there? No, of course not. But if there hadn't been, then why was
someone back there now in this retelling of events? How could that be
possible?

*"It's possible because your mind is using its broader powers to
explore the full spectrum of possibilities,"* suggested that voice. *"Perhaps there was someone spying on you at that time, a person your
subconscious saw and noted but who your conscious mind failed to
acknowledge."*

I looked over my shoulder, checked back there again. The woman
was now moving forward, approaching the altar. She certainly seemed
real, walking about just like everyone else here.

*"Then again, perhaps your imaginal subconscious is merely giv-
ing form and shape to—"*

To my paranoia.

*"Perhaps."*

But if so, I pondered, if that woman over there was merely an
imaginal representation of what I feared, what difference did that really
make? None, for I knew that just as a hypochondriac's pains were
every bit as real to him as to a genuinely sick person, my fears were
just as legitimate whether or not I was actually being followed. In
either case, however, I knew that I couldn't let this continue, that I had
to be proactive rather than reactive. I could do that, couldn't I? In this
mesmerized retelling of the murder of Lev, couldn't I use my other
powers to explore other avenues?

*"Such is the beauty of hypnosis."*

And so I froze the images of Lev's funeral, turning away from the
reality of that scene and taking off in pursuit of my darkest fear.

# Chapter 14

I slipped into a fantastical aspect of the story, leaving the funeral behind and making my way to the front of the cathedral and toward some greater truth. I pressed my way along, knowing that I hadn't done this before, the first time, when all this had really happened, but I was most certainly doing it now in trance, and there she was. The mysterious woman, her head bowed, was praying before an enormous, gold and jewel-encrusted icon of the Virgin Mary to the left of the altar. I wondered why the spying woman was doing this, why she would be praying when she was supposed to be watching me, unless of course she had accomplices and this was some sort of trick, a way to lure me into some dark corner where they could overwhelm me. My eyes darted about. An old man was on his knees and bowing his head to the floor. A young mother, holding a girl by the hand, quickly scurried across the vast chamber.

The spy turned from the icon, lifted up a long, golden beeswax candle, and held its wick to a burning taper. Once it was lit, the woman in black set the candle in an enormous brass candelabra, which held maybe a hundred burning candles, then bowed her head as if praying for someone. I watched all this, tried to see her face in the golden light as I continued stalking her. Would she talk to me? Would she reveal her intentions?

I passed around a huge column that rose from the floor all the way up to the ceiling of the cathedral, and as I passed around it, I lost sight of the strange woman for a mere few seconds. When I emerged on the other side of the column, she had totally disappeared. A babushka now stood at the candelabra, snuffing out old candles and picking at dried wax, but the spying woman had vanished.

Hurrying forward, I went up to the babushka, demanded, ''There was a woman just here all dressed in black. She had brown hair. What happened to her? Where did she go?''

At first I didn't think I'd get an answer. Using an old bent butter knife, the old woman snuffed a nearly finished candle, then started scraping away melted wax that was dripped about the stand. Her fingers were thick and gnarled, her face puffy and worn, and one of the lenses of her glasses was broken and patched with peeling tape. Finally she looked up at me, squinted, made some disdainful face, then lifted up the old waxy butter knife and pointed to the back of the cathedral.

''You can catch her, perhaps, but I'm not sure you want to,'' she muttered in a cracked voice.

I caught sight of the last of the spy at the cathedral's entrance, just as she hurried out. Breaking into a run, I dashed through the church, weaving around a couple of kneeling babushkas who were prostrate, their foreheads pressed to the cold stone floor as they recited a litany of prayer. Off to the left, Lev's funeral service continued, the priest swinging the incense holder, the choir singing its mournful Gregorian chant, Tanya crying.

I charged out first one, then the second door, hurried past the horribly ragged begging women, and came to the top of the steps. I looked off to the right, saw no sign of the woman rushing down the gravel path and out the main gates. On my left was a large gathering, a procession headed by a suited groom and a bride in white, waiting for Lev's funeral to conclude so they could enter the cathedral and holy matrimony. One of their mothers was nervously clutching the two crowns they would wear during the service. Or would the young couple proceed now, would the ceremony simply take place in another corner of the never-quiet institution?

Looking through the cottonwoods and the gravestones, I saw her racing away, cutting across the middle of the monastery courtyard cum cemetery, darting in and around the headstones. I leapt down the steps two and three at a time. She'd gotten away before, but I couldn't, wouldn't let her get away now, and I charged down a gravel path, then cut between two graves. The stranger glanced back once, and though I couldn't make out her face, there was something oddly familiar about her. I racked my memory, tried to place where I'd seen her before.

Was it possible that someone I'd known here in St. Petersburg, another student perhaps or one of Tanya's friends I'd met at her place, was now haunting my every move?

She reached the long low building on the other side of the courtyard, a structure with deep red stucco walls and arching windows. Hesitating at a pair of doors, she glanced back. What was this? It appeared almost as if she wanted to make sure I'd seen where she was going, that she wanted to make sure I'd be able to follow. I slowed slightly, not caring at all for this. All too easily, this could be some KGB trick, a plan to entrap me. When she disappeared inside, I was tempted to call this off, to retreat to the safety of Lev's funeral. But I knew of course that this dark spy would be back again and again, treading around the edges of this story, picking at my paranoia and tormenting me. So I had to find out. I had to keep pushing at this until I discovered either pain or resolution.

I came to the double doors of the monastery building, opened one half of the entrance, and passed inside. Seated on a tiny chair was a babushka, wearing a blue robe over a dress and a white kerchief snugly over her big round head. Her thick brown stockings had slid nearly down to her tired ankles.

"Where's the woman who just came in here?" I demanded.

The babushka moistened her lips, smacked her dry mouth as if she were about to speak. She said nothing, however, instead raising a hand and pointing down a dark hall that disappeared into blackness.

Did I dare go down there? I took a few steps, and then I heard something creak about twenty feet ahead. I paused. The ceiling was low and arched, and I couldn't see much of anything. Even though I knew I shouldn't, I pressed on, moving slowly down the hall and finally reaching a doorway. The door was slightly ajar, and I heard faint movement from within. Oh, no, I thought. Not another one of these. The closed door. The mysterious noise from inside. Turn around, I told myself. Don't go in. Get out of here. Run.

But how could I?

I was trapped in my desperation to know, to understand. I put one hand on the latch, pulled. It was a heavy door, though narrow. Probably this had been a monk's room once. Or a cleric's office. Someone hidden away. And now there was a truth waiting inside for me. But how painful would that knowledge actually be? I knew I had to proceed, and so I pulled it open. The chamber inside was as black as a cave. But it wasn't empty. Staring into the darkness, I could tell that much. She was in there, the spy. In there and waiting for me.

I entered the darkened room, taking four or five short steps. Out of nowhere an eerie breeze came up, blowing shut the door and trapping me in here. Unable to see in the darkness, I stood perfectly still. Gradually, however, my eyes adjusted and I could barely make out the outline of a window off to my right, an opening that appeared covered with a heavy curtain, a thick, old velvet one. I turned slightly and realized I could see her. She was just ahead, this woman who'd been spying on me, and I studied the faint outline, the dark shape of her body seated in a chair directly in front of me. Oh, shit, I thought, she could be holding a gun, aiming it right at me.

There was something eerily familiar about her, and I asked, "I know you, don't I?"

"Yes."

"Who are you? Why have you been following me?"

This was a dream within a trance, I told myself. It was some mesmerized part of me playing out a fantasy that held more truth than reality. Or something like that. As Maddy would say, this was a way to a greater truth.

Again, I demanded, "Why have you been spying on me? Why are you so interested in what I'm doing here?"

"You know why."

Oh, Christ. Was all this nothing more than a game, a riddle?

I asked, "What do you mean?"

"I mean exactly this: I must know all that you do."

What? I searched my own mind, tried to imagine what this was all about, what she could be talking about, what I could possess that someone else would want so desperately. After all, I hadn't come to Russia as an agent or double agent or anything so ridiculous.

"I only came here to see my friends. I have no other intentions, no other plans," I replied in my defense. "You're not KGB, are you?"

"That's not important."

But to me, of course, it was. Very much so. I thought back. Could all this in fact be tied to the documents I'd inadvertently smuggled out as a student? Or had I on this trip become involved in something much more sinister, something connected to Lev's murder or perhaps even to the store Tanya and he had dreamed of opening?

I couldn't stand it anymore, and so I rushed compulsively over to the window and with a huge heave yanked back the thick, ancient curtain. Harsh bolts of sunshine immediately stabbed into the dark chamber, and huge, billowing clouds of dust rose all around me.

Squinting and coughing, I spun around, anxious to see the truth illuminated by the bright sun.

But the chair was empty. The spying woman had vanished.

My heart churning, I saw that the door was still closed. I turned and turned. There were no other doors, no nooks, nowhere for her to hide. Only four solid walls. She'd vanished like a ghost.

The next instant something was brushing up against my leg. I jumped back, nearly screamed out. It was an animal, a cat. Not too large. All white. And the thing was nuzzling and cuddling up against me, begging for affection. My brow blistering with nervous sweat, I bent down, stroked its long supple back.

My voice shaking, I asked, "Do I have anything to fear?"

And if that creature had been able to talk, I knew it would have responded, Yes, you most certainly do.

pranks and simple plays on words. And, I guessed, it was no wonder, for ever since she'd lost her sight in her early teens she'd been so fucking mature, so unbelievably stoic. But she had to have lost so much of her childhood. No, she had to have stuffed it, and the little girl in her crept out from time to time.

I just stood there staring outside, my eyes open unusually wide. The yellow and red leaves swirled in the windy afternoon. The blue lake heaved and swelled, rising into whitecaps.

Wait. Was it afternoon or wasn't it? And what day was it? I was a mess, stretched not only all across the planet but between the conscious and the subconscious.

A note sounded, floating high into the third-floor ballroom cum trance room. Then came a whole series of notes. No, it wasn't from Maddy's stereo, but from her new polished ebony grand. Some romantic piece rose up, surrounded me with its warm music. Ravel? I didn't know, but it filled me, warmed me. I bowed my head against a glass pane, let the sun sink into me, and listened as that entire huge room bloomed with a sound that churned like the autumnal day outside. I took a deep breath. Everything was going to be okay, wasn't it?

My eyes burst open. Christ, when did that witchly Maddy learn to play the piano, let alone like this, like a real master? I whipped around, Maddy, of course, was no longer by the recliner. But she wasn't at the keyboard of the piano either. Yet the keys were moving, rolling up and down, gushing with gorgeous music as if played by some virtuoso ghost.

I shook my head, certain that I was more screwed up than I thought. Was this still a trance of some sort? Or had I broken from hypnosis and stumbled into a dream or perhaps the beginnings of a nightmare? I took a step. Holy shit, I suddenly feared that the spy or the remains of Pavel himself had followed me into this world.

"What do you think?" called a bright Holly Golightly voice. "It's great, isn't it?"

I took a step away from the door, cautiously peered down to the far end of the room. There was my sister, some fifty feet away, a huge grin on her face and a remote control held in one hand.

"It's the very latest, an all-digital player piano. You just put in these discs, and off it goes. It mimics everything perfectly, right down to the pressure on the keys." She giggled, said, "I can make it louder or faster, too."

With the touch of a couple of buttons, she did both, the music booming and increasing in tempo. This was prime Maddy, the blind crip, the tragic one who'd taken her huge insurance settlement, exploded it into forty or fifty million dollars on the stock market, and the one who'd created an island world that she ruled over and controlled, a world that was equally magical and mesmerizing. On the one hand, I was fascinated by it all, this place, this piano with its keys tinkling as beautifully as if an invisible angel were playing. On the other hand, it was tragic.

"Maddy, you do need to take a trip."

"What?"

"Turn that thing down."

"Oh, Alex, you really are so stuffy sometimes."

I'd failed her, I realized, as she turned down the grand with a wave of the remote. I hadn't succeeded in getting her off the island. This sandy, pine-studded island that was capped with this glorious house was, for Maddy, merely a gilded prison, a fact I'd known for some time and the very reason that had precipitated my trip to Russia.

"I really wish you'd come with me," I said.

"Don't be ridiculous. Russia's got to be the least handicapped-accessible place in the world. Were the sidewalks in as bad shape as the roads?"

Actually, they were, for not only had a great deal of them been torn up and not repaired, but I'd also seen a couple of open manholes. Not amusing for a sightless person. I wasn't going to tell Maddy about all that, though. That wasn't the point.

"It would've been big fun," I lied, because it surely would have been a hellish experience, trying to cart her around that crumbling city and all.

"Right," she replied, not convinced.

She drifted into the music, her body swaying as her new toy, that piano, played on. I didn't get it. I didn't understand why she was way down there at the far end of the old ballroom, so distant from both me and my trance. Was she just spacing out for a while, taking a break from the trance and me, or . . . or was she scheming? Or was I just being paranoid of my own sister?

There was a knock on the door and Solange entered, carrying a tray. She was a striking woman, her cheeks high and well defined, her posture always assured, confident. Even though I'd been on the island for a number of months, I hardly knew her. On the other hand, she and Maddy were very close. It wasn't that the two women talked so much, for I hadn't witnessed that really. Rather, they seemed to converse in some unspoken way.

"Thank you, Solange," I said as she set down the coffee.

She smiled slightly, said in her lush Jamaican accent, "I made it plenty strong."

"Good, I need it." Trying to sound casual, trying to sound, well, cheery, and even a bit interesting, I added, "I want to stay up late so I can get back on this time zone."

"Certainly."

That was all she said, and then she was gone. As soon as the door clicked shut behind her, Maddy was wheeling across the room. She stopped just short of her recliner, then reached out into the air.

"You're about two feet short," I volunteered. "And then the table's on the other—"

"Alex, I'll let you know if I need help."

Her tone was stern, a tad testy, so I thought, fine, go ahead and grope all you want. I just stood there, not ten feet away, and watched as she inched her wheelchair forward, felt the back of the recliner, then maneuvered around the back of it and blindly reached out for the small table. I could have told her not only where everything was on the tray, but what was in fact there.

Maddy, however, somehow knew.

Even though she hadn't requested it or Solange hadn't made mention of it, my sister knew not only that there was a tall glass of iced tea, but a plate of sliced lemons. And she knew where they were, right on the upper left side of the tray. She reached for her drink—obviously Maddy was still hoping for a strong Indian summer, for when the truly cold weather came she'd switch to hot tea—all so casually and with so little hesitation that it crossed my mind that she was faking it, being blind and all.

She took a deep whiff. "The coffee's quite strong."

I stepped over and took my coffee, which was so black that I couldn't see the sides of the white mug. With any luck, I'd be awake for hours, I thought as I retreated to the French doors.

"So are we done for the day?" asked Maddy. "Or are we just pausing?"

"Pausing." Turning this conversation down quite a different path, perhaps one that Maddy had been hoping to avoid, I took a sip of coffee and casually asked, "So tell me, what do you think of Pavel and the woman from the restaurant?"

132 R. D. Zimmerman

Placing the glass into a holder on the right side of her chair, she turned her wheelchair, pushed away from me. And then stopped, still and quiet for the longest time.

Finally she said, "I remember that about Pavel, that he was very aggressive with women. When he was in Chicago he touched me a lot. And, frankly, I liked it. Very few people touched me. I was blind then, of course, so people would often take me by the arm and such. But very few touched me in a normal, noncontrolling way. They were afraid to. Yet Pavel wasn't. In fact, he did so with an awful lot of confidence."

"In other words, you could see how he could do something like that, seducing that young woman?"

"Sure, if that's what actually happened. Pavel was always a little inappropriate." Maddy turned around, faced me, and took her iced tea and sipped it. "But how much of that is cultural? I mean, do Russians just touch a lot more than Americans?"

"Yeah, they do. They're a lot more openly affectionate on every level, actually." Wanting to keep all this on the odd target, I probed, "So what do you think about that? What do you think of him for—"

"Oh, Alex, if he did sleep with one of his clients, it was wrong. Absolutely so. That's what I think. That kind of thing is terribly unethical, and in the States, at least, illegal. But dear God, I hope he's not going to be killed because of that. Tell me that, won't you? That woman with the baby's not going to shoot him, is she?" She shook her head, momentarily confusing my present trance-induced telling of the story with the one that had already played out. "I mean, she didn't, did she? That wasn't what happened, was it?"

I thought about the whole, broad picture. Sure, I knew who did it, but I was only halfway through the story. Maddy was going to have to wait, hear everything else because there was so much more.

Diverting her, I took a jab, tartly blurting, "Hey, that guy really got to you, didn't he?"

"I . . . I suppose so." She hesitated, then added, "It wasn't just that he was attentive, it was that I felt . . . felt . . ."

"Taken care of?" I asked, wondering if Pavel had been able to do for Maddy what she wouldn't let anyone else do.

She nodded, for it was hard for her to admit, and she bowed her head and blushed. "I heard from him almost daily. I'd turn on my computer in the morning and there was a message from him. Of course, there'd be something about hypnosis—a theory, an idea, a new induction method, something about creativity—or maybe something about a movie. He loved movies, as you know, and he was always interested in what I'd just seen, what films were coming out, which ones might be up for an Oscar. But then there was almost always something else. Something special about me. You know, something personal. At first maybe he'd just ask about the weather, how it made me feel that day. Later he'd ask if I thought my insights were different because I was blind. So, yes, he really did reach in and touch me.''

''And you liked that?''

''Of course I did. Do you know how lonely I get? I mean, it's wonderful to have you here—Solange and Alfred, too, of course. What I'm trying to say is that while I'm not alone, I'm lonely because I'm stuck inside my body.'' Maddy gazed upward and, as if she could see right through the roof and see exactly what it was like outside, said, ''The sky's so beautiful. And so are the clouds. Cottony puffs of white against the blue. Those are the kind of things I miss.'' With a sigh of defeat, she lowered her head. ''I don't know how to put it, Alex, except that there are very few people who can hypnotize me.''

''He did that?''

''Yes.''

''You mean, when he was in Chicago?''

''No, recently.''

''What? How?''

''I called him and he did a wonderful induction.''

''Oh, my God. You had phone . . . phone trance with him! Was that all?'' I moaned at the possibilities, turned away, didn't want to know the answer. ''I bet you that call cost a fortune and I bet you paid for it, right?''

''So what if I did?''

''Maddy, what you're telling me is that there are very few people who you'll let into your life, who you're comfortable letting down the barriers with. Or rather, you're comfortable hypnotizing people because then you get to direct things, yet there are very few who you're willing to let have that kind of control over you. And Pavel was one of them.''

''He . . . he just kind of marched right in.''

''Pushy and domineering. That was him,'' I quipped. ''And I see why in the beginning, when I was planning the trip in the first place, you even entertained the thought of coming with me. You didn't want to go to St. Petersburg to learn about hypnosis per se. You just wanted to see him.''

She nodded.

"So you sent me instead so that I'd ferret back as much information as possible." I saw her devious scheme in full now. "What were you planning all along, to hypnotize me so that I could tell you about my grand, glorious trip to Russia and it would seem as real as possible to you? You were, weren't you? You'd planned, didn't you, to put me under and then follow me into a trance so you'd see it all in your mind's eye? You wanted me to expound on St. Petersburg and Pavel so that you could suck it all up, so that my memories would become your memories."

"Alex, please. You make me sound so . . . so calculating. I just wanted to see him and the only way I can see anything is in hypnosis."

"Maddy, you should have come with me. It would have been hard, but you should have gone to Russia. And I suspect you would have made the trip but for the fact that you didn't know how to tell him about that little incident with the bus." I was shaking, I realized, as the coffee and my anger fused. "You never told him you'd been paralyzed, did you?"

"I knew," meekly confessed my sister, "that he could entertain the thought of me sightless. I knew that didn't repel him. I just didn't know what he'd think of me in a wheelchair."

"Oh, Maddy."

I was suddenly flooded with sympathy, and I wanted to rush over, to hold her, to try to convince her that the difference between her sitting down and standing up was only a concept. But Maddy was never to be held. She leaned over, quickly placed her glass on the floor, then spun around and gave herself a big push, shooting far and away from me. I chugged the last of my coffee, scurried over and picked up Maddy's glass—when she got agitated she could really get zipping around up here—then put both of them safely out of the way on the tray.

Suddenly she braked to a stop in the middle of the room. Taking the remote control from a pouch on her chair, she zapped the piano from a schmaltzy piece into another zippy one.

"So as long as we're playing truth or dare," ventured my sister, "why don't you tell me about you and Tanya?"

I turned back to the window, peered out. She'd caught me off guard, for there was a good deal I hadn't told her about my times at the university. And why should I have?

In response to my silence, Maddy taunted, "Well?"

"Well . . . well, what do you think of her?"

When there was not a word behind me, I turned around. Dear Sister was sitting still, her sunglassed eyes locked on me.

"Oh, I didn't know," she said.

"Know what?"

"You just never told me you care for her in that kind of way."

"No, I guess I never have." I decided to fess up completely and added, "But I do. That's the trouble."

"Trouble?"

"I don't know what to do about it."

"Does she feel the same way about you?"

"At one time she did."

"Did? What do you mean?"

"I mean she's confused right now, but the feeling was definitely mutual when we were students." I took a deep breath, decided to come clean. "Lev and Tanya were already dating when we met, but . . . but . . ."

"Oh."

I snapped, "What do you mean, oh?"

"I mean, I'm no dummy just because out of this trance of yours I'm a blind crip."

"Maddy, don't talk about yourself that way."

"Well, I'm not. My God, you should have heard some of the stories my patients used to tell me. Trust me, you hear a lot of dirt when you're a shrink. And when you're a good one, as I was, I might honestly add, you hear it all. I think my patients used to really open up to me in part because I was blind. You know, like they could confess to me and not fear how I would look back at them. Granted, I do have an excellent poker face."

"No shit."

"So you and Tanya had an affair."

"Do you have to put it like that?" I asked. "Is it really an affair when you're in your twenties and you meet a girl and sleep with her even though she's dating someone else? Tanya and Lev weren't married yet, after all."

"Did Lev know?"

"Hell no." And, I realized, now he never would.

"Yet the three of you were doing things together?"

"Well, yeah." I stared at the wooden floor, started pacing. "That's who I hung out with. Like I said, they would barely let go of me."

"Still, somehow you and Tanya found some secret time to—"

"Maddy, stop it! You're making it sound so seedy. We were just a couple of kids."

"Alex, it's not simply a question of semantics. If Lev didn't know, and if you were his friend and she was his fiancée, then I'd call it an affair."

I retreated, turning my back on my sister, and said, "Maddy, I'm not dating anyone. I like working for you, I like living with you, but it's an island. We live on an island and, like, I'm not meeting anyone."

"Alex, what's your point?"

I took a deep breath. "I want to invite Tanya to visit us. Russians can get out now. I might have to send a formal invitation and sign something assuming financial responsibility for her, but I want to see what would happen between us. Maybe even the three of us could go on a trip. Maybe to New York or San Francisco. Or Hawaii."

"No."

"What?" I said, totally stunned.

"Three's a crowd. The two of you could go somewhere, but I think it'd be best if I passed on that trip as well. Thanks but no thanks." She added, "I think it would be good for you, Alex. You do need to get away. You do need to see people. I love having you all to myself, but, hey, I understand. You should be dating."

"Maddy, I'm almost forty. Most people my age are already married."

"Of course."

"And it's not like I'd be rushing in, rushing after the sad widow. I mean, apparently Lev and Tanya hadn't had much of a relationship."

"No, not for years."

"So I think it would be good for her to get away from St. Petersburg. Living there's just so stressful. I'd love to show her—"

I cut myself off, drifted away in thought. What had Maddy just said? She knew that Tanya and Lev had had marital troubles for some time? But how? I racked my brain. I'd covered a lot of ground so far, but I hadn't gotten to that yet, had I? No, I was sure I hadn't. Suddenly I was filled with panic.

"Maddy," I challenged, "unless you're a total psychic, you should only know what I've told you about Lev and Tanya. And to the best of my knowledge, I haven't said word one about the quality of their relationship."

"Oh, Alex, I just meant . . . I don't know. I just meant . . ."

This was just like her, evading any sticky points. From the way she was dancing around the question, I knew this was something major too. As if to raise my concerns even more, she rolled over to the grand, placed her hands on the black ebony.

Above the rolling music, she nearly shouted, "The vibrations are almost as good as the music."

I stood firm, demanded, "Maddy, turn that thing down and answer me. How do you know that about Tanya and Lev?"

"Alex . . . Alex . . ." She reached for the remote control, softened the volume. "Would you please use your brain?"

"No, Miss Smarty, I want you to spell it out."

"Don't you understand? Pavel and I were in touch."

"Of course you were. So?"

"Stop being so dense." She moved away from the piano and zeroed in on me. "Alex, I knew almost everything that Pavel was thinking and doing."

"What are you saying?"

"Just that while you were there Pavel was telling me everything." She shook her head in disbelief. "Don't you get it? He was sending me E-mail two or three times a day."

"What?"

"We were discussing Lev's murder."

"You're kidding?"

"No. And he did a little research on Tanya after the two of you had visited him. That's when he found out about Lev and her."

"Shit," I muttered, "you knew almost before me."

"Sorry."

I was such an idiot. It had never even occurred to me that Maddy and Pavel would have been in touch while I was in St. Petersburg, that they would have been bantering electronic thoughts and gossip back and forth during my entire visit. I didn't like the thought of it either, the very idea that they'd been talking behind my back.

"God-damn-it, Maddy, why do you always pull stuff like this on me? I always want to be there for you, but I don't like being used."

"Good grief, don't be so self-centered. I wasn't using you."

"Well, you've got to start leveling with me."

I clenched my fists, wanted to burst. Just when I was beginning to feel independent from her—I'd actually left her island and made the trip—I realized that my role and relationship with my sister were just as intertwined as ever. Would I never get beyond it?

"Maddy, you don't know how upset I am." Forcefully calming myself because I feared the answer, didn't want to betray my worries, I asked, "How much else do you know?"

"I don't know. Not much."

"Oh."

I left it at that. I didn't want to get into it, so I shut up. It might all come out in due time, but I hoped it wouldn't. There wasn't any real need for Maddy to learn every dirty little detail, was there?

Maddy inched herself forward and said, "Alex, I really do need to know who killed Pavel."

"Believe me, I understand that more than ever."

"So tell me."

I shook my head in frustration. My sister. She was so fucking persistent. She could never just let things alone. I ran my hand through my hair, popped an audible sigh. There was no getting around this one. No way. I'd started it, and now it was time to finish.

"It was all so complicated, Maddy." I stepped around, sat on the edge of my recliner. "But I want to do it all your way. I want to tell you under hypnosis. I insist on that, actually. And I want you to go into a trance as you listen to me, too. You probably were before, but I just want you to see exactly what I did. I want you to come at his murder from the same angle, at the same speed." When she didn't move, I lay down and pleaded, "Come on, let's go."

Reluctantly, she wheeled herself over and climbed onto her recliner, and soon, as she chanted along, I was blasting off, returning to Russia, that tortured country that was wrapped in a mystery inside a trance.

# Chapter 16

I stood staring at Lev's ghostly white face, my eyes teary not simply with the memories of my friend, but also from the incense swirling around me, and I pondered how sick I was with Russia. This was a morbid, melancholic country, haunted by the horrors of Ivan the Terrible, Stalin, and an endless series of deathly tragedies that had killed tens of millions in this century alone. Yet I felt like this was my place. And they felt that as well, for it was Lev himself who had once said, "I don't know why, but you belong to us."

I should have left Russia right at the conclusion of Lev's funeral, but of course I couldn't. Even though I could've gone to the airport at any time and fled to the luxuries of the West—what was I doing here when the charm and warmth of Amsterdam and the beauties of Paris were waiting?—I knew instinctively that I wouldn't leave until my visa expired and I was forced out. And then once I was gone I was aware that I would miss this . . . this huge dysfunctional country. No, that wasn't right. Russia was more than a country. It was a state of mind.

So I stood in that church, my feet rooted to the stone floor, as the service went on and on, the priest chanting in Slavonic, the choir rising and falling in dramatic swells. The choir, the priest, the dark cathedral filled with the haunting icons, all mirrored the pain of Lev's death so perfectly that it didn't even occur to me that just a few years ago it wouldn't have been like this at all. Nothing religious. No, instead it would have been something hideously Soviet, that was to say not simply banal but horribly bland and out of sync with the realities of human emotions and needs.

After Lev was carted away and just as the bridal procession started to parade into the church, I left them all, strolling into thought. I passed from the haunting courtyard of the small cathedral, back over that small bridge, beneath the heavy trees of the cemetery, and onto Nevsky Prospekt. My pace none too fast, I walked all the way up Nevsky, eventually passing the Moscow train station, the small street that led down to Tanya's hoped-for store, and on and on, through the crowds, past the palaces, until a good while later I finally arrived at the Winter Palace, the Neva River, and a handful of questions regarding Lev's death. Staring across the flat waters, I knew what had to be done next.

That night I made a couple of phone calls, and the following morning I emerged from the Pribaltiskaya Hotel at ten and found, as once again arranged, Pavel's Volvo and chauffeur waiting for me. I climbed into the backseat and the driver nodded a gruff good-morning, starting up the car and driving away without saying another word. As we made our way up the center of Vasilevsky Island, swerving around craterlike potholes, I decided this was stupid. I doubted I'd get much out of him, but I couldn't miss the opportunity.

Sitting forward and grabbing onto the back of the front seat, I said, "I'm Alex. What's your name?"

His dark eyes glancing suspiciously at me in the rearview mirror, he replied, "Misha."

"So, Misha, who was that woman?"

"*Kakaya?*"

"The woman with the child. The one who was outside the TV studio."

"That one?" He shrugged. "To hell with her."

"But who was she?"

"Just a gypsy wanting money."

"That was a gypsy?"

"Of course."

"But I saw her at the hotel too. She was the one who threw the *kasha* all over Pavel."

"Then she was a prostitute. I don't know. They're all whores at the hotel." In a typical whiny Russian voice, he added, "To hell with them."

I caught his face in the rearview mirror, tried to ascertain his reaction when I asked, "What's her connection to Pavel?"

As if I were the KGB, he shut down, his eyes, his brow, void of expression, and he shrugged, uttered some sort of grunt. It was clear I wouldn't get anything else out of him, that he was the devoted sort. Or obligated. Studying the back of the burly driver, I didn't doubt that Pavel had found him in some Siberian backwater. He'd probably worked on BAM, the new trans-Siberian rail line, or perhaps in the endless, hopelessly antiquated oil fields out in Kazakhstan. Or perhaps he was an ex-criminal, someone who'd been banished to the Far East. Whatever. It was just clear he wasn't a St. Petersburg native—he was much too coarse—and that in exchange for obtaining a housing pass for this man in the city Pavel had in turn received his utter obedience. And it was quite clear that I had transgressed some boundary between him and his master, that I shouldn't be asking about the woman with the baby, and that I certainly wouldn't get anything more out of the driver. Absolutely. This man was not only Pavel's chauffeur but undoubtedly also his bodyguard. I leaned forward again, scanned the front seat for a gun or knife. One of the two had to be tucked under the seat or in the glove compartment.

I sat back and hung on as we continued into town, across the river, and back around the rusting construction equipment that filled Hay Market Square and made it appear like an abandoned amusement park.

Motioning toward one building, I said, "It's that one."

Misha dropped me at the entrance to Tanya's building, and I jumped out, darted through the front door and all the way up some five flights. Huffing, I knocked on her door.

"*Da?*" came a voice that was clearly not Tanya's.

"It's Alex."

Several bolts were snapped and the door was finally opened by Sveta, who offered a subdued, "*Privyet.*" Hi.

"How is she?"

"*Normalno.*" Okay.

"Is she ready?"

"*Da, da.*"

Sveta, who was staying with Tanya indefinitely, stepped out of the way, and I saw Tanya sitting by the window, staring out over the red metal roofs. She'd agreed to this last night. I just hoped that it was a good idea, that this wasn't too soon after the funeral.

"Tanya," I said, seating myself on the couch next to her, "how are you doing? You know we don't have to do this, especially today."

She turned to me, her eyes vacant, her lips pursed tight. Every death was a crisis for those left behind, yet when I searched her eyes for that truth, certain that I'd see it mirrored there, her gaze was murky. Concerned, I stared at her, studied her face, and she turned away as if there was something she didn't want me to see. Her voice soft, she replied, "Of course we have to." So we started out. I helped her on with her raincoat, the pleated one from Sweden, and we set off.

Standing in the doorway like a hovering babushka, Sveta looked at me sternly and chided, "You take good care of her and bring her back soon. She's awfully tired. She didn't really sleep last night."

I nodded, took Tanya by the arm, and we headed down to the car, where Misha, clearly irked by my earlier interrogation, didn't bother to open the doors or even acknowledge us with a word. Instead, just as soon as Tanya and I had climbed in the back and shut the door, he revved up the engine and took off. Racing through the streets, we cut back to the broad and bustling Nevsky Prospekt and across the Fontanka River. As we drove along, I wanted to ask Tanya about the store and just what I might have actually seen the other day. Glancing at her drawn face, however, I knew this wasn't the time.

When we turned onto Rubinshtein, she quietly referred to the city by its nickname, saying, "This is the best street to live on in Peter."

I looked out at the drab five-story buildings, their once ornate façades pockmarked with despair, and hid my amazement in a bland, "Really?"

"It's right off Nevsky, it's quiet, the apartments are big. I'm sure there are some who've lived here since the Revolution, but the rest are all rich *biznizmeni,* like your friend who has his own television show."

If this were the best, I would have hated to see the worst. I noted one babushka lugging a lumpy string bag of apples, a woman in a jeans skirt pushing a shiny Western stroller, and then some boarded-up windows, a broken-down car. Wait, no. There was a BMW parked up to the right, yet had this been America I would have assumed that it was a drug pusher's car stopped in front of a crack house.

Misha pulled to an abrupt halt in front of a couple of ratty double doors and mumbled, "Second floor."

We got out on the curbside, and Misha took off at once, speeding down the street. I glanced up at the old structure, which had definitely seen better days some hundred or hundred and fifty years ago. I pulled open one of the short, thick doors, and Tanya and I stepped into a cavelike entryway that was dank and dark and far too acrid smelling. Some old wooden mailboxes hung on the left, a naked bulb hung from a wire, and we made for the broad stone staircase. So this, I thought, was a swank building on St. Petersburg's Park Avenue. We hadn't mounted more than two or three steps when I heard the clunk of a door being opened.

"Come up, come up, my friends!" bellowed a voice.

When I'd been a student here I'd always heard it said that you knew you could really trust people—i.e., they weren't KGB stooges— only when you either met their family or they invited you into the sanctity of their home. There was nothing more sacred in Russian culture than friendship, yet as we ascended past an open pail of garbage that was brimming with potato peelings, I wondered if that still held true in this post–Cold War era. Or was Pavel's eagerness to help merely a way to pull me deeper into his web, a calculated means to ensure his bond to my sister, the great Maddy?

"Come in, come in," called Pavel.

He stood above us like a modern Grandfather Frost, his salt-and-pepper hair pushed back, his beard brushed, and his large stomach stretching beneath a white shirt. I was suddenly worried, for I distinctly remembered how difficult it was to introduce different circles of Russian friends to each other. Such was the competition for Westerners. I distinctly recalled having made that error when I was at the university; each group had taken me aside and called the other prostitutes and thieves.

"*Zdrah'stvooite.*" Hello, I said. "This is my friend Tanya."

"The poor widow." Pavel tugged on his beard and shook his head. "Such a pretty woman. I'm sure your husband was handsome and smart. I'm so sorry, my dear. You must be terribly heartsick."

Tanya said nothing, only raised her hand, which Pavel captured and took in both of his. He stroked her thin wrist, then as if this were a scene from *War and Peace,* bent over and kissed it. Oh, brother. After witnessing his television show I certainly had my doubts; whether or not this was a mistake would be evident soon enough.

"You must let me help, my dear Tanya," demanded Pavel. "I'm sure I can. Have you ever seen me on television?"

"Of course," she replied.

"And did you like it?"

"*Da, da.*"

"Good, then you're aware of the strength of hypnosis and you know what I can do."

Pavel ushered us out of the horribly dingy stairwell and through a thick door, which he locked tightly, closing no less than three bolts. Even at first glance, this was an expansive apartment. The ceilings were at an easy twelve feet and we stood at the beginning of a long, broad corridor with a series of doors that led off on either side. Pavel slipped off Tanya's tan raincoat and hung it on a mahogany coatrack, then took my jacket as well.

"What a nice place," I said, for it was already apparent this was the most luxurious home I'd ever seen in Russia.

Tanya glanced in one doorway and surmised, "It's so big."

"Yes, isn't it? Six rooms."

That, I understood, meant without the kitchen or the bath. And that also meant it was indeed huge by Russian standards, where the minimum housing was prescribed as a few scant square meters per person.

"This is the way the building was originally built, two apartments per floor," explained Pavel, the proud property owner. "Then in Soviet times the bastards chopped it all up. There were two communal apartments, four families in one, five in the other. Over twenty people lived here, can you imagine? My mother lived in one half, and I bought out everyone else three years ago. Then last year I bought out the other bunch—very complicated, I had to find them all other places to live—and had the two communal apartments rejoined and the renovations done. Now I have an office and plenty of room to live like a civilized human being."

This was as vast as I imagined a Kremlin apartment would be, and I had to indeed think that Pavel was quickly on his way to becoming the Oprah of Russian television. Perhaps his show had made him a ruble billionaire, though with inflation running at the speed of a race-horse, that wouldn't mean so much. Nevertheless, to afford a place like this I wondered how much *valuta* he had stashed away.

"Well, let's get to work." Starting down the hallway, into some unseen chamber he called, "Mama, we'll have some tea!"

As we proceeded, I glanced through a slightly cracked door on my left. Catching a brief glimpse of a bookcase, I saw that the shelves were not lined with books but videotapes. So Pavel wasn't joking. His great love and escape was film.

We entered Pavel's office, which held a huge oak desk, a few chairs, and then a long couch off to one side. The walls were covered with a deep red wallpaper, and it felt confining yet warm and secure in there. Pavel took Tanya by the hand and escorted her to the couch, then pulled up a chair and sat next to her. I took a wooden chair facing them both.

Pavel's mother entered, a short gray-haired woman wearing a

blue housedress and slippers. She silently carried a tray, set it down on a side table, and was about to pour tea.

"This is Mama Luda," said Pavel, introducing his mother. "We'll get it, Mama. That's all for now."

She smiled and obediently left, seeming more like an indentured maid than the matron of the house. As she left, she carefully shut the office door behind her, sealing us in Pavel's trance room.

Ignoring me, Pavel again stroked Tanya's hand, saying, "Would you like some tea now or later, my dear?"

Tanya blushed. "Later."

"*Xhorosho.*" Good. "Tell me, Tanya, have you ever experienced hypnosis before?"

"*Da.*"

"When?"

"Recently. I'm taking an English class and that's the method the teacher uses. She puts us into a trance and the lesson begins."

"And do you find it helpful?"

"*Da, da.*"

"Good, then you know the strength and power of hypnosis." He paused, then asked, "Can we begin?"

Glancing nervously at me, Tanya replied, "Sure."

"Then please lie down on the couch and get comfortable."

She hesitantly did so, stretching out on the couch, adjusting a pillow behind her head, while Pavel rose and turned on a small light on his desk and shut off the overhead one. He next pulled heavy curtains across the windows, and we were enveloped by a deep gloom. Then he moved the chair closer still to the couch and planted his left hand on Tanya's shoulder, pinning her down. It was immediately clear how things could stretch beyond acceptable limits; I could easily imagine that waitress lying there with Pavel's large, secure hand stroking her. In fact, I wondered how many he'd slept with. Certainly there had to be more who'd fallen too deeply under his magnetic influences.

"Now, my dear," he began, voice large and strong, "you've suffered a horrible tragedy, but you must know that all is safe here. You are with me, Dr. Pavel Konstantinovich Kamikov, and I will offer you only security and insight. Do you understand?"

"*Da,*" meekly replied Tanya.

"Good. We will begin the hypnotic process now." Like a healer, he ran his right hand over her head, down her neck. "I'm taking the tension away from you now. Simply let go of it and I will absorb it. That's right, breathe in, breathe out. Relax and let go. Give up all of your tension. Deliver it to me. In trance you will be safe and secure. I will make sure of that.'' Pulling back his shirtsleeve, he held out his right wrist. ''I want you to find my pulse and focus on it. I want you to follow the rhythms of my heart.''

I watched as Tanya reached out, took his wrist in her hand, coupling her being to his. Within a minute or so, her chest began to rise and fall peacefully as the tension spilled out of her. All this was in a way similar, of course, to a trance Maddy would have introduced, but, just as at the television studio, it was also fundamentally different. I tried to tell myself that it was all cultural—namely, this pulse thing—that what was appropriate in America might not be so in Russia, and vice versa. But I still didn't care for it. I had far more confidence in Maddy and her methods, but only hoped that this would work, that Pavel would be able to dredge up any overlooked information regarding Lev's murder.

Careful to keep his right wrist in Tanya's clutches, he lifted his left hand from her shoulder and made a fist, which he lifted high above her face. I watched the spectacle almost in shock, studied them both as the beginnings of a trance swirled about and into the room. And I could feel it, that ethereal energy sweeping in there, gathering force, preparing to strike and pass through Pavel and into Tanya.

''I hold the sun in my fist and you look at it. Look at it, Tanya! Look at it and feel the power and strength emanating from me. As you feel the beating of my heart beneath your fingertips, you look up at my other hand and feel a deep warmth beaming down upon you. And as my fist descends, so does the sun. And as the sun sets, you feel a deep relaxation enter your body. Watch the sun go down. Your eyelids become heavy. Your eyelids begin to close.'' He slowly reached over and placed his left hand over Tanya's eyes as if he were an undertaker sealing shut the eyes of a dead person. ''Sleep. Let my power come over you . . . and spat . . . spat . . . spat.'' Sleep . . . sleep . . . sleep.

Not unlike the Russian Orthodox priest's at Lev's funeral, Pavel's voice chanted on, rising and falling with unusual emotion and conviction. I stared at his face, saw his own eyes close, witnessed as Pavel himself descended into a trance of his own making and pulled Tanya in after him. The induction went on another five minutes, and like lovers holding hands, they jumped into a dark abyss, leaving me behind to sort out what and how and why.

Finally Pavel's eyes half opened in a sleepy, almost drunken stupor, and he said, ''My Tanichka.'' My little Tanya, he called, using the terribly endearing form of her name. "I have taken you into a deep trance. I have put you there. And in trance everything is quite clear. You will tell me all that you see, won't you?"

Her lips moved, at first not a sound emerged, and then, "Absolutely."

"I want to know about your husband."

Her voice small, she whispered, "Lev."

"*Da, da, da.* Lev. He was your husband."

"Was . . . was . . ." she mumbled. "He's dead now."

"That's right, Tanichka. He was murdered. Go back to that time. That day. Return to that scene and look at it once more." Pavel's eyes drifted shut again, he reached down, wrapped his left hand over hers, and commanded, "Go back to that time and take me with you. Lead me there, my little one. Make me see what you do. Go back . . . back . . . Use my power to go back through time to that afternoon."

I watched as Tanya's entire body began to writhe on the couch.

"I'm holding you, Tanichka. I'm with you. There's nothing to worry about. What is it, my dear? Tell me what you see."

"I can't see much."

"So it's dark."

"It's dark and I'm moving quickly."

"Go on, run! I'm with you!"

"Lev's hurt. He's crying out!"

"I can't hear him. What's he saying?"

"Pain. He's screaming in pain. There's a gunshot."

"And what do you see?"

"Darkness. I'm running through a passage. And then . . . then there's a car. It's up ahead."

"Good, Tanichka. What color do you see?"

"Light."

"Is the car white?"

"*Nyet.* It's . . . it's darker. Like brown."

"The vehicle's brown?"

"The inside is brown. I'm looking right inside it. The door's open."

"Yes, my dear. I see the vehicle in the courtyard. It's parked there. The door's open. You see that and then . . . then what?"

"Lev!" screamed Tanya.

I jumped in my seat. Tanya was lying physically on the couch. Her body was here. But the rest of her was back there in that courtyard, witnessing the death of her husband all over again.

"Lev's on the ground!" she sobbed. "There's blood. All this blood!"

"What else, Tanichka? Look around. What do you see?"

"Lev. He's on the ground."

"*Da, da, da.*"

"A noise. A noise and then . . . then nine . . ."

When Tanya's voice trailed off, Pavel burst in, demanding, "Nine? Nine what? I can't see it. Tell me! Tell me what you see!"

"Nine . . . four . . ."

"Go on!"

"Nine . . . four . . . zero . . ."

"What else, Tanya? Give me more! More!"

Pavel's demand extracted a horrible scream, and a huge, pained cry burst from Tanya's mouth. I leapt to my feet, stared at my friend as she doubled up, rolled to her side, and disappeared into an hysterical burst of tears and sobs. This was too much. Too coarse. Too crude an exercise.

"Tanya!" I called, rushing to her side.

I bent over the couch, reached out for her. Sobbing, Tanya was doubled up, her knees pulled up to her chest. I looked over at Pavel, saw him just sitting there, eyes wide in shock.

"Get her some water!" I shouted.

He hesitated, couldn't move.

"Go on!"

He quickly rose and scampered out. Once I'd gotten rid of him, I knew I had to back her out of it. To hook her and coach her back to the here and now.

"Tanya!" I called. "It's me, Alex. I'm here, it's all right."

"He's . . . he's hitting me!"

She was reliving the attack, suffering the blows, and she moaned and her face flushed red and her body twisted. Oh, shit. How would Maddy the wise and conniving handle this? What angle would she take, how would she twist things so they came out right?

"Tanya, I hear your scream! I'm in the car, sitting there. Remember? Remember? And I hear your voice, so I get out, and now I'm hurrying down the sidewalk toward you." I took a deep breath, prayed this would work. "I'm going to count from five down to one, and when I reach one I'll be there. I'll reach you and bring you back here to the present."

"Oi, *bozhe!*" Oh, God!"

"Five. I know something's wrong, so I'm hurrying as fast as I can. Four. The man hears me. He knows I'm coming so he stops. Three.''

"Car!''

"Yes, he hears me coming so he's in his car and he's speeding away. I'm in the passage and . . . and two! I'm almost there, Tanya. And when I reach you you'll be all right. You'll be back in the present. Again, two. I'm just seconds away. Here I come. Here I am . . . and one! One, Tanya!''

Just as I called the number, I reached out. And right on command, she burst out of the past, twisting into me, grabbing me, begging to be pulled back into the present. I wrapped my arms around, held her firmly, as she opened her eyes and drank in the red wallpaper, the desk, the curtained windows, and everything else of this time and place.

I heard steps behind me and looked back. The large figure of Pavel stood in the doorway, a glass in hand, and his face blanched with fear. He looked scared as hell, for certainly it was a rare day when a trance got away from him, a hypnotist of his command and repute.

His diminutive mother, her hand to her mouth, poked her head around him, and Pavel pushed her back and snapped, "Not now, Mama.''

He moved into the room, closing the door behind him, took a drink of the water, then looked at the glass and handed it to me. I passed the water to Tanya, who took a short, nervous sip and then eyed Pavel either with fear or distrust.

Pavel pressed back one of the curtains, peered out, and in a voice smaller than I'd ever heard from him, said, "I was there.''

"What?'' I said incredulously.

"I don't know what you call it or how even such a thing is possible, but I was there,'' he confessed. "Just now, just in trance, I mean. There was so much energy passing from Tanya to me that I saw all that she did.''

Holy shit. I'd brought Tanya here because I'd hoped that Pavel could do as much as my sister. I knew I could have attempted to hypnotize Tanya, that I had a broad familiarity with uncovering techniques and could have gotten something out of her, but I'd wanted the best for her. Now, however, it was not only clear that I could have done better than Pavel but that he was stretching the realm of reality beyond the possible.

"And I'll tell you what our Tanya saw,'' began Pavel, still staring out the window. "She heard her husband's cry for help and so she hurried down the sidewalk. Turning into the passageway that led into that courtyard, she was immediately struck at how dark it was. Isn't that right, Tanya?''

Next to me, Tanya nodded, said nothing.

"Of course it is," continued Pavel. "There was something up ahead in the courtyard, though. Something bright. It was a car, a brilliant piece of machinery. But not a white one. No, I think it was beige, and she was looking right at the side of it. Looking right in the open driver's door. It was brown inside.''

"Yes, it was brown," muttered a convinced Tanya.

As Pavel spoke, Tanya pulled away from me. She wiped at her tears, pushed herself up, all of her focused on Pavel's reconstruction of the event, every bit of her wanting the truth that had eluded her.

"So Lev's murderer had perhaps a white but more likely a beige car with a brown interior. Tanya saw all that. And she also saw . . .'' Turning to us slowly like an omnipotent sorcerer, Pavel pronounced, "And she saw a series of numbers, which was undoubtedly a license plate bearing nine four zero.''

This was much too much like a church revival meeting, and I glanced at Tanya, tried to ascertain her reaction, what buttons this might push. Nodding her head ever so slightly, she lifted her left hand to her mouth, seeing it all again as interpreted by Pavel.

"*Da, da.* That's right. Absolutely. That's what I saw.''

"Of course it was.'' Beaming smugly, Pavel added, "So that should give the police something to go on. Of course, three numbers would mean the car had come from Helsinki or perhaps the Baltics. Or maybe she only saw some of the numbers. Then again, that could have been some sort of diplomat changing money, someone with special plates. Whatever, with this to go on, it shouldn't prove too difficult even for our police.''

I stared at him in shock. This wasn't how Maddy would have handled this. Not at all. No, this was a sorcery of a different kind, one that I didn't care for and that actually made me feel quite uncomfortable. What shocked me was how poorly Pavel had conducted this, how woefully lacking he was in the field of forensic hypnosis. He hadn't carefully and gently led his subject back to the scene. Instead he'd dragged her back, kicking and screaming, then rubbed her nose right in it. And then worst of all, he hadn't enabled her to recall what she'd actually seen but had suggested it in a way that made Tanya believe his own vision was 100 percent.

Tanya was the perfect escape. She was clearly exhausted. Obviously worn out. So I made excuses. Sure, I did have to get her home. But really what I wanted was to get out of there. And I told Pavel we'd be in touch, then helped Tanya to her feet and out of that room of ill trances. Still in shock, she let me do it all. I helped her on with her raincoat, fastened the belt.

"You're right, absolutely so," confided Pavel to me as we stood in the doorway. "This has been far too stressful. She must get rest. And lots of it."

We bid him farewell, then retreated from that huge apartment, down that hideous stairwell, and out the front, where Misha, Pavel's chauffeur, was miraculously waiting for us. We clambered into the car, Tanya and I, and as we were whisked away, I self-righteously thought how smart I was to see Pavel for all his showy stupidity. But in fact the shoe was on the other foot. I was the stupid one, the one who'd been duped.

A voice out of nowhere burst in, calling, *"Alex, what are you saying?"*

I didn't learn it until later, but Pavel had of course been controlling and manipulating it all, making sure Tanya saw only exactly what he wanted.

# Chapter 17

It was early afternoon, the sun was stabbing through the gray sky, and the most expedient way to Tanya's apartment was up the broad and bustling Nevsky. The two of us sat in the rear seat of the car, a numbing cloud of confusion having engulfed us. What were we to say to the police? That all of what Pavel had conjured up was fact, that they should at once start looking for a light-colored car with a brown interior and license plate number 940? Or were we to say nothing? A horrible thought struck me. All too easily I could imagine the famous and pompous Dr. Pavel Konstantinovich Kamikov descending upon the police and pronouncing that he had solved the murder. Or, shit, maybe he wouldn't go to the police at all. Maybe he'd just make it all part of his show and reenact the whole thing. That was what I feared. Absolutely. I feared that we were nothing but stooges, that Pavel would use us to make him appear great and magnificent on *Mesmerizing Moments*.

None of this was sitting well with me, and when we finally turned off Nevsky toward Hay Market Square, I leaned forward.

"Misha, would you mind stopping here?" I said to the driver.

"*Shto, shto?*" What, what?

"Please stop here. We'll walk the rest of the way."

As Misha quickly pulled the car to the curb, Tanya looked at me, her brow wrinkled with confusion.

"There's something I want to look at," I said to her, leaning over and opening the door. "Don't worry."

I thanked Misha and hustled Tanya out and onto the sidewalk. Misha leaned over, cranked open the passenger window, asked what we were doing, if there was somewhere else we wanted to go. I assured him that all was fine, that we could get home. He shrugged, grunted something, and I watched, standing there on the curb, until the vehicle had turned a corner and was out of sight. And then I took Tanya by the arm and steered her toward a narrow side street.

"Alex," she said, "where are we going? My apartment's back there."

"I know."

"We're going the wrong way."

"No, we're not."

"Then where are we going?"

"To that courtyard."

Knowing at once that I was referring to the murder site, she stopped, placed a hand on her heart, dramatically gasped, "Oi."

"Tanya, we have to. It's just a few blocks away."

"But, Alex, I—"

"Something doesn't make sense. There are a couple of things that Pavel brought up that I don't understand. I know this might be difficult, but we have to go back while it's still fresh."

Fear and concern riddled her face, and again she muttered a long, pained moan.

"It'll be all right," I assured her, even though I had no idea what this might trigger or what we might dig up. "Please trust me. This is something we have to do."

Russians were never ones to hide their emotions, particularly if they were being pushed into something, and Tanya's face puckered into a childlike pout. I paid her no attention, taking her again by the arm, pulling her along. I couldn't quite identify what, but there was something all wrong about Pavel's re-creation of the crime scene.

"Please," I nearly begged. "We won't stay long. I promise."

Tanya gave in, and I closed in on the courtyard like a bloodhound, making a right at the first corner, then a left, and finally another right. Within minutes we emerged on that short street, and of course we both flashed back to that afternoon, to that quick car ride in from the airport, our gabbing, our driving along and parking there, right up there, not suspecting a thing, not realizing that Lev was about to be shot to death.

As before, the street was quiet, a desolate few blocks free of any commercial activity and little pedestrian traffic. I heard one car up ahead, that was all. The buildings were drab and dark, muddy brown and green structures that barely looked inhabited. This was a perfect place to change money.

No, I realized, it wasn't at all pleasant coming back here. I could almost hear Lev's laugh, see him jumping out of the car and rushing down the sidewalk. I glanced at Tanya, saw her face numbing with wretched memories. We had to get through this quickly.

"So we parked here," I said, stopping at the approximate place. Tanya stared off, gazing at nothing.

"Tanya, isn't this where we parked?"

"I guess so."

"And then what?"

She didn't reply.

I said, "Lev got out of the car." I stepped off the sidewalk, went out into the street, started to retrace his steps. "He said he was going to change money, told us to wait, and then he headed toward that passageway."

As nearly as I could, I followed Lev's path, moving down the sidewalk and heading some thirty feet toward the opening that led into the courtyard. When I reached the passage, I stopped. Tanya had barely moved.

"Was there anything else out on the street?" I asked. "Any other cars or anyone suspicious lingering about?"

Tanya looked back at the place where we had parked. Then she glanced up the street. Looking across the way, she focused on a building where three steps led up to an arched entrance.

"No, I don't think so," she finally replied as she walked toward me.

"I don't either. At least not that I remember."

I took a deep breath, looked into the passageway, a low arched opening that curved slightly as it led to the heart of the building. It was dark. The perfect place for things to rot and rats to gather.

I reached out for Tanya, put my arm around her, said, "You and I were sitting in the car, talking. For how long?"

"Ten minutes perhaps. Maybe a little longer."

"Right. And then you got out because he was taking so long. You thought Lev was having a cigarette."

"He liked to smoke. He'd stand around talking and smoking with just about anyone."

I smiled because of course Lev would. He loved to gab. How

many times had he and I stayed up into the late hours, arguing politics? I said, "Then you heard him cry out."

We went through it all, her breaking into a run, my leaping out of the car, how she'd rushed into the passageway, which had seemed so dark. As we talked, we walked through it, moving some ten feet into the dark opening. Then Tanya stopped, her eyes staring into the open courtyard ahead.

"I . . . I was about here when I saw it."

"The car?"

"*Da, da.* It was parked up there, right in the middle of the courtyard, and there must have been some sunlight coming down."

"Of course. That's why it would have looked so bright." I jogged ahead of Tanya, stepping directly into the open-air courtyard. "Where was the car, about here?"

"*Nyet,* over a meter or two to your right."

I went over and stood in the indicated place. Off to the left was another passage, this one leading to a different side street. Obviously the money changer had escaped via that route. Sure.

"Tanya, what else about the car?"

"Well, the door was open. And the inside of the car was brown. I'm sure of that."

"Was it the driver's door or the passenger side?" I suggested, "Close your eyes, try to picture it again."

She did so, bowing her head, trying to recall the image. She seemed lost in thought. Suddenly she looked up.

"I remember a steering wheel. Absolutely. So it had to have been the driver's door."

"Okay. You were looking at the side of the car when he sped off. Which means—"

"*Nyet* . . . I didn't see him drive away." She slowly moved forward. "There was the car. And . . . and then Lev. I saw him on the ground, right there," she said, her eyes fixed on the very spot. "That's when I shouted out. When I screamed. I started running . . . and . . ."

Right on the edge of the courtyard she stopped. She looked to her right. The left. "He came from over here. From this side. I didn't see him. He just jumped out of nowhere and that's when he hit me."

"But you didn't see him?"

"*Nyet.*"

"You're sure?"

"Absolutely. I didn't see anything. Just this fist that came out of nowhere. And then nothing."

I hadn't come long after that. I'd heard her scream, started rushing. In the distance I'd heard Lev's murderer racing off, his car roaring as he exited through the other passage. And then I'd seen Tanya lying there, an unconscious heap. Lev, too, his body collapsed into a pool of blood.

"Something doesn't make sense," I said.

I went over to the spot where Tanya had fallen, looked back at where the car had stood. Next I went over to where we'd found Lev's body. Staring at the large granite cobblestones, I saw that they were darkened. Was that his blood? I shook my head, broke away. And then studied how the money changer must have escaped. It didn't add up.

Tanya said, "Alex, what is it?"

"If you came in that way and were looking at the driver's side of the car," I began, "the vehicle was obviously pointed toward the other entrance over there. Right?"

"Why, sure. That's exactly how it was."

"And then out of nowhere came this fist that hit you in the face. Are you sure you were knocked out right away?"

"Absolutely. I don't remember anything after that."

I went back to the point where she'd fallen and where she now stood. This was all wrong.

"Tanya, there's no way you could have seen the license plate from here."

"What?"

"Well, you were looking at the side of the car when you came in, so you couldn't have seen it then."

"No . . . no, I suppose not."

"And how could you have seen the plates after that if you were unconscious?" I asked.

Her face flushed with concern. "I . . . I don't know. Maybe I . . . maybe I looked up when the car was speeding away."

"No, Tanya. You couldn't have. When I found you, your body and head were facing that way toward Lev's body. Not that way toward the other entry." I shook my head. "Tanya, there's no way you could have seen that guy's license plate."

From up above, from some second-floor space, I heard a window abruptly creak. I looked up, saw the last of a thick figure melting into the darkness. Shit, someone had been there the entire time, listening to our whole conversation, spying on us. As the sound of quick steps disappeared into the heart of the old building, Tanya and I exchanged a nervous look. Who in the hell had that been?

"Alex, we shouldn't be here," she urged, now keeping her voice low.

Terribly confused, I glanced up at the window. Just then I heard the roar of a car engine in the distance. Someone coming after us? The killer returning, now ready to gun us down?

Tanya was absolutely right, and we quickly joined hands and hurried out of that rathole of a courtyard and back onto the street.

# Chapter 18

Tanya and I wasted no time. As directly as we could, we hurried back to her place, which was just the other side of Hay Market Square. We hustled around the huge construction site that swallowed most of the square, past dozens of tiny kiosks—squalid shacks which looked more like icehouses than retail outlets—that were selling everything from Nescafé to caviar to Pig's Eye Beer all the way from St. Paul, Minnesota. Finally clambering over temporary streetcar tracks that were laid on the street atop a long ribbon of rock, we came to Tanya's street and her building, which was unremarkable in every aspect.

I just assumed that Tanya would invite me in. That there would be no question about it. We had a lot to discuss, a good deal of it personal, and I'd supposed we'd spend the evening together. When I'd been here before, I'd had trouble, if the truth be known, getting rid of Tanya and Lev. They'd not only sucked up all my free time, they'd acted like jealous lovers, wanting to know what I was doing when I wasn't with them, who I was seeing, where I was going, trying to ascertain if I might like someone else better. They'd also expressed great, compulsive pleasure in taking care of me. Did I have everything I wanted? Was I getting enough to eat? Come, eat some borscht with us. Drink some vodka. This is the best, the tastiest. We got it just for you. Only for you, our Alex. Our dear friend from America, whom they had treated like a real treasure.

So I didn't consider otherwise. I was sure Tanya would ask me in for tea and a snack of cucumber and sausage and black bread. Something like that. And then we'd just sit around and talk. When we reached the door of her apartment building, however, she stopped. And said, "Thanks, Alex."

I came to an abrupt, awkward halt, saw how she had grasped the door yet not pushed it open, her arm blocking my path. I was no dummy. I'd been on a number of dates that had ended at the threshold. Yet this time I didn't know what to say. When I'd been arranging the trip, anticipating the days here, I had planned very little, so sure was I that all my time would be gobbled up by Tanya and Lev. It had been so long since we'd seen each other. There was so much to catch up on. And really I had so little time here. Just a few days. Granted, Lev's murder was a horrendous turn of events, but now more than ever Tanya and I had something to discuss. I'd simply thought that this afternoon would bleed into evening, that Tanya wouldn't let me go, that instead she'd cling to me more strongly than ever—in exactly which way I was desirous to know—and that afternoon tea would turn into a few shots of vodka, which would in turn lead into dinner perhaps with Sveta and her boyfriend, Igor. When I'd departed from the hotel this afternoon, I was certain I wouldn't be back until well after midnight. If at all.

Yet here was Tanya implying: You're not invited up. I stared back at her, so stunned that I didn't know what to do or say.

Finally she reached out and caressed my cheek, asked, "Alex, can I see you later?"

"When? Later tonight? Can we have dinner? Can I take you out to a dollar restaurant?"

"Maybe tomorrow. Right now I . . . I just need to be alone for a while."

That was ludicrous. Since when did a woman of the great Soviet collective begin to talk as if she were from California? Things had switched all around. I shoved my hands in my pockets, turned away from her. Christ, now it was I who wanted to know what she was doing, if she was going to be meeting with someone else.

"Tanya," I said, my voice slow, untrusting, "is everything all right? Do you have other plans?"

"Alex, I just need some rest. That's all." As if she were anxious to get rid of me, she added, "Let's get together tomorrow."

This sucked. I studied her face, noted that she was obviously exhausted. Dark circles stretched beneath her eyes, and she did appear sad, her mouth small and flat. But she wouldn't look at me. Her head was bent, her eyes flitting at the street, the sidewalk, her hand. She wasn't simply barring me entry to her apartment, but also her life. What was she trying to keep from me? Or was I all wrong, was I being too harsh, too distrustful, was she truly the spouse in deep mourning? If so, why was she keeping me at arm's length?

"Will you give me a call in the morning?" she asked.

I wanted to say if I felt like it, if I wasn't off doing things with other people, if I wasn't busy having too much fun doing God knows what. But I was not only too Midwestern to be that direct, I was too proud to show my hurt.

"Sure."

Clearly relieved that I wasn't pressing her any further, she leaned forward and kissed me on the cheek. I held her, kissed her back. Squeezed her. You can trust me, Tanya, I wanted to say, for the two of us shared not simply a long history but a complicated one. How odd it was, I thought, that when I'd been a student here at the university, our common enemies—the Soviet state, the KGB, the CIA—had brought us closer together, bonding us as one in a conspiracy of defiance and friendship. In these times, however, the enemy was no longer black and white.

She said, "Thank you for taking me to Pavel's. That was *ochin interesno*." Very interesting.

I pulled back, stared at her, tried to see beneath her mask of grief. *Ochin interesno?* Shit. We'd just been sticking our fingers in Lev's murder, stirring everything up as if we were mad finger painters, and all she had to say was *ochin interesno*? Oh, please, am I crazy?

"Tanya, is there anything wrong?"

"*Nyet, nyet,*" she replied curtly. "I just need to go up. I have to lie down. I hardly slept last night."

"Sure. Okay. I'll see you tomorrow." I thought better of that and asked, "I will see you tomorrow, won't I?"

"Absolutely. Call me in the morning, and then we'll spend the day together, just like old times."

But Lev wouldn't be there, I thought, as I said to her, "Sure." I studied her face. "Tanya, what's going on with the store?"

She hesitated, then said, "I'll explain tomorrow."

"But—"

As if she were escaping from me, she quickly slipped inside without another word, without another embrace. How unemotional and for that very reason how very un-Russian. I just didn't get it. Looking at this picture, I knew something was wrong. But what?

Feeling rejected and confused, I started to walk away, to wander off in search of a taxi. I crossed the street, passed down the block and onto the edge of Hay Market Square, where taxis were flitting about like annoying mosquitoes. Had Tanya really been wanting to get rid of me so she could get some rest? The resulting lack of hospitality was just so unlike the smothering concern that I'd anticipated that I couldn't believe it. I'd come to expect star status here in Russia. An American. They adored us. Wanted all they could get. I was from the land of fortune and opportunity, from that dreamy, gold-ridden place. Yet here was my Tanya turning away from me. Furthermore, she wasn't even asking how I was going to get back to the Pribalt, what I would do for dinner, how I would amuse myself. Nor had she even arranged any kind of *kulturnaya programma;* she hadn't arranged for a friend of hers to take me to a museum or play, film or any such thing. Her negligence most certainly could have been due to Lev's death and the horrible shock. Yet I didn't think so. Tanya was clearly distressed by the murder of her husband, but she didn't look devastated, didn't seem as if the light of her life had just been snuffed and her world had gone dim.

*"If there's another reason, Alex,"* beckoned a wiser voice, *"now would be a helpful time to acknowledge it."*

Of course there was another reason. One that, albeit mysterious, certainly wasn't a mystery for very long. Just as I melted into the crowds milling along the edge of the square, I glanced to my right, searching a side street for one of those small green cabs. My attention was caught by something else, though, which I noticed because it was so clean and shiny. So brilliantly gold. I stopped, totally fixed on the vehicle. Anything that clean and that new stood out in the economic ruins of old St. Petersburg. It was the Mercedes, that very same one. Had they followed us back to her place and now that I had left, were they circling in, getting ready like crows to dive in and claw apart Tanya?

I spun around, desperately pushing my way through the crowd. I had to go back, had to see if Tanya was in any kind of danger. The mafia was now headed toward her house, and I cursed myself. I'd been stupid to let her avoid the question of the store. She'd put me off the other day when Lev's father had been up in her apartment, but I'd had ample opportunity today and I'd let it slide. How stupid. At some point this afternoon I should have asked her exactly what that had all been about at the Springtime Beauty Salon. Surely she knew.

The big gold Mercedes sped down the street, zipping right toward Tanya's building, and I chased after it. I had no idea what I could do, how I could intercede to protect her. I had no weapon of any kind. Perhaps I'd be able to make enough commotion, though. Something to screw things up. Something to attract the attention of the police.

I was nowhere near as fast as the car, but fortunately it wasn't that far, and I was a mere half block away when the vehicle pulled up in front of her building, when I saw the rear door of the car quickly swing open. My heart clenched. Were a couple of thugs with guns going to leap out and charge up to Tanya's apartment? Were they going to go up and drag her out? Was my old friend about to meet the same fate as her husband?

No, instead a short man in a blue coat climbed out, smoothed back his thin, graying hair. Before he could take a step, however, the door to Tanya's building was hurled open and Tanya herself came charging out, rushing this man and going immediately on the attack.

Wait. No. I froze in shock. Oh, shit. I ducked around the corner of a building, sulked in the shadows. Tanya wasn't attacking this mafia guy. No, she'd gone flying into his arms and now she was kissing him wildly. Spying on them, I stopped in shock. Tanya, who had only minutes ago appeared the grieving, worn-out widow, now had changed into a glitzy red and black dress. Everything about her, from her face down to her shoes, had brightened dramatically.

And after a long, obscene kiss, she and this mafia man in the blue coat climbed into the back of the chauffeur-driven Mercedes.

# Chapter 19

For the longest time I couldn't move. I was so dumbfounded that I simply stood there staring. Then, to my shock, I watched the glitzy robber baron car pull a smooth U-turn and head toward Hay Market Square.

What was I supposed to do? The car passed by me, and I hurried into the street, stared after it. And then I was jogging. It didn't occur to me that I'd never be able to keep up with it, let alone catch it. All I knew was that I was desperate to find out what this was all about, why Tanya would move so quickly from a dead husband to a mafia thug, why she would push me out of the way to be meeting this guy this afternoon.

I was jogging after them, and as the car accelerated, my pace quickened into a run. They started to pull away from me. I was going to lose them, be left in the dust of confusion. Then one of the sacred cows of Russia, a bent babushka, emerged from the square, stepped into the street, moved right out in front of them. The car skidded to a quick stop. Oblivious, the babushka paid them no attention, moved on. I gained on the halted Mercedes, but it was still useless. They took off in a second, and I scanned for a taxi, saw none, only a handful of cars, one of which pulled up on my right side. I glanced over and the driver, his teeth bent and cigarette-stained, smiled at me through an open window.

"Need a lift, *tovarish?*" Comrade.

What did it look like, I was training for the Olympics? People with cars trying to earn an extra ruble here and there were common, though slightly illegal. And I knew, of course, how to assure I got a ride.

Employing the magic word as I ran along, I said, "I'll pay you in dollars."

The car skidded to a halt, the passenger door was hurled open, and I ran around and squeezed in. It was a Moskvich, the tiniest of Soviet cars, this one a real rattrap that was rusting and falling apart. There was barely enough room for my legs.

I pointed to the Mercedes. "Follow them."

With a grin he said, "Just like in *Our Man in Siberia*. Did you see that movie? It was great."

The guy punched on the gas but not much of anything happened. Still it was quicker than running and definitely easier, and fortunately the Mercedes wasn't going all that fast.

"You an *Amerikanets*?" he asked as he shifted gears.

I nodded.

"One of our Russian girls giving you troubles?"

"Something like that." The Mercedes turned to the right. "Just don't lose them."

He laughed. "I'm sure she's not worth it. A smart girl would be chasing after you and your *valuta*."

I paid him no attention as his small car tailed the Mercedes like a mettlesome fly chasing after a bird. Somehow we managed never to be more than a block behind them; as it turned out, they weren't going that far either. The gold car twisted its way through a series of side streets, emerged alongside the crumbling Gostiny Dvor, that huge old department store that was closed for repairs, then turned down Nevsky before taking a right and pulling up to the Grand Hotel Europe.

"Don't get too close," I told my nameless driver as we turned off Nevsky.

The hotel, just a block from the palatial Russian Museum, loomed on our left like a jewel, a pre-Revolutionary structure that now sparkled as the result of a total renovation. I'd heard it was a Swedish company that had taken it over and that it was now as good as the very top hotels in Europe. Surely this and the recently redone Astoria were the best in St. Petersburg, and by the glimmering exterior, the waving flags, and the uniformed doorman, I knew, of course, that rubles were just not an acceptable currency. Which was why I watched intently as the chauffeured Mercedes pulled up to the main entrance, the driver jumped out and opened the rear door, and Tanya and the man in the blue coat climbed out. A wave of distaste passed through me. They weren't going to check in for a late-afternoon quickie, were they? Whatever they were doing, I knew Tanya wasn't paying.

"How much?" I said to my driver.

He sucked on his cigarette, thought for a moment, and pronounced, "Twenty-five dollars."

Surely that was more than this guy made in a month. And surely, I thought, studying him, he had no idea the true value of twenty-five bucks.

Pulling out my wallet, I said, "Here's five."

He smiled, exposing his browned teeth, didn't utter a word of protest as he accepted my money. *"Spacibo."* Thank you.

So maybe that was his gimmick, ask for the moon and get just the sky, which was still more than plenty. It didn't matter if I'd been taken, though, and I leapt out of the car, made my way across the street. All up and down this short street was the largest collection of Western cars I'd yet seen in St. Petersburg, from freshly washed Honda Civics to Mercedes-Benzes, BMWs, and a bright red Saab. I saw only a couple of Finnish license plates, so it was clear that these belonged if not to the burgeoning mafia then to the very-upper-crust wheeler and dealers, the *biznizmeni* of these post-Soviet times. Off to the left, on the corner of Nevsky and built into the base of the hotel, I saw the Sadko, one of the hippest restaurants in town and now supposedly a real mafia hangout.

Tanya and her friend had disappeared into the main entrance of the hotel, and I hurried to the wide doors. As I approached, I saw the doorman scrutinizing me, observing that my clothing was not of top Western style. Clearly he wasn't sure if I was Russian or American, and hence he wasn't sure if he should allow me entry.

So I spoke in English, beamed a nervous smile, and said, "Good afternoon."

"Good afternoon, sir," he replied in accented English, opening the door and allowing me passage.

I'd last been here as a student when this had been called the Evropeskaya, and back then it had been anything but grand, a rundown hotel, a remnant from tsarist times that had more closely resembled an ancient YMCA. Now, however, the interior radiated elegance, from marble floors to glistening atrium. I climbed a short staircase, turned right, checked the front desk, which looked like a reception desk of any fine New York hotel. Tanya and her friend weren't there.

I turned the other way, headed for the bar, which I recalled as a dark, dismal little place. Now, however, the bar had been scrubbed and redecorated, and the art nouveau interior shone with elegance. But Tanya and her beau were not to be found there either.

I saw a sign indicating that the Caviar Bar was open, and I hurried down the hall, up a broad staircase, left, and into a large two-story room. In a quick glance I could see why counts and princes had once dined here, for the elaborate art nouveau decor had been faithfully restored, the tables were set with white linen and fresh flowers, and the private second-floor dining rooms that overlooked this hall screamed intimacy and seduction.

At the far end of the room, a woman played a harp for the only two guests, Tanya and her friend, who were just sitting down to a waiting bottle of celebratory champagne.

A hostess appeared to my right, asked in perfect English, "Would you care for a table, sir?"

"No."

Storming past her, I walked directly toward Tanya, who was reaching over to that guy, lifting his hand, kissing his knuckles. For all the right reasons and a few of the wrong, my body started shaking. And just after she had planted a luscious smack on that jerk, Tanya glanced my way, saw me coming. She dropped his hand, sat back, fear in her eyes.

As the harpist strummed out some flowery, heavenly tune, I went right up to Tanya and demanded, "What the hell is going on?"

"Alex, I . . ."

Suddenly there was a huge, hulking figure behind me and an enormous hand grabbing me by the shoulder.

Seated across from Tanya, the man in the blue suit waved away his chauffeur and bodyguard, saying, "It's alright, Sasha. This one's harmless."

I glared at him, then to Tanya said, "I thought you were going home to get some rest? I thought you were exhausted and worn out?"

"You don't understand."

"I think I understand enough." Why in the hell had I ever come back here? "I understand that for someone whose husband just died, you certainly don't look very sad."

Tanya bowed her face into cupped hands. I was glad. She should cry. She should feel shame and disgust. And maybe, by the looks of this little tryst, I wondered if she shouldn't feel guilt for Lev's death as well.

The guy across from her was laughing, and I stared at him. Balding, hair graying, he was short and plump. And beautifully groomed. Cleanly shaven, a crisp white shirt, tie. An Italian suit. So who was he ripping off? What company had he stolen to reap so much money that he could afford to eat in a place like this when most of his countrymen couldn't afford a banana?

"You Americans," he said, dismissing me and another two hundred-plus million people. "You're so righteous, so superior and presumptuous." He laughed and spurted the classic pat phrase, "Yankee, go home."

"Who the fuck are you?" I demanded.

"My name's Viktor. And can you not appreciate how hard our lives have been? Can you not see how we have suffered?"

I couldn't believe I was hearing this, turned back to Tanya, asked, "Just what are you involved in?"

She looked up at me, her eyes swollen and red. She started to say something, but her lips were quivering and she bit down on her lower lip.

"*Radi boga.*" For God's sake, continued Viktor. "Can't you see that your friend is about to have everything she's ever wanted? Soon she'll have her very own store and an apartment—"

"All to herself," I interrupted, shouting above that stupid harp music. "Is that what you wanted, Tanya? To be rid of your husband?"

"Alex, you . . . you don't understand," she muttered through her sobs.

"Just tell me one thing. Are you out here celebrating Lev's death?"

And when she just sat there, her hand to her mouth, her eyes clenched shut as the tears rolled out, and said nothing, my worst fear was realized. I didn't know what to say, what to do, so I just turned and walked out of there, hoping to God I'd never see Tanya ever again.

# Chapter 20

I exploded from the Grand Hotel, rushing out of there and bursting onto the sidewalk, my heart twisting with confusion and anger. The late northern sun was softening to a dusky gray, and I hadn't taken more than five steps when a huge figure was rushing into my face.

"You need taxi?" asked some guy in rough English.

I angrily waved him away, turned from him and a bunch of other guys and the bustle of Nevsky. I stormed down the sidewalk. Yes, this was just like the old Russia. Nothing had changed, nothing improved. This was still a warped place. And just as before, I still didn't know whom to trust. In a place where friendship meant everything, it also meant nothing. You were totally dependent upon your friends until they'd done all they could for you, until someone else came along who could do more.

Leaving the hotel behind me, I quickly reached the end of the block, then trotted across another street and to the small circle where the statue of the revered poet Pushkin stood. A handful of red carnations lay strewn at his feet, the petals wilting with sadness. Were trust and honesty to be found anywhere, I wondered, or were they only romantic notions, visions of utopia that would and could never exist? I hated the fucking Soviet Union, detested it for warping the mentality of all these people, making them so desperate for a normal life that they'd sell their own mother for a pair of blue jeans or Ray • Bans. Would integrity ever return to Russia or had it been permanently stomped out?

Moments later I was standing at the black wrought-iron gates of the Russian Museum, the former palace of some prince that now housed so many great paintings. I stared at the huge thing, a sprawling classical structure with huge white columns. My fingers clung to the bars and I hung there. What was I supposed to do now, go back to the hotel, pack up, and head for the airport? Probably. I didn't know what Tanya was involved in, hated to imagine what role she might have, could have played in Lev's death. I didn't want to know either. I was sick of this. I just wanted to go home, retreat to the isolation of Maddy's boring island.

I started walking, heading toward a canal, passing a long pale yellow building that looked like the former stables of the neighboring palace. Reaching the granite-lined strip of water, I looked to my left, saw Dom Knigi, the House of Books. To my immediate right towered the Cathedral of the Blood, an exotic, fanciful creation of brick and onion domes that stood on the exact spot where Alexander II had been assassinated, his legs blown out from underneath him. After thirty years of being covered by scaffolding for a supposed renovation, the brick structure had only recently been liberated; now its multicolored and gold onion domes sparkled like jewels against the darkening sky.

Heading into the shadows of the church, I made my way toward the huge park behind the Russian Museum, hoping that somehow I'd figure this out, that if I thought hard enough it would all make sense. Instead, I began to feel worse, as if a dark wave had not only swept over me but was pulling me under. I should be wary, should be afraid, I sensed. I shouldn't be out here. There was danger crawling much too closely.

That voice called, asked, *"What is it, Alex?"*

It was a sense that I had then. A fear that came out of nowhere, that started prickling the back of my neck.

*"Can you be more specific?"*

As I turned a corner, headed into an opening in the fence and into the park, I glanced back. Someone was lurking along the granite embankment of the canal. It was a figure, thick and dark, who seemed oddly familiar. Where had I seen this person before? Back by the hotel, milling in that group of people by the entrance? I couldn't distinguish a face, but there was something oddly familiar.

*"Who is it, Alex?"*

I started down a gravel path lined with statues and benches, a path that curved beneath large, old trees. Having gone some hundred feet into the park, I checked behind, saw that figure now lingering by the entrance to the park. I was being followed, wasn't I? I quickened my pace, turned down another gravel-laid passage, then stole a look over my shoulder. The person was now dipping into the park, subtly keeping an eye on me. Whether this was someone from Viktor's gang, that elusive, imaginal spy I'd encountered before, or perhaps someone else, I didn't yet know. Nor was I sure I wanted to.

*"Take a deep breath and look beyond this time. Look into the future, Alex. Who's following you?"*

I thought I knew, but I wasn't sure that I could grasp that knowledge.

*"In hypnosis there is no simple present tense, but rather something much broader. The past, the present, and the future all blend together into something much more three-dimensional. So look back in the park. Look back as if you were looking back into time from the future. Who's following you?"*

I couldn't be sure. I wanted to say it was that vision of a woman whom I'd chased at the monastery. Or perhaps a colleague of hers. Yes, I feared it was tied to all that messy business. On the other hand, this could be something very real. It could be Lev's killer stalking me, couldn't it? Absolutely.

Instinctively I knew I had to get away, and I broke into a run. The path curved and twisted, and I wasted no time in making my way toward the other side of the park. I didn't want to be trapped in here, and I saw a gate on the other side, rushed toward it, passing a babushka and a small boy, then a young couple cuddling on a bench. I hesitated about halfway through the park, pausing near a statue of a naked woman and noting the huge Russian Museum that loomed at the far end of the lawn. There were a handful of people strolling through the park. But the person was gone. Then again, maybe not. By a huge, ancient lilac bush something moved. Yes, there, lurking in the shadows.

I didn't look back again. As fast as I could I ran toward the other gates, where I left the park and burst onto a quiet street. To my left was a busy intersection, and I jogged down there. Standing anxiously on the curb, I found a free taxi, and as I jumped into the cab, I looked back, saw no one. Still, I sensed my tail was close by.

The driver turned around, blurted, *"Kooda?"* Where to?

*"Gostinitsa Pribaltiskaya,"* I said, asking for my hotel.

And we were off, shooting through the streets, across canals, over the Neva, and to the far end of Vasilevsky Island, where the large hotel loomed over the serene Bay of Finland. The driver tried to make conversation but I ignored him. I simply sat in the backseat, bouncing around in my confusion and dilemma, hoping that I would find some sort of peace in the privacy of my hotel room.

Yet there was more to come that night. More to add to this pile of problems. After reaching the hotel and paying the taxi driver, I mounted the broad granite steps in front of the hotel and entered the lobby. I hadn't even made it past the reception desk when I saw someone rushing through the dimly lit space.

"Alex!"

Crap. This was the last person I wanted to see. It was Pavel, his large figure plowing toward me. How long had he been hanging out in the dollar bar waiting for me, and what was he going to chide me for now?

"Alex!" he called again. "I've been looking for you."

"I . . . I . . ." But I didn't know what to say or even where to begin.

He looked me up and down, couldn't hide his concern. "Where have you been, my friend? Is everything all right? You look terrible."

It was only then that I noticed that my face was all sweaty and grimy, my shoes covered with mud, and my shirt soiled and barely tucked into my pants. I looked like I'd just been in a brawl.

"It's a long story." I didn't want to divulge too much, so I merely said, "Tanya had some problems."

"I'm not surprised." He took me by the arm, led me to the side of the lobby, and in a low voice said, "That's what I wanted to tell you about. This woman, this friend of yours."

Here it comes, I thought. The lecture. And the nasty words of my friend. The one whom I could no longer defend.

"What are you talking about?" I feebly asked.

"This Tanya, of course. After you two left my apartment, I did some checking. As I told you, I'm under my cousin's *kreesha*. He's very powerful in this business of protection, and he asked around. Unfortunately, I have to tell you that she's trouble. To put it frankly, she's very involved with the mafia here in St. Petersburg."

My head was pounding so hard that I thought it would crack. I didn't want this, particularly now.

"Is that why you're here?" I snapped. "Did you come all the way out here just to tell me that?"

He took a half step back. "Actually . . . actually, no. My television commercial is running for the first time tonight. It'll be on at nine. I was wondering if you wanted to get a drink and watch it with me in the bar?"

"Listen, Pavel, I can't." Oh, God, get me out of this, I thought, shaking my head. "I've got to take a shower and get some rest. I'll call you in the morning."

Before he could say anything else, I retreated from him, scurrying to the elevator and up to my room.

# Chapter 21

Russia had to be the least restful place in the world. Granted, it was among the most interesting, but by the time I nabbed some hard-boiled eggs and sausage and bread at the *boofyet* on my floor, then returned to my room, I felt like I'd been drugged with exhaustion. Eating my makeshift meal, drinking a couple of cans of beer, I sat by the window, staring out at the flat, gray sea, and thinking, Tanya, Tanya, Tanya.

Eventually I turned on the television. The station didn't carry endless reports on the wheat harvest in Ukraine, no information on the decision of the Communist Party. Nothing like that. Not even any documentary footage of the Great Fatherland War and how many millions and millions of people had died in the struggle against the Hitlerites. Instead the first channel I turned to was all telemarketing. A soft, well-spoken woman's voice told all about a shiny white Siemens dishwasher as the camera slowly circled the machine. Next was a large plastic bottle, simply called Kola, a beverage from Poland that could be had for a reasonable amount. After that, the camera switched to a Korean stereo.

I changed channels, landing on a soap opera, a Mexican one. I wondered it if was the famed *The Rich Also Cry*, which was all the rage in Russia, construction workers and babushkas alike skipping work to watch it. Whatever it was, the characters were all having bad hair days. Massively so. The women had futuristic beehives, the men poofy, weird cuts; I hated to see what hair was going to look like across Russia in the next year. When a commercial came, which was an altogether new concept in this formerly socialist country, it was for Orbit gum, with lots of pictures and diagrams showing the *zona riska* and how this gum was good for your teeth. Then came something about Tix laundry detergent.

I stayed fixed on the soap opera all the way to the end—of course it was about money and jealousy—and just as I leaned forward to switch it off, a familiar woman popped onto the screen. She had a perky face, spiky hair. That, I realized, was none other than Pavel's assistant. And this was Pavel's television commercial.

"At the Hypnosis Institute of St. Petersburg, Dr. Pavel Konstantinovich Kamikov can not only help you achieve your dreams, but make big money," promised the enthusiastic woman. "Just watch the doctor himself as he exhibits his strange and mesmerizing powers."

With that, the camera cut to Pavel, who was dressed in a plain white shirt and standing next to a window. He was moaning, perhaps chanting something. Just to assure the viewers that he was in a deep trance, the camera closed in, exposing the whites of his eyes. And then in one brash moment, the good doctor swung out his fist and smashed the window. It broke, of course, into a multitude of pieces, yet he kept swinging at it, shattering it into ever smaller bits. Finally he scooped up some glass and squeezed it in his hand. When he opened his palm, however, the camera zoomed in, and Pavel had not a single cut, not a drop of blood.

His assistant's voice proclaimed, "*Da,* the power of the mind is great. Call the Hypnosis Institute of St. Petersburg today and find out how you can be richer, stronger, smarter."

The camera cut to another scene. Two women, their eyes closed, were sitting about two feet apart on a small couch. Pavel then appeared, approaching the two women and kneeling before them. He took them each by the hand, bowed his head, muttered a few odd things in a deep, strange voice.

And then he commanded: "*Or'gazm!*"

I couldn't believe it. Of course I understood what he said. There was no missing it. And as if that weren't particularly clear enough, the two women on the couch started shuddering and moaning. With great pleasure too. Holy shit, I thought, totally transfixed by the writhing women. This was on prime St. Petersburg TV, right here for Lenin and everyone else to see. I burst out laughing, unable to believe it.

Pavel let them fall into ecstasy for some ten seconds, and then he ordered: "*Or'gazm vyuikloochil!*" Orgasm off!

With that both women uttered a postcoital-like moan, their heads dropping forward into a state of bliss. I half expected Pavel to offer them a cigarette. Instead, the spiky-haired woman came back on the screen, going on about the Hypnosis Institute, call today, great results, here's the number, you need it, we can help.

When another show came on, I flicked off the television, went over to a chair by the window and stared out. Had I really just seen that? I started laughing all over again. God, I thought, wait till I tell Maddy. *Or'gazm!* No, I realized, my big sister would not think it funny. Not at all. She'd be appalled that someone would exploit hypnosis in so strange and undoubtedly false a way. And she'd be horrified that the exploiter himself was none other than her treasured Pavel. But it was funny, horribly so. Just as it was a horrible sign of how this country was struggling and stumbling to re-create a Western way of life. Good grief.

I don't know how long I sat there, but it was dark, which meant that in this northern land of the midnight sun, it was indeed late. Finally rising, I stripped off my clothes, stumbled into the bathroom, where I stood in the shower for a good long while, the hot water beating down on me. When I finally climbed in bed, my head sinking into the soft, feathery pillow, I had this horrible sensation that I wasn't going to be able to fall asleep. My eyes were open, I was staring at the ceiling. And Tanya just kept flying around in my head, thoughts of her swooping back and forth like a bat trapped in a room that was much, much too small. But then everything went black and I don't think I dreamed about anything or anyone, in particular her, all night long.

I was woken the next morning by pounding at my door, a relentless banging that went on and on. An eager maid? Doubtful in a country where initiative had been all but obliterated by the communist system. I was sure I knew who it was, though, and so I didn't get up. Didn't want to. I rolled over in bed. Had I come to any conclusions? Did I know what I was going to do yet? Hell no. A night of rest had not brought me any clarity. I was going to have to think of something, however, because by the horrible racket I was sure my dear Pavel had returned.

When the pounding only grew more forceful and determined, I called, "Just a minute."

I rose, rubbed my eyes, pulled on my jeans and a T-shirt. I wanted coffee, maybe some toast. I was certain it was Pavel, come to inquire if I'd seen his commercial. The last thing I wanted was to see him first thing. Shit, I thought, feeling horribly cornered, what could I say? I'd told him that I'd call this morning, so why was he here now, yanking me from such a deep, escapist sleep?

I stumbled to the door, unlocked it, twisted the knob, and was slapped with surprise. "Oh."

Tanya looked like hell. Her blond hair jumped this way and that, and her dress—the same black and red one she'd been wearing last night—was creased and crinkled. Whereas I'd fallen into a hole of rest, she looked as if she'd been up all night, pacing away her problems.

I asked, "What do you want?"

She glared at me, and it was only then that I saw the fury in her eyes. Brushing past me, she crossed through my room, marching right up to the windows.

"Viktor was right," she snapped, her back to me. "You are just another pompous American."

I shut the door, didn't move, stunned at her arrogance. "What the hell are you talking about?"

"You really don't understand anything."

"I understand what I saw."

"You only saw the tip of things."

So this was how it was going to be. A war of words. I caught my breath, tried to wake myself fully. I had to be sharp when I only felt dull with grogginess.

"Viktor's mafia, isn't he?" I asked.

"Of course he is," she snapped back as she looked out at the Bay of Finland. "The mafia's the only thing holding this country together right now. They're the only ones providing law and order. And they're the only ones trying to get us out of the pit that we're in." As if I were a village idiot, she condescendingly added, "What do you expect in a country without a constitution? You should try really living here, Alex, instead of coming in and looking at us just because you find our situation amusing."

All this, I thought, was amusing? "I wonder what your dead husband would say about this, about you going out with some other guy and smooching it up the day after his funeral?"

Tanya was motionless at the window, her back to me. "Lev wasn't my husband."

In Russia black was white and white was black. I couldn't move. Had I heard right? Was I still asleep? Or could this possibly be some sort of dream?

"What?"

Tanya turned around, stared at me, her eyes blooming once again with tears. "Lev was a very dear friend. I loved him very, very much. But we weren't married."

Frozen in disbelief, I stared at her. Since the moment we'd first met, Tanya and Lev had been the only ones I'd ever believed in this country. When they'd explained the Soviet Union and its twisted history, their viewpoint was the only one that I could accept. When they'd told me their dreams, their aspirations, I heard the pleas of an entire generation. They were my grounding rods here, the ones I returned to over the years in thought, in theory, in heart, and this time in person.

Like a jilted, betrayed lover, I finally managed to mutter, "You're right, I don't understand."

"Alex, all I can say is that our marriage just came to an end. It stopped, you know."

"So you two had been married?"

She nodded. "We were divorced almost three years ago."

"Oh, fuck." Rubbing my forehead, I went over and dropped myself on the bed. "But you were still living together, weren't you?"

"Sure."

"But—"

"Do you know how hard it is to find a place to live in St. Petersburg, Alex, particularly in the center of the city? I could've moved way the hell out into the suburbs, but Lev was nice enough to let me stay."

"You were divorced and yet the two of you lived in that tiny one room? I mean, wasn't that . . . that . . ."

"It was his aunt's apartment first, so it belongs to his family, really. I couldn't ask him to leave. But he let me stay. We divorced and started dating other people, and over time we went back to what we were best together, who we were best—just friends."

"I can't believe it. Why didn't you tell me?"

"Because things are so different here we weren't sure if you'd understand. We were friends, and that's all that mattered. And you were our friend and it had been so long and . . ."

That sounded like a horrible reason. Some kind of sick logic. I put my elbows on my knees, leaned forward, rubbed my eyes. Tanya and Lev were smarter than that, weren't they?

"And what?" I asked, looking up at her. "What else is there, Tanya?"

She hesitated, glanced at the floor. "The store."

"The store?"

She came over and sat on the bed opposite from me. Sighing, she shook her head.

"It's so complicated, I don't know where to begin. These are such strange times in this very strange country."

"Go ahead, give it a try."

"You know I used to be a hair dresser at the Springtime Beauty Salon."

"Of course."

"Well, there were three of us who worked there. Three women. And when the shop closed, all three of us had control of the lease for fifteen years. That's by law. Lev wanted very much to own a business. He was sure that was his future, the only way to get ahead. And I wanted to have a store, someplace where I could sell clothes that make Russians look like normal human beings and not guinea pigs. So you see, that's when Lev came up with his plan."

"What plan?"

"Lev decided he would give me the money and I would buy out the other two women. We paid them and—"

"How much?"

"Twenty-five thousand American dollars each."

"Just for the right to lease it?"

"Fifty thousand dollars isn't so much for real estate here. A store such as we planned—and in that space right by the subway stop— would earn that much back in just a few months. You might not realize how hard it is to legally control a property, Alex, and how much money you can make here. Now that I bought out those women, I own one hundred percent of the rights. Once I get that store open, I'll make a mountain of rubles."

In its own convoluted way, this story behind the story all made sense. Lev and Tanya were just trying to take that initiative, to pick up the pieces left from the collapse of their country and make something for themselves. Okay, so I got it. But why was she telling me this?

"Tanya, what does this have to do with why you didn't tell me about your divorce? I don't get the connection."

"Lev borrowed the money."

"From whom? Friends?"

"Alex, don't be silly. Fifty thousand American dollars is more than fifty million rubles. And that is a lot of money, you're right. Very, very few ordinary people have that kind of money."

But someone did, and the words jumped from my mouth. "He borrowed it from the mafia, didn't he?"

Tanya bowed her head, nodded. All of a sudden the bigger picture started appearing. It was all fitting together. I understood why that gold Mercedes had been hovering, tailing us right from the moment I arrived at the airport. And I knew why I was more valuable than ever to Tanya and Lev.

"Lev borrowed the money and he couldn't pay it back, could he?" I began.

"He thought he could borrow it from one of our new banks but . . . but it didn't work out." She shook her head. "Where was he going to get that kind of money? What was he supposed to do?"

"So you had no place to get it . . . except from a rich American."

"It's an incredible investment, it really is."

"Okay, so you wanted me to pay back the loan and become your partner."

"Exactly. We were late paying back the loan and these thugs started to harass and threaten us."

"And you didn't tell me about the divorce because you didn't want to scare me away?"

"As a team, Lev and I were solid. We weren't sure if you'd understand, but we knew we could count on each other and that's all that mattered."

"And this Viktor and this group knew about me?"

"*Da, da.* We told them you were our very close American friend who was coming in to look at the store as an investment."

"How much was I thinking of investing?"

"Two hundred thousand dollars. Sixty to pay back the loan— that's with interest—plus seventy to renovate the space and buy lights and shelves and mirrors, and seventy or so to buy inventory in Sweden. That's really not that much, particularly from a Western view of what it takes to start a business. The store would earn out like that," she said with a snap of her fingers.

"Of course."

But it was still a hell of a lot of money, even though that wasn't the point. And I didn't like this. In the recent chain of events, money and murder were orbiting much too closely.

Praying it wasn't too late, I simply volunteered, "Tanya, if you need fifty thousand or even two hundred thousand dollars, it's yours. I'll get it from my sister. She's loaded. And she trusts me. All I have to do is call her and she'll wire the money. We could have it by tomorrow."

"It's too late."

"Viktor's your new partner, isn't he?"

She hesitated, barely nodded her head.

"What did he do, cancel the loan?" I suggested. "And what are you, fifty-fifty?"

"Actually, he's fifty-one percent. Viktor's wife wanted a store, something to do with fashion and clothing, so she and I will manage it together. Somehow it will work. We're supposed to go to Sweden to do the buying together. I don't know, she wears too much makeup. Her clothes are too showy. I think she has awful taste." Tanya sat back on the bed and wouldn't look at me. "I had no other choice, don't you see?"

"So the other day that really was you I saw coming out of the store and getting into Viktor's car?"

"*Da, da.* I think he wanted to make the deal before you and I could talk. That was when he offered to void the loan and . . . and when he invited me to come under his *kreesha.*"

"So now you're under his roof. That's just great. Congratulations."

Her voice tight and high with desperation, she pleaded, "But, Alex, I didn't have any choice. If you'd become my partner, we'd still have to come under someone's *kreesha.* We'd have to pay a lot for protection, thousands of dollars a month just so we wouldn't be burned out or killed. There's no other way to do business here right now. And if you and I had become partners, then I don't know what Viktor would have done even if we'd repaid that loan. There would have been all sorts of problems. I didn't want to put you in that kind of danger. You're too . . . too important to me. I love you too much."

"How do you love me?"

"Alex, don't."

"Like you loved Lev? Like the closest of friends? Or differently?"

"Stop."

But I couldn't, not until I'd captured the truth by its slimy tail and pulled it out, and I said, "So to protect me you've become Viktor's mistress?"

"Lev and I made a mistake!" she shouted. "I should have sold out like those other two women. I should have found another buyer and taken the money because this is too big, too much. But I created the problem and now . . . now that Lev's dead I don't want to get anyone else involved."

"So that's how it works. As long as you sleep with Viktor everything's okay. He lets you be his partner. You just spend the evenings with him and the days working with his wife. And you get your store."

Tanya was crying.

"You're never going to last, Tanya. I really don't think you will. In the end you've got too much integrity." I got up, moved across, sat on the bed next to her, put my arm around her. "You might have been a Pioneer when you were a kid," I said, referring to the communist youth group. "But in the end, you didn't sell out to them. You saw the ugly truth."

"It was . . . it was just a beautiful dream that could never be, no matter how hard they tried to force it on us."

"Of course. And now you're seeing the ugly side of capitalism. You were lured into a trap by the glitter and excitement, and now you're caught. At least for the time being."

"But you know, *dorogoi moi*," my dear, she said, putting her head into my chest and crying, "I'm not sure if I was lured into the trap or pushed."

"What are you saying?"

"I don't know what Viktor had to do with the situation."

Which was exactly what I was fearing. "You mean Lev?"

She nodded and confessed, "I'm afraid Viktor had Lev killed just to get control of the store and . . . and . . ."

"And control of you?"

"*Da.*"

# Chapter 22

I knew what to do. My sister had taught me well. Whenever there was a nagging dilemma, it was important to pay attention to that. To stop everything and take a good, long look at it simply because things begging for attention usually required it. So as Tanya and I sat on the bed, confined in that room and in our confusion, I knew our next step, what had to be done, if we were to figure any of this out.

"Tanya," I began, my arm still around her, "I want to go back to the place where Lev was killed."

"Oi, again? Alex, we shouldn't. It's too dangerous there."

"No, I don't mean physically. I mean, here, now."

"What?"

"There's something that Pavel brought up when he hypnotized you, something that doesn't make sense. Will you let me put you under?"

After seeing Pavel's commercial, I not only distrusted the information he'd mined from Tanya, I doubted his professional skills as well. I was sure I could do it, too; I knew enough to safely induce Tanya into a trance and probe her memory.

"Don't worry, I've hypnotized my sister before. And I've been put under about a zillion times."

She said, "What, do you think there's more? Didn't we get it all at Pavel's?" She looked away, not eager to return to that nightmare. "I'm not so sure. Do you think we should?"

"Tanya, Pavel used a method that is different from what I've seen. It's something more Russian." Now was not the time to tell her what I'd seen last night on television; I needed to gain her confidence in hypnosis, not undermine it. "I want to put you into a trance and look at things more like my sister would. It won't take long. And maybe seeing things from a different angle will turn up something different. It can't hurt."

"Well, I suppose not."

It was that simple. We talked another few minutes, I promised her I'd bring her back if things got too rough, assured her that, of course, I'd be right here, right by her side. I couldn't promise we'd find anything new, I told her, but things weren't coming together in a simple, logical manner. Tanya uttered more doubts, then finally lay back on the single bed, positioning the pillow behind her head, stretching her arms straight. I sat on the edge of the other bed, took a deep breath. I could do this.

*"Of course you can."*

I'd gone under countless times. All I had to do was take it slow and easy, do it just like my big sister. Just find the holes and make them bigger. And then let the information seep out.

"You've done this before, Tanya," I began. "You've been hypnotized, so you know that state of relaxation and calm. And you're going to return to that state once again. While you're lying there, I want you to roll your eyes up, look up as high as you can. That's one."

Then I went to two. The part where I coaxed her to close her eyelids while still looking upward. I talked on and on, lowered my tone, tried to seduce her with my words. Told her she was getting more relaxed. And then three. I asked her to relax her eyes, to breathe in and let go as she entered a wonderful, deep state of hypnosis. That was the beginning of it, the first of Tanya's journey. I told her how a numbing, relaxing sensation was creeping up her legs, beginning first at her toes, overtaking her feet, then seeping upward.

Next using the deepening technique my sister most frequently used on me, I suggested, "And now imagine you're stepping on an escalator. I'm going to count again because you're up at the top. You're on the very first step, and as I count down from ten to one, you'll fall deeper and deeper into hypnosis." I paused, took a slow, deep breath. "The escalator's moving, carrying you down. One. You feel yourself descending, being carried deeper and deeper . . ."

I chanted on and on, closing my eyes, opening them, watching Tanya, ascertaining what and how far, how fast. It crossed my mind that I should reach out, stroke Tanya's arm, her forehead. Not out of lust. Not craving the sensation of her body. But wanting to assure, to coax. I thought of Pavel. He'd done it. I could too. I could just reach out and pull Tanya deeper into trance. I understood more of him, then. Why he would use such a technique. To lead someone into that other world. Yes, that was a dangerous boundary. One that could be transgressed for all the wrong reasons. But . . . but . . . I couldn't do that. Couldn't touch Tanya.

*"That's right. You are only to suggest and then to follow. Never lead, Alex. You must follow and then let the information be revealed."*

So Tanya rode deeper and deeper on the elevator, and I finally counted, "Ten."

At that moment it was clear she was down in that world of blackness that was nothing but illumination. I could tell by her gentle breathing. I mumbled on, spoke of tranquillity, clarity. My words drummed along, encouraging and mesmerizing, suggesting peace and calm.

"You're there, aren't you?" I finally asked, sitting on the outside and across from her.

Her voice was low and breathy, *"Da."*

"Good, Tanya. Now there's something for you to look at. Something that happened a few days ago. Do you recall the courtyard?"

"Lev was killed there. He was murdered."

"Yes, he was."

I recounted how she and Lev had picked me up at the airport, how we'd driven in to town, past the store, up Nevsky, then down the side street. I described the street because I was there as well.

And then Tanya cut in, blurting, "Someone came after him in that courtyard. I saw it all."

"Yes, you were there. Now be there again." I breathed in and out, tried to telegraph relaxation. "Return to that scene. It all becomes amazingly clear to you once again. See it as if you were seeing a movie being replayed."

"Lev!"

"Tell me what's happening, Tanya."

"I'm running down the sidewalk. I hear Lev. Lev! Something's wrong. There's a gunshot! I thought he was smoking. But I know something's horribly wrong. And I'm running, can't get there fast enough."

"What do you see when you turn the corner and start into the courtyard, Tanya?"

"Dark! I can't see anything. Wait. A car. There's a car up there."

"Hold that image. Look at it. What color is it?"

"Like white, but not."

"A color such as . . ."

"Light brown."

"And what part of the car are you looking at, Tanya?"

She confirmed again that she had first seen the side of the car, its door open. And that the interior was brown, maybe tan. Lying there on the opposite bed from me, Tanya went through it all once more, running the sequence of events once again through her mind's eye. The steering wheel. Then Lev. His body was there on the ground. I kept as quiet as I could, not wanting to infer or imply anything as she recounted everything just as she had at Pavel's, not varying more than a word or two. Once again, there it all was. The passage. The courtyard. The automobile. The blood seeping onto the cobblestones.

Then suddenly she blurted out, "Nine-four-oh."

"What are those numbers, Tanya? Where do you see them?"

"There. Right there in front of me. I—"

She screamed as a fist came hurling out of nowhere, hitting her, sending her into a sea of blackness. After that she started crying, either out of pain or shock. Perhaps the horror of seeing it, feeling it, all again yet again.

"Tanya, I'm going to count down to one," I quickly called to her. "I'm going to count from five to one, and when I reach the number one you'll be back up here. The trance will be done. Finished."

Rushing right in, I started the numbers, fishing and hoisting Tanya out of the trance and back onto the surface of consciousness. She stirred painfully as I counted until finally her eyes burst open. She stared up at the white ceiling, glanced at me, her eyes filled with resentment, then rolled away, moaning and shaking her head.

"*Bozhe moi.*" My God, she mumbled.

I went over, sat on the edge of the bed, reached up, and massaged her neck. It certainly seemed as if there was nothing new, that we had nothing further to go on.

"I knew it then," she said.

"Knew what?"

"That I didn't see the license plate."

"What do you mean?"

"Pavel was just so forceful, so strong. I . . . I remember. It's just like now. I woke up with the vision of the side of that car."

"Why didn't you say so?"

"Because Pavel started telling me what I saw. And . . . and I was so upset. He just started telling me what I saw, what it meant. It was like he was interpreting my dream, so I believed him. I just wanted someone to make sense of it, and that's what he was doing. Or so I thought."

Pavel the domineering. Pavel the mesmerizing magician. What he'd been doing, I thought, was not coaxing the images out of Tanya's memory, but arranging the situation so it fit his expectations.

I shook my head. "If those numbers only made sense. If we could only figure out where you saw them. Any ideas?"

"It's useless."

"Just try."

She moaned, glanced away. "I don't know. On the side of the building or inside the car. Maybe I saw something on the front seat. Maybe that's all. Maybe some paper or something."

"Where else do you see numbers on a car?" I asked.

"I don't know. Sometimes . . . sometimes . . ."

"That's it, just relax," I said, echoing Maddy. "Close your eyes and simply let the ideas come and see what fits."

"Sometimes you see them on the side of the car. You know, if the car belongs to a company, they—"

Tanya cut herself off. Next she quickly rolled over, looked up at me. Was this it? The key?

Her voice hushed, she said, "If a car belongs to a company, sometimes they have the address painted on the side."

We were getting close, I sensed, as I added, "Or the phone number."

I got up, started pacing. This wasn't a hypnotically exorcised vision but again conjecture. Granted a logical one. And definitely one worthy of pursuit. Nevertheless, while this might provide a real clue, I knew we should treat this possibility of an address or a telephone number on the side of the car as a possibility dredged up not from the subconscious but the conscious. Just as Pavel should have done. After he'd hypnotized Tanya, the very most he should have done was suggest she might have seen a license plate. Instead he'd claimed it as fact. And right now, putting everything into perspective, I found that particularly disturbing, and I went to the window, stared out. Down on the rocky shore there were a handful of people letting their dogs run free.

Yes, I thought, Pavel should have definitely known better. And, somehow I was certain he actually did. Despite his quirky, quacky approach to hypnosis and that ridiculous television commercial, he'd visited Chicago, had given lectures as well as attended them. He was no dummy. He had a ton of experience. Hadn't Maddy said he'd visited a California college or university as well for nearly two months? Obviously, then, he knew a great deal about the hypnotic phenomenon and he knew exactly what he was doing. So why had he steered Tanya's attention toward the idea of a license plate? What was this calculating man, this friend of my sister, trying to prevent my friend, my Tanya, from remembering and seeing?

There was no time to waste. Even though I felt as if time were ticking toward an inevitable conclusion, I had to corner Pavel, demand to know not only what he was trying to conceal, but whom he was trying to protect.

# Chapter 23

Drained and exhausted, Tanya dozed off on the second bed in my room. I, on the other hand, was suddenly and completely awake. Disappearing into the bathroom, I jumped in the shower and let the water drone down on my neck and back as I tried to suppose where these new ideas might lead. By the time I'd dried off and dressed, I knew my next step.

I took Tanya out for breakfast at the Swedish Table downstairs, where both of us fell ravenous on the long line of food. I went back three times. Tanya twice. I was catching up not only for missed meals, but loading up for the day. Who knew what would happen. There were no cute little sidewalk cafés in St. Petersburg. Only a few stands selling piroshki, the greasy meat pies. So I ate and ate, scanning the restaurant periodically for the young woman who'd nailed Pavel with the kasha; I was eager to learn the source of her anger. Failing to spot her, I wondered if she'd been sacked. Then again, she'd only flung food at another Russian, not a Westerner, so halfway through my meal I went to the kitchen door and peered into the back. An older, heavy lady with brown hair and an easy smile came out, and I inquired if Pavel's assailant—I was careful not to put it in those words—was about. *Nyet, nyet,* the lady told me, eyeing me suspiciously. She wouldn't be back until next week.

Tanya and I barely talked, not as we ate, nor as we shared a cab back into town. I told her what I intended to do, then dropped her at her apartment near Hay Market Square.

"Call me," she said as she got out of the taxi. "Tell me what he says. What you're doing. And come over for lunch. I'll be waiting."

This was more like the old Tanya, the one who'd barely let me go, who wanted to smother me in her embracing friendship, and I kissed her on the cheek. I promised to be back soon, then gave the taxi driver the next address, the one on Rubinshtein.

It was almost eleven when the cab turned off the busy Nevsky, taking a right on Pavel's street and pulling up in front of his building. I glanced up at the second floor. I had no idea if he was home, but it was worth checking out, so I gave the driver a fresh five-dollar bill, instructed him to wait, and he eagerly muttered, of course, of course.

I really didn't know what I hoped to learn from Pavel, what he might be able to tell me about Tanya's trance, or rather, specifically about the numbers she had recalled. Perhaps I was just desperate, pulling at nothing in hopes of discovering something about Lev's death. But this was leading somewhere, I sensed. The events were unfolding like chapters in a book, and I was sure Pavel was wiser and craftier than I'd given him credit for.

Pushing open the heavy door of the building, I once again entered the dark lobby of Pavel's building, my eyes straining to see as they adjusted from the sunshine outside to this dim entry. I glanced to my left, saw the mailboxes, heard movement ahead. Looking deeper into the building, I saw the ghostly image of a woman at the bottom of the staircase, her pale face surrounded by a bunch of thick, light hair. I could barely see her, but there was something terribly familiar about this figure. She was short, I could tell. And there was something furtive about her. Perhaps it was the way she moved so quickly, the way she shifted as she stared at me.

My eyes unable to drink in enough light to see, I blinked long and slow. When I looked back up, she was gone. For an instant I wondered if I had only imagined it, but then I heard her steps as she scurried away. Next a door opening and closing. Who had it been? Just another resident of the building, someone perhaps waiting for a visitor? Evidently so.

*"But it wasn't, was it?"*

I made my way across the cool stone floor and to the base of the staircase. To my left was a short hall, several doors leading off from there. I suddenly felt dizzy, reached for the iron railing. A horrible vision was streaking into my mind. A forethought. A future thought.

*"So it was her, the waitress, and she was already back there, behind one of those doors, waiting for Pavel, stalking him."*

Yes, and she was avoiding me because she assumed I was with him, that I was his friend. But . . .

I shook all of that away, pushed it out of this time, as I mounted the stairs, moved up and around to Pavel's apartment, where I pushed a buzzer to the right of the door. When there was no reply, I pressed again, and heard some quick, short steps scurry down the hall.

An older woman's voice called *"Kto tom?"* Who's there?

"Alex Phillips."

*"Kto?"* Who?

I further identified myself, explaining that I'd just visited, and so on, tossing in that I was the American. Oi, she replied. Of course. And heaving aside several bolts and latches, Pavel's elderly mother, Mama Luda, pulled open the heavy front door, where she, dressed in a pink housedress and slippers, greeted me with a warm smile.

"Is Pavel here?" I asked.

*"Nyet,"* she lamented, a hand to her chin. "He's out."

"Do you know when he'll be back?"

Mama Luda shrugged, gazed toward the heavens. "Who knows? Pavel, that son of mine, keeps himself so busy. I'll have lunch on the table for him but who knows if he'll remember to come home to eat with his mama."

She went on to suggest I try the studio. They might be taping a show today, then again, they might not. Pavel hadn't said. But if I had a car, advised Mama Luda, I could check where they make Pavel's program.

I thanked her, retreated back down the stairs, outside and to the taxi, where I asked the driver if he knew of a television studio on the edge of the city. He thought for a moment, said he knew of several.

He asked, "Which one?"

"It's a big white building, fairly new, with a big antenna on top. It's where they film the show, *Mesmerizing Moments.*"

"Oh, that one. *Da, da, da.* Sure, I know. I just took some woman out there the other day."

Without further word, he shifted into gear, and we were off, charging through the straight streets of St. Petersburg, out of the historical center, and into the broader and far blander suburbs. It was a quick twenty-minute ride, one that I hoped would be fruitful. It had started to rain lightly, and as the driver pulled up alongside the white building, I saw a few cars but no sign of activity. I scanned the area, searching for Pavel's driver and Volvo, when I was struck with a horrible thought. Pavel's car was a tan sedan. And I recalled seeing three numbers emblazoned on it. What were they? Wasn't the car a 740 Turbo or something? Could those be the numbers Tanya had seen?

"I'm looking for someone," I explained to the taxi driver. "Let me check inside."

My interest burning stronger than ever, I had to go in, see what I could find. Perhaps Pavel might be doing some work. Or perhaps the woman with the spiky hair would be here and she would know where I could find her boss. So I quickly walked to the building, up the short set of steps, and to the doors, which were open.

Either Pavel had contracted for security only during taping sessions or the *kreesha* Pavel was under was not a very good one, for there was no security man to stop me at the door. Freely entering the building, I found the place oddly silent. There were no voices. No sound of movement. I glanced in the studio where Pavel's show was filmed, but it was black and empty, a huge empty cave of a room.

Continuing down the corridor that ran along the windows, I called, "Hello?"

I was about to give up, but then I heard a deep, low voice droning on and on. Slipping closer, I tried to discern the words.

Someone muttered, "Sure. Of course. I understand."

I slowed. Was it Pavel? I couldn't tell, nor could I hear if there was someone else, if there were in fact two people down there. I followed the sound, hoping that I'd found him.

"No problem," continued the voice. "I'll take care of it."

Up ahead I saw an open door and a room with a light on, and as I approached I realized I didn't recognize the voice. It proved to be a lone person, too. Someone speaking on the phone. He said a couple of more things, muttered good-bye. He'd been on the phone, I realized, as I heard him drop the receiver into its cradle.

"Hello?" I called louder, announcing my visit.

*"Da?"* he called back. "Come on in."

I entered a small, smoky room and found a young guy in his twenties, sitting at a console in front of an entire wall of video equipment. I glanced up, saw the machines whirling, tapes moving. Obviously this guy worked as a technician of some sort.

"Hi, Pavel's not around, is he?"

The guy smiled, took a long drag on his cigarette. "You're the

American, aren't you? Pavel's assistant—you know, the one with the funny hair—pointed you out to me the other day.''

I nodded. "Yeah, I was here when you taped the show. You haven't seen Pavel, have you? He's not here by chance, is he?''

"Sorry, he's not. He came in earlier to drop off these tapes, but then he left. Don't know where he's gone, either. I don't think he'll be back until tomorrow. I'm Yuri.''

"Oh.''

My attention was caught by a small cardboard box on the console in front of him. A small carton, colorful and covered with photographs. I recognized it.

Yuri saw what I was looking at, volunteered, "You brought us this, didn't you?''

He lifted up the cardboard container of the hit *Aladdin* and I saw that it was empty. My attention was quickly caught by a TV screen, and there it was. Yuri was running the film, and the cartoon characters were traipsing across the screen. But they were doing so in complete silence.

I asked, "You're not watching the movie, are you?''

"I watched it the first time, but not now. I just sit here all day and make the copies. This is the second time through. It's a good film, though. I'm sure it'll be popular.''

"What?''

Yuri took another long drag. "Only another ninety to go for today.''

It didn't make sense until I looked up and saw that virtually all the equipment in front of Yuri was VCR machines, three or four rows of them stacked on their sides and mounted up the wall. I quickly counted at least ten machines. All of which were whirling away.

"Wait a minute, are you copying that tape?''

"Sure, I am.'' Yuri parked his cigarette between his lips as he adjusted a dial. "Ten at a time.''

"But . . .''

Proudly Yuri turned up the volume of the master machine, and all at once I heard that familiar music rising and pulsing with joy. But the voices of the characters played by Robin Williams and others were only faintly to be heard in the background. On top of them, overshadowing them and their American English, was another voice. A deep one, speaking continuously in Russian.

"See, we already have it dubbed.'' Yuri looked at me proudly.

"Pretty quick, aren't we? We have an excellent translator, and then this same guy does all the dubbing for us. He's pretty amazing. He does all the voices for all the films. I must say, the copies we make are very high-quality. Pavel made sure all the equipment was top-class. He bought them all in Amsterdam just last year."

Stunned, I could barely speak. "But . . . but that's copyrighted material."

"What?"

"I'm sure that movie's under copyright."

Yuri shrugged, wasn't even phased by the question. "Maybe in the West it is, but here in Russia no one pays attention to that." He laughed. "We're a free country now!"

My first instinct was to go over and pull the plug. To play the righteous Boy Scout and scold this guy for stealing *Aladdin*. I quickly recovered, though, for I understood Yuri was just an employee. He was simply doing his job. I couldn't stop him from doing anything. I could only disrupt his work. All that I could do now was garner information, and then take that information and my disgust to Yuri's boss, my dear friend Pavel Konstantinovich Kamikov.

"How . . . how many copies are you making?" I asked.

"Hopefully I'll do one hundred today. Then another hundred tomorrow. Pavel wants two hundred and fifty by the end of the week."

"What about the other films I just brought? Is Pavel having you copy them, too?"

"Of course. *Under Siege* is next. I love Steven Seagal, and that's one of his best films—all that shooting and killing. It will be very popular here, particularly in times like these. I think it's already been translated. They should start dubbing the film tomorrow."

"And *A Few Good Men*?"

"We probably won't get to that until next week."

"*Home Alone 2*?"

Yuri started laughing. "Do you see how much work you made for me? You brought all these great movies and now I'm going to be working fourteen hours a day for the next three weeks!"

I rattled them all off. All fifteen movies that I'd brought to Pavel from my sister. They were all to be translated, dubbed, and copied. Holy shit. I asked Yuri about a couple of other films, the ones Maddy had air-expressed last month—at quite a large cost—including *Chaplin* and *Last of the Mohicans*. *Da, da*, those ones were already copies, replied Yuri. They were sold months ago.

I stopped him. "What do you mean, sold?"

"To the video stores. We have them now, too, where you can rent a movie. They're everywhere."

I didn't even know what to say. I got some more bits and pieces out of Yuri. A few little facts. But he didn't even get how illegal this would be in the West. Or if he did, it didn't make any difference. International copyright laws? So what. This was money. He was paid well. Business was good.

Yes, I thought. Movies were Pavel's business, not his passion, and business indeed was good, in large part because he had an excellent supplier, namely, my sister. Over the past couple of years Maddy had sent Pavel well over a hundred films. Not just any old ones either, but the very latest, the most popular, all of which Pavel surely had dubbed, copied, and then sold, surely receiving top ruble. Finally I understood the source of all Pavel's money, or at least a large part of it.

As I turned to go, Yuri said, "What about that big movie that came out this past summer, the one about the dinosaurs? I heard about it on Voice of America."

I shook my head, said nothing because I didn't want to help him, not even in the least. Besides, I had to leave. There was someone I had to meet for lunch.

*"Dear God,"* moaned a distant voice. *"I thought Pavel cared for me. I really did. I mean, he lavished me with all these words, all that attention. And here he was just . . . just using me."*

Poor Maddy. She was going to be pissed as hell. Maddy, who'd never been blind to anyone and his motives before. She hadn't seen this one, though. Not at all. Yet I couldn't help but gloat, for I'd expected something like this, proving that just once I was a tad smarter than she.

# Chapter 24

Not even a half hour later I was back, jumping out of the taxi, tromping through the rain, then going up and pressing the buzzer. When there was no response, I started pounding on the big thick door. Finally I heard the small steps again scurrying down the hall.

And again, *"Kto tom?"*

"It's me, Alex."

"Oi."

All at once I heard the long series of locks snapping, and then the door was pulled back. Mama Luda, Pavel's mother, stood there, blotting her mouth with a napkin.

"Any word from Pavel?" I demanded as I walked right in. "Do you know where he is?"

"Of course I do. He's here. He's eating lunch. Please come in. I made some nice borscht. We have cutlets too." And then down the broad hallway, she called, "Pavlusha dear, you have a guest!"

I stepped past her, ducked into the first room on the left. Before I'd only glanced in here, seen one bookcase filled with videocassettes. But upon stepping into the large room, I saw that all the walls were lined with tall cases. And all of them held cassettes of movies. It was an entire library. Or rather, an entire video store's worth of movies. Thousands and thousands of films. I also noted that the two windows were covered with bars. I thought of the heavy locks on the doors. No wonder the security measures, for on the black market this had to be a fortune's worth of film.

"Alex, what a surprise. Won't you join us at the table?"

I turned. Pavel stood in the doorway. Gray dress pants. A pressed blue shirt. The sports coat and tie removed for lunch. And his big gut sticking out. Still chewing his last bite, he held a piece of half-eaten black bread in one hand.

"So these are the originals," I said.

"My film collection. It's quite large, isn't it?" He forced a proud smile. "Now come, *droog moi*," my friend, "I'll show you all of this later. My mother is a wonderful cook. Her borscht is the best in Petersburg. You must have something to eat. Have you eaten at all today?"

I didn't budge. "You make the copies from these. How many have you done altogether? Hundreds and hundreds of thousands, right?"

"*Shto shto?*" What, what, he asked hesitantly, stroking his gray beard.

"I just came from the studio. I went out there looking for you."

He was silent, eyeing me, wondering how much I really knew.

"I saw your technician, that young guy," I continued. "He was copying *Aladdin*. Don't get me wrong, I've made a few illegal copies in my day, but you do know about international copyright laws, don't you?"

"Alex, what in the world are you talking about? You look so upset, so serious."

"He showed me the equipment."

"Let's just have some vodka and—"

"Pavel, I know what you're doing. You're pirating all these movies, you're stealing them," I said, running my hand over a row of cassettes. "And that's not to mention you've been using my sister to get the latest films. She's not going to like this, I can guarantee you that. Maddy's rather judgmental, particularly when people use her."

"Movies are my pastime, my hobby, and—"

"This is no fucking hobby. We're talking about a business. A pretty big one, I bet. You must really be raking it in."

"Please, calm down. I've just been making a few copies. That's all."

"Two hundred and fifty copies of *Aladdin*? Jesus Christ, it hasn't even been released in the States yet."

Pavel took a deep breath, closed the door to the room. Setting the piece of black bread on a shelf, he started searching one of the bookcases. Finally he pulled one out and held it up.

"Look here," he said, holding the video toward me. "Here's your *Dick Tracy* with Madonna. Madonna, your huge, huge superstar. How many millions and millions did they make on this film?"

"Pavel, that's not—"

"What do you think their profit was? Fifty million? One hundred million? And wait, here's *Batman*."

"Courtesy of Maddy."

"*Da, da,* you're right. Courtesy of Maddy. She sent it to me last year or the year before. And what did she tell me about the film? Didn't the actor Jack Nicholson make over sixty million American dollars on it?"

"I have no idea." But it was, I thought, sitting down on a window ledge, something obscene like that. "That's not what I'm talking about."

"But you're accusing me of stealing something. So tell me, my American friend, where is the crime, with an actor or even a Hollywood company that makes hundreds of millions of dollars, or with me, who's just trying to keep a few people employed?"

"Pavel, you're twisting things."

"They've made enough money on these movies."

"How Soviet of you."

"Well, haven't they?"

"That's not for either you or me to decide. They're earning all that money on an investment they made."

Pavel waved me away like an irritating fly, stomped across the room, blurted, "All I know is that Hollywood doesn't need my rubles. But the people here do. You know how much I pay that young man you just saw back at the studio? I pay him, let me think, it would be about thirty-three dollars a month. That's his income, and he's happy with it."

"But you're running a business here with stolen merchandise. Look at all these movies. This is incredible. What are you, the biggest film supplier in St. Petersburg?"

"Actually . . . that's about right. I don't sell to Moscow, there's someone else down there. But I supply the Petersburg region and north." Pavel rolled his eyes. "Surely you, Alex, of all people know the problems we have here. Surely you know what we must do to exist. I have a staff of almost thirty people I must support. They depend on me for their food. Every month I have to come up with enough money so they and their families can eat.''

"But you must make a lot on the show, especially if it's so popular.''

He burst out laughing, rubbing his stomach like Santa Claus. "One hundred.''

"What?''

"That's right, I make a hundred thousand rubles a month, which is not quite one hundred American dollars.''

"That can't be.''

"Of course it is. Why would I lie about such a pathetic sum of money?'' He added, "But the show is valuable to me because people come to me to study hypnosis, and for that they pay a good amount. That's where I earn my money.''

"And the movies.''

"Sure, sure. How else can I do it, Mr. America? How else can I pay for this apartment, for food for my old mom, for all of my staff, not to mention for my Hypnosis Institute, which is the thing that I care the very most about? How? With these videos, naturally. Now, of course, that I've sold my show to Mexico and Thailand, things are very different. Now that I'm earning hard currency abroad, I'm able to buy a few things, bring them into the country and—''

"A few things like more movies.''

"*Da, da,* like more movies. I must make it all grow. Isn't that the American way, after all, bigger, bigger, bigger?''

"Then again, why buy the movies, when you can get a nice blind girl to send you the movies for free?''

"Alex, shame on you. Don't talk about your wonderful sister like that.''

I started shaking my head as I walked away from him, saying, "Pavel, it's not up to you to determine how much is enough for a film company to make. Obviously you know it's wrong. Otherwise you would have told my sister what you were doing. You wouldn't have told her you were merely collecting films.''

"*Radi boga,*" for God's sake, he exploded, "you're making it all so complicated. Your sister and I are just a couple of film lovers discussing what we've seen.''

"Bullshit.''

"Alex, please, just calm down.''

I looked out the barred windows. Shit. I didn't know what to think. Pavel wanted to talk about movies with Maddy because of what he could learn. Maddy wanted to talk about movies with Pavel because . . . because of the attention he lavished upon her. This was all so twisted.

I said, "I put Tanya under."

"I beg your pardon?"

"I hypnotized her. I know how to do it. Actually, I know a lot about hypnosis."

"I'm sure you do. You must have picked up a great deal from Maddy. She's really quite brilliant." Pavel started for the door. "Now come on, Alex. You must eat. Come join us at the table. We'll have some vodka and relax. Please, I promised your sister I'd look after you."

"Oh, and we went back there too."

"*Shto?*" What?

"After Tanya and I were here we went back to the courtyard and walked through the whole thing."

Pavel rubbed his forehead, rather quietly said, "You shouldn't have done that."

"Why? Is there something we might have found?"

"*Nyet.* Don't be so ridiculous." He caught his breath. "It was just too soon after the trance. It must have been very traumatic for her."

"It was," I said, "particularly since there's no way she could have seen the license plate."

"I don't understand."

"Oh, I suspect you do."

"Alex, I'm tired of these games. I'm tired of you accusing me of things. What in the world are you talking about?"

"What I'm saying is that you're a much better hypnotist than you let on. After your show and after seeing how you handled Tanya—not to mention that ridiculous commercial—I thought it might have been because you weren't much more than a stage hypnotist. I thought it might have been because you really weren't very good at pulling things out."

"Are you calling me a fraud?" he snapped, his face flushing red.

"No, not really. All I'm saying is that the protocol for forensic hypnosis is very strict simply because it's so easy for the hypnotist to influence the subject. And obviously you know that because that's exactly what you did. You didn't want to help Tanya discover what she really witnessed."

Pavel closed his eyes, shook his head.

Searching for his reaction, I said, "You knew that Tanya didn't see the license plate, didn't you?"

"Of course she did," he snapped. "You heard her as well as I did."

"No, I heard you telling her what she saw."

"Stop being ridiculous."

"Then stop lying to me."

"Now you're offending me," he said, raising his voice. "I open my house to you, I invite you to lunch with me, and all you do is insult me. This is absurd. Absolutely absurd. Your sister wouldn't approve of this, the way you're treating me."

"Just tell me, why are you so afraid of what Tanya saw? You know exactly what she witnessed, don't you? Pavel, what does that number mean?"

"Like I said before, she saw a license plate. Those were the numbers on a license plate. You should give the information to the police. I'm sure that will enable them to find the killer of Tanya's husband."

I shook my head, said, "No, that's not information, that's conjecture. Your conjecture." I started for the door. "I'm going to have to put Tanya in a trance again, aren't I? I'm going to have to take her back to the day her husband was murdered, right? And, you know what? This time I'll probably get it out of her."

# Chapter 25

"So after the studio, I went to his apartment," I explained to Tanya and Sveta. "And by then he was there. He'd come back to have lunch."

*"Bozhe moi,"* my God, gasped Sveta.

As I sat on the couch in Tanya's apartment, I went through the rest of it, how Pavel's mother had answered the door, how I'd found the room with all the videos and what I'd said to Pavel, what I'd learned of his business operations. The two women shook their heads in disbelief, were astounded by the number of films as well as our conversation.

"Of course he's making a fortune and of course all of that is illegal," said Tanya. "Copying all those movies is totally wrong. That's stealing. He's an educated man and he's been in the West, too, so he knows perfectly well what he's doing."

Sveta shook her head in disgust, added, "Now you see what we're up against here. For seventy years we were cut off from civilization, and people just don't know how to behave in a normal manner. Not long ago I heard about a publisher who sued a man for pirating a book that they had published two years earlier. The jury let the man go, even though he'd printed fifty thousand copies and sold every last one of them. Our Russian jury said the publisher had already made enough money on that book. Can you believe it? It was perfectly clear that the original publisher still owned the rights, too."

"It's going to take us decades to come out of the dark ages and enter the twenty-first century," bemoaned Tanya, expressing her fatalistic outlook, which in itself seemed altogether Russian.

She rose and went to the tiny kitchen in the corner, where a kettle was rumbling with a boil. Pouring hot water in three teacups, Tanya then added a thickly brewed tea concentrate. Finally she scooped two teaspoons of precious sugar into each cup.

"*Shto dyelat?*" What are we to do? she asked, handing me one of the cups. "Is it useless? Hopeless?" She clucked her tongue, shook her head. "And this business with Lev. I think that's truly hopeless. His killer must be long gone by now."

"I suppose you could go to the police and tell them these numbers," suggested Sveta. "Maybe they'd know what to make of it all. They must have a detective working on it."

I took a sip of tea. "Or we could try hypnosis again."

Sveta purposely said nothing. Only drank some tea and stared at her friend. Tanya, cup and saucer in hand, went to the large window. The rain was falling hard now, the drops large and heavy, and she stared out over the red and green metal roofs of St. Petersburg.

"In the beginning, Lev was my best friend," she mused. "And then he was my husband. After we divorced we became very close again. Like in the beginning. So now, in the end, I just want to do the right thing for him."

"Of course," I said.

Tanya turned toward me. "But I don't know. We've already tried hypnosis, and what have we learned?"

"Well, if we just push at a couple of things, we might figure it out." Knowing it was by no means pleasant returning again and again to the murder scene, I added, "It wouldn't take long."

"I just don't think I can do it, Alex. Not today."

Sveta anxiously took a large swallow of tea, then started to get up. "Maybe I'll leave."

Tanya looked at her, said, "But it's raining."

"I think you two need to talk." She rose, hunted for her purse. "Listen, I'll go out and get some food. Some sausage or something. Some fruit too. I saw some kiwi just this morning. Alex is our special guest."

I glanced at Tanya, who was making no moves to stop Sveta. And neither would I. Tanya and I had been bouncing from crisis to crisis, never taking the time, perhaps purposely so, to talk about that other important subject. Us.

"Here, Svetochka," said Tanya going to a hook by the door. "At least take my raincoat and a scarf."

As if they exchanged clothes all the time, which they probably did, Sveta slipped on Tanya's raincoat, the pleated one from Sweden. Next Sveta tied Tanya's scarf over her head and beneath her chin, then turned and quickly kissed Tanya on either cheek, saying she'd be a half hour, not more. But that wasn't the truth. I feared it even then. I wasn't just being nervous. I sensed it beforehand, was overwhelmed with a hideous premonition.

Shutting the door after Sveta, Tanya looked at me, said, "Alex, what's the matter?"

Unable to be specific, I replied, "Nothing."

"She's right, you know. We do need to talk." Tanya returned to the tiny kitchen. "Would you like some more tea?"

"No thanks."

It was probably only a few seconds but it seemed much longer. We were there, the two of us, in that tiny apartment, and there was complete silence. I wanted to talk, to say something if only to fill the void, but what? I ran my hand through my hair, shifted from foot to foot.

As Tanya was refilling her own cup, I finally blurted, "Is it really too late?"

"Too late for what?" she replied over her shoulder.

"An investor in the store."

"Stop it, Alex. Don't be silly."

"I think I should buy out Viktor's share."

"Alex . . ."

"Seriously, I could offer him a good profit, so he'd probably sell. You could run the place—that could be your contribution—and then we'd be fifty-fifty."

I watched as she stirred two teaspoons of sugar into her cup. Even as she returned to the main room, she was shaking her head.

"No, I won't do it," she tersely said. "Do you know the difference between Americans and Russians?"

I could hardly wait for this one, I thought, taking a place on the couch opposite her. "No."

"Americans are weak."

"Don't be silly."

"Alex, you don't know what it's like here. You really don't. Russia is trapped between Europe and China, and we're a very strange people because of that. Trust me, you should keep your money in your pockets and run."

"But there's a lot of money to be made here. Even Lev said it. He called Russia a real Klondike."

"Lev . . . Lev was a dreamer." Tanya shook her head, took a long, pensive sip of tea. "Russia is in the early stages of capitalism, and it's a very ugly, very cruel time. You've only seen the surface of things. The corruption is hideous, particularly in the government."

"Tanya—"

"Alex, forget about it. It's just too dangerous. I won't let you invest here. Russians are either good or they're bad. There's nothing in between, and right now I'm afraid. I really am."

"But if I invested here—maybe not in the store, maybe in something else—I'd come over more often." This was going to be a hard one to win, I sensed, so I went directly to my real motivation. "I'd get to see you more often."

She set down her teacup, looked away. "Alex . . . don't."

"Tanya, think of it. I'd come over every couple of months, maybe I'd even stay for a month at a time." The idea, springing from the seed that had been planted so long ago, was blossoming quickly and eagerly. "And you could come to the United States, too, either to buy clothes for the store or . . . or something else. Think about it, Tanya. Think how wonderful it could be."

"Stop it, Alex . . ." She quickly came to her feet, started pacing. "Don't make me say it."

"Say what?"

"You stupid American, don't you understand?" She turned away, went to the window, stared out into the heavy, gray rain. "I don't want you to invest in anything here in Russia because . . . because I don't want to see you again."

Too stunned to say anything, I sat frozen on the couch. Holy shit, what had I misunderstood, misread, not noticed? Was I that dumb, that thick? I thought back over the last week, all the nuances. What about the way she'd embraced me at the airport, the way she'd looked so deeply into my eyes, the way she'd clutched my hand so tightly when we'd sat in the backseat of the car?

I leaned forward, rubbed my forehead with both hands. Could it be time to leave, to put all this behind, to—?

"I don't want to see you again," continued Tanya, "because it's too hard."

I lifted my head. "What?"

"You fly in here and look at us like we were monkeys in a zoo. Then you fly out, saying, My, how interesting that was." She shook her head. "That's not what I want. I don't want to be your animal behind bars, waiting for your generosity."

I had to clear my throat. "Tanya, that's ridiculous."

"No, it's not, Alex." She turned to me, her eyes red and tearing. "Do you remember when we first met? You were lost on the street, and Lev and I came over and asked if you needed help."

"I was trying to find the main post office. And then you took me home and fed me so much I thought I was going to die."

She laughed and wiped her eyes. *"Da, da.* That's how it was." She took a deep, almost soblike breath. "Maybe it was fate, meeting you, but it poisoned my life."

I started picking at the fabric on the couch, and said, "You Russians are so damned dramatic. What the hell are you talking about, Tanya?"

"Alex, don't you see? Don't you understand?" she said, staring down at me. "I fell in love with you back then. You entered my life with that curly hair and those white teeth and that big smile and . . . and I've never been happy since. You were like this big bright sun that came into my life. That entire summer was something different because there you were, this wonderful, handsome person from the West. It wasn't just hearing about all the material goods you had or could have. It was your attitude. Your outlook. I remember how you were going to go traveling after leaving Moscow."

"To Greece."

"Exactly, to Greece. You didn't know how long you were going to stay or what you were going to do afterward, but that didn't matter to you. And that was what amazed me. Just how open and free your mind was."

I came to my feet, moved around a low table. "Tanya, please, let me—"

"Alex, listen. We spent one night together, and then I thought about you everyday. I mean, every single day after you left. I thought about the back of your neck. Your wrists. Your energy. I couldn't stop thinking about you, even when we didn't hear anything from you for almost a year after you'd gone."

"You were with Lev, Tanya. You two were a couple. And you were going to get married. It was all set before that summer." I'd done it all wrong, hadn't I? I went over to a radiator, ran my fingers along its fins, trying to ascertain if I'd been stupid or young or self-centered. Or all three. "You know, when I left I wasn't sure what I really meant to you or even Lev for that matter. I was afraid I was your American friend, the ultimate status symbol. I didn't know what you really felt for me, personally. And I was scared of how much I felt for you. I didn't write because that would have meant writing to both of you, and I really didn't know what to say. I should have written just to you, though.''

"Don't, Alex." She lifted a hand to her eyes.

"No, that's what I should have done." I asked, "Do you know how much I wanted to come back, how many times I almost did?''

She turned to me and yelled, "Then why didn't you? Instead you left me trapped in this . . . this zoo! I would have come to America if I could have. Don't you see, I married Lev because I didn't think I'd ever see you again!''

Part of me wanted to say she was ridiculous, blaming me for her marriage, her divorce, her unhappiness. We'd been kids then. Our countries were in a cold war of words and false moves. If I'd returned, if we'd dated, how could I have ever been sure that Tanya wouldn't have been using me as a means to get to the West?

I moved through the silence that hung between us, cautiously came up behind Tanya and said, "I'm sorry. Perhaps I should have done things differently. Perhaps we both should have. But we didn't. And I'm here now.''

"It's useless, Alex." She shook her head. "I'm different. I've changed. I'm no longer young and . . . and I've become too hard. That was why Lev and I were divorced. He said I'd changed, and he was right.''

I reached out, touched her on the shoulder. She didn't respond, but she didn't move away either.

I said, "Your life's not over, Tanya. You may be a little bit more thick-skinned, but it's a whole new world.''

Slowly, almost painfully, she turned around. I embraced her, and she rested her head on my shoulder, right against my neck. At first she was scared to hold me as well, but then she wrapped her arms around me, clutching me tightly. I felt her trembling as she started sobbing for what might have been but wasn't.

That was what was so horrible. Tanya and I were just finding some peace, some hope. We were just getting to a kind of middle ground. But then there was that scream. It came from outside. A distant plea that was sharp and full of pain. I wondered if perhaps it was a car screeching to a halt. Or a child who'd fallen on the sidewalk. But no. There it was again. A woman's scream, long and terrified.

Horrified, Tanya pulled away from me, begging, "Not her, too."

# Chapter 26

The scream echoed endlessly, and what we feared was so horrible that neither Tanya nor I could move. Sveta was out there, on the street, in the rain, and we both knew it. That had been her shriek.

"Oh, shit," I finally muttered in English.

I rushed to the window, saw a handful of figures running through the rain and toward the front of the building. They were scurrying toward the scene of a tragedy, I knew. Those wishing to help as well as witness. It was the same all over the world.

When I turned from the window, Tanya was already reaching for the door. I stumbled past a chair and hurried out after her. Not speaking, we raced down the staircase and outside, where the rain was falling in thick straight lines. Dashing through a wide puddle, we cut immediately to the left and toward an alley alongside the building. Several people were rushing to the same point, while one was hurrying away, perhaps to call the *militsiya* or an ambulance.

My heart was twisting with fright, and I glanced at Tanya, whose blond hair hung straight and flat and totally wet. Her face was tense and pale, horribly drawn. Sure, she knew. It was only a question of how bad.

She screamed: "Svetochka!"

Racing to the alley, the steady rain drenching our clothes, we reached the huddle of people. But we couldn't see, couldn't tell. There were so many gathered. Everyone struggling to see.

Tanya started desperately calling, "Sveta? Svetochka? Is that you? Are you hurt?"

She started pushing, madly so. Heaving everyone aside. Pushing them back. Cutting through the crowd. She was crazy with fear, trying to see what and how. I was right behind her, fighting my way as if pushing upward through a mad stream. Suddenly everyone understood that we might be related to this victim, and they parted. Stood back. And exposed the victim, the body of a young woman lying facedown on the ground. Recognizing her own raincoat and scarf, Tanya screamed. She darted forward and dropped to her knees, tentatively reached out to the bleeding body.

"Svetochka!" sobbed Tanya.

There was blood, a good deal of it, seeping into muddy black puddles, dancing in the rain, and washing away. I dropped to the other side of Sveta. She'd been stabbed, most definitely so. I could see the torn coat, the slash dug deep into her right shoulder. Horrified, I stared at her, tried to ascertain if there was more than one wound, when miraculously I saw movement, the heaving of her back, the struggle for air.

"She's alive!" I shouted.

"Sveta, Sveta! I'm here!" called Tanya, fearfully reaching out and touching her friend.

Behind me I heard someone say how awful. How terrible. Such violent times. But not to worry, an ambulance had been called.

An older woman, a babushka with a soft, wrinkled face and tiny eyes, pressed forward, pushing aside a boy, and saying, "I was a nurse. I know these things. You must be very careful with her."

Not hesitating, the woman knelt down on the ground, dropping to her knees as she'd probably done hundreds of times at church. She wiped the rain from her brow, then with thick, worn hands, she felt Sveta in several places. Next she pulled back the raincoat, exposed a blood-sodden mess of jagged clothing and flesh.

"I saw worse in the War," she said, referring to the war against the Fascists. "Here, let's roll her over so she can breathe more easily. We must get her head up and loosen her scarf. And all of you people, back up! Move away, do you hear? This poor girl's been hurt and she needs air!"

Obediently, the gathered bunch of people backed away. But not enough.

"Get back, I say!" snapped the bossy woman.

Once the crowd was at a good distance, the babushka took hold of Sveta with gentle authority, then with Tanya's help the two of them turned her over. Someone handed me an umbrella, which I held over Sveta, shielding her face from the rain.

Tanya loosened the scarf on Sveta's head, pulled it away, and kissed her forehead, saying, "I'm here, Svetochka. Everything's going to be okay. I promise."

Sveta opened her eyes, gazed up at Tanya, tried to say something, but her words were as faint as they were mumbled.

"Quiet, Svetochka. Everything's fine. Don't talk. An ambulance is one the way. You're going to be just fine."

"Of course she'll be all right. She just needs to be sewn up," added the babushka, dabbing at the blood on Sveta's shoulder with a handkerchief. "What lawlessness we have now. Hooligans everywhere. Not like the old days. Where has all the order gone? What has happened to all the control? Oi, oi, oi. And where have all our good citizens gone?"

A man stepped forward, his blue shirt soaked, and boasted, "Some of us are still here. She wouldn't have been all right if I hadn't seen him and started shouting."

"What?" I demanded.

"I frightened him off."

"How much did you see?"

The man pointed to a first-floor window across the street. "I was just looking out, seeing if it was still raining because I wanted to go for a walk with my dog. That's when I saw a man jump out of the alley and attack this woman. He grabbed her from behind and pulled her into the alley. By the time I could get my window open and shout at him, I think he'd already stabbed her. I don't think he took her purse or any money. He just attacked her."

"No, he didn't take anything!" shouted a boy from the crowd. "There's her purse. And a bag of food."

Off to the side, thrown against the wall of a building, lay a black purse and a string bag holding a handful of kiwis.

"See, the attacker didn't even steal anything from her," said the man.

I anxiously demanded, "But did you see him? What did he look like? Do you have any idea?"

"Well, I really didn't see his face."

"What about his clothes? What about—"

The man looked down the alley. "He dropped her when I started shouting, and then he took off that way, out the other end of the alley, so I only saw the back of him. I remember that he was bald, though. I could see his head, the back of it, you know.'' He delved into his memory. ''Oh, and he was wearing black leather boots.''

A bald man with black leather boots. Dear God. I looked down at Tanya, who was staring up at me. Who could that be? I certainly remembered Sveta's boyfriend, Igor, and his boots. But he hadn't been bald, had he? Or could he have had a bald spot on the back of his head?

Tanya looked at me, muttered, ''Pavel's driver is bald.''

I raised my head, stared down the alley where Sveta's assailant had fled. If by some bizarre chance it had been her boyfriend, Igor, what would prompt such an attack? No, Pavel's driver made more sense. For whatever reason, Pavel could have sent him after our heated confrontation.

My head was spinning. I didn't understand what this was all about. What was going on. None of it made any—

A good ways down the alley I saw something black. Something dark in this deeply gray afternoon. The thing moved. It was a figure, I realized. No one else saw that person. Of course not. In this telling of the story no one but me could see that spy, the one who'd tailed me at the hotel, at the monastery, perhaps through the park. Yes, it was the very person who'd been secretly observing me throughout this entire venture.

In the distance I heard a siren barking and slicing through the rain. I twisted toward the street. The ambulance was perhaps just a block away. Yet when I turned back, when I looked down the alley once again, the spy was gone, perhaps already knowing the horrible truth.

# Chapter 27

Once the ambulance had gone, Tanya and I were left standing in the rain. The downpour had slowed, yet both of us were as soaked as if we'd taken a shower.

"Let's go change and then head to the hospital," I suggested. "She's going to be all right, don't worry."

Staring at the spot where her friend was attacked, Tanya mumbled, "She was dressed in my clothes."

I knew what she was thinking. I knew what she was going to say. What other assumption was there to make?

"Alex," continued Tanya, verbalizing what we both knew, "I was the one who was supposed to be attacked. I'm sure I'm supposed to be dead now."

She was right, of course. It only seemed too logical, too obvious. So what was it that Tanya knew that was so important? And to whom was it of importance? It all pointed, of course, to only one person.

Anger and fear flushed through me—was I next on the list?—and we made our way back to her apartment, climbing up the steep, narrow stairs. When we entered, she didn't reach for a towel or for dry clothes. Instead she went right to her black telephone and started dialing.

"Who are you calling?"

She turned her back to me, spoke into the receiver, "This is Tanya. I need to speak to Viktor."

Oh, shit, I thought. Not him again.

"What do you mean he's not there?" she demanded into the phone. "I have an emergency. I have to speak to him."

I whispered, "Tanya, what the hell are you doing?"

She put her hand over the receiver, pointed to a small closet. "Lev's clothes are in there. Put something dry on."

"But—"

Quite irritated, she said, "Fine, then I'll call him on his mobile phone. What? What do you mean I can't?" As she listened, she shook her head angrily. "Well, if he calls in, tell him something terrible's happened. My friend Sveta was attacked. Of course it was awful. Tell him I think it was arranged by Pavel Kamikov and that I want Viktor to do something about it."

Tanya launched into an other angry tirade, demanded that Viktor be found and call her as soon as possible. And then slammed down the receiver.

Even though we might not have had a choice, I questioned, "Tanya, is it best to get Viktor involved right now? Maybe we should go to the police."

"That idiot forgot his mobile phone," she ranted, not paying me any attention. "I can't reach him. And his assistant at the office isn't sure where he is. He's going to try reaching him at a restaurant where he was supposed to have a meeting."

I didn't have a good feeling about this, didn't like where this was leading. Everything was getting dialed up. Bringing in a mafia guy would definitely take it up another notch.

"What's Viktor supposed to do about this?"

Tanya looked at me, simply said, "Tell Pavel he'll be killed if he or his chauffeur harms me or any of my friends."

"You're talking about putting a contract on him."

"No, I'm talking about warning him for now. If I wanted Pavel killed tonight," she said, crudely, "that would cost a thousand American dollars. That's the going rate in Russia these days. It's not much but I don't have it, not unless you want to give it to me."

"No," I replied, quickly realizing my limit, at least for now. "I mean, we're not absolutely certain that Pavel is involved. What if it was someone else?"

"Well, if it was then everything will be fine. Don't worry. Viktor's very smart in these matters. He'll know how to get the truth out of Pavel."

She wouldn't talk any more about it. Almost as if I weren't there, she went to a closet, took out a brown skirt and tan blouse, stripped and changed. Oh, my God. I couldn't believe this. Here I was in Russia, not fearing the KGB, but instead talking about hits and killings. It was outrageous. This entire fucking country was outrageous.

Tanya tossed me a yellow shirt and a pair of Lev's jeans, and I held them up and was able to see that they were a pretty close fit. Slipping out of my own clothes, I was just putting on those of my dead friend when the phone rang. Tanya scooped the receiver up on the first ring.

*"Da?"*

I could tell it was Viktor's assistant, reporting what he had learned. And it was perfectly obvious Tanya didn't like what she was hearing.

"Well, as soon as you find him, you tell Viktor he has to help me."

The conversation lasted only another few seconds, and then in a great huff, Tanya slammed down the receiver. She stood still, lost in desperate thought, one hand pinching her hair to the back of her head.

I asked, "What did he say?"

"Viktor already left the restaurant. And now his assistant doesn't know where Viktor is or when he'll call in."

Good, I thought. That might give us some time. Things might cool down.

"Tanya, we're close to something," I ventured, trying to slow things a bit.

She was rummaging through a dresser drawer. "What?"

"I think it's worth another shot at hypnosis. I think we need to push at it again. If we take it step by step, you might recognize what those numbers meant. Where you saw them."

"To hell with that."

"Tanya, we have to try again."

*"Nyet."*

"Come on, just one more time."

She stopped, both hands in the drawer, and looked at me as if I were crazy. "Someone killed my ex-husband and just attacked my best friend. I could be next. You can forget it, Alex. Hypnosis just hasn't worked. I need some direct answers, and the only person I can get them from right now is Pavel."

Her hand obviously struck something. Reaching a little farther into the drawer, she took hold of an item, then withdrew it.

"Oh, shit, Tanya," I moaned upon seeing a dark pistol with a wooden handle. "Where did you get that?"

"One of Lev's friends gave it to me after he was killed." She rubbed the black barrel. "It's just a gas gun."

"You Russians are crazy."

She shrugged, simply asked, "Are you coming with me or aren't you?"

# Chapter 28

I wasn't going to let her go by herself. Of course not. So when Tanya slipped on another raincoat and hurried out the door, I was right behind her, wearing Lev's clothes and hoping that we'd find the truth without getting ourselves killed in the process.

The rain had stopped when we emerged from the building, the day had turned dark, and we turned to the right, crossed to Hay Market Square, wading through the mud and wet trash. Spotting a free taxi, I dashed into the street and flagged it down.

"The corner of Nevsky and Rubinshtein," snapped Tanya as we climbed in.

As we raced along, I couldn't believe it. Lev had been killed just days ago. Sveta had just been horribly knifed. And it all seemed to point to him. To that one person. That asshole Pavel. I didn't know his complete role in this, but he certainly played a major part. The main question at the moment, though, was whether or not he'd still be at home.

Minutes later the taxi stopped on Nevsky, pulling up just short of Rubinshtein, and the cab driver asked, "*Zdess?*" Here?

"*Da, da,*" replied Tanya.

For our own safety it was better to get out and walk the two blocks. If Pavel was indeed home, if he had indeed ordered the attack on Sveta, then we had to proceed with caution and a good degree of stealth.

I felt the tension mount and twist within me. As we turned the corner, I looked back on Nevsky, scanned the street to see if there was a car or perhaps someone on foot. Anyone could be tailing us, spying on our activities, which was what I feared the most.

As we proceeded down the street, I glanced at Tanya, saw the anger swirling within her, the emotion bursting tearfully from her eyes and reddening her cheeks. Shit, I thought. She was loaded with fury, ready to fire at any second.

"Tanya," I demanded, "give me the gun."

She shook her head, barely so, as she pushed down the street.

"Tanya."

"*Nyet,* Alex."

"We have to be careful. You're too upset, and besides, what if he sees that this is a gas gun?"

"There's no way. It's a very good replica."

"Well, what if he has a real gun?"

She paid me no attention, virtually ignoring my concerns as we pressed down the street. It was late and getting dark quickly, and while I knew this was a ritzy neighborhood, it looked awful. All the potholes. The stucco peeling from the buildings in great, huge scabs. The only thing that betrayed the wealth hidden behind these walls was the small handful of imported cars—a BMW, Honda, two Volvos—that were sure to be stashed away as night and the gangs descended upon the streets.

Tanya said, *"On doma."* He's home.

Looking up at his apartment building, I saw the front windows of his expansive apartment burning with light. That had to be him. Certainly his mother wouldn't be so wasteful with both energy and light bulbs.

Suddenly I heard tires screeching around a far corner, and I looked down Rubinshtein, saw a marauding pair of headlights. It could be nothing, just some up-and-coming young *biznizmeni* out for a hot ride in their hot car. But I didn't think so. There was something far too menacing about this. I grabbed Tanya by the arm, pulled her into some doorway, and pressed her into the deep shadows.

"Don't move!" I ordered.

Hidden there, we peered down the street. It was a light-colored car, I could see. But whose? Could Viktor have received Tanya's message and come directly over? I didn't know, couldn't tell if that was a Mercedes or not. As the powerful car slowed in front of Pavel's apartment building, I only knew that this was getting far more complicated and because of that, far too dangerous.

To my surprise, however, the auto didn't come to a complete stop at Pavel's front door. Instead the vehicle slowed, then suddenly took off in a burst of speed, whizzing rocketlike past us. It was only then that we recognized it.

Dismayed, Tanya said, "That was Viktor. Why . . . why didn't he stop?"

I was only glad that he hadn't, and as the Mercedes turned with another squeal onto Nevsky, I said, "Maybe he called from his car phone. Maybe Pavel's not there."

Tanya shook her head, her determination only briefly dented, and simply said, *"Poshlee."* Let's go.

She took off again, darting out of the darkness, across the street. As the few streetlights struggled to life, I darted after her. I didn't like this. None of it. Pavel had quite possibly caused a great deal of death and tragedy, and I certainly didn't want to meet the same fate. But I wasn't going to abandon Tanya, not now, not by any means.

I looked up to his apartment, thought that one of the lights in his window had just gone out. Be that the case, if in fact he was on the way out, that might make things easier. At least then we wouldn't have to force our way into his apartment. Instead we might be able to intercept him in the lobby, corner him there and force the ugly truth out of him.

Moments later we were ducking through the front doors of his building, entering the dank lobby that smelled so thickly of stale urine. Just as we approached the stone staircase, we heard a door up above, then voices. That of a man and woman. They were bidding each other farewell. One of them was most definitely Pavel, the other clearly a young woman. Who was she, yet another client he'd seduced? Or just some *valuta*-hungry slut?

Tanya stood firm, reached into her coat pocket, lifted out the gas gun. Oh, this was going to be great. Pavel was going to come down the steps, and here we were going to stand, just a couple of goons. No, it would be far better if we—

From outside came the roaring of a car as it raced down the street, then braked to a quick halt right in front of the building. I tensed. Crap. Who was this? I heard one, then two doors open and shut. It could be Viktor and his bodyguard, come to our early rescue. Perhaps they'd just gone around the block, gone after something or someone else, and then returned. Then again, it could very well be someone else, and here we were between them and the descending Pavel.

Tanya's face suddenly washed with fear, and I nodded to our left, down a short corridor. We pressed down the passage, disappearing into the darkness. I discerned several doors behind us and tried one of them, finding it open. If need be, we might be able to escape out the rear of the building.

We heard the lobby door open, then several sets of brisk, heavy footsteps. Of course they were on a collision with Pavel.

And in response to their arrival, Pavel called from somewhere above in the building, "Is that you? Sorry I'm late! I'm coming, I'm coming!"

Next to me I could sense Tanya trembling. Hearing Pavel's voice flicked a switch in her, and I could sense the anger rise and physically boil within her. There was nothing I could do. I couldn't hold her back. In a burst, Tanya jumped out of the darkness, gun pointed at the figure descending the last flight of stairs. I followed right behind her, saw not only Pavel frozen on the steps but Viktor and his driver, Sasha, stopped in the lobby not fifteen feet away from us.

"*Bozhe moi!*" My God, shouted Pavel.

Staring at him, Tanya shouted, "You killed Lev, didn't you?"

"What? No, that's not true."

"And what did you do, order your driver to attack me? Well, he's an idiot because he went after my friend instead. Or was it you who stabbed her?"

"You don't understand." Pavel looked at me. "Alex, please this is all some sort of mix-up!"

Tanya glanced desperately at the two men in the lobby, shouted, "Viktor, Sveta was just attacked. She was knifed. And . . . and I think he killed Lev, too!"

Viktor was clearly stunned by the scene he'd just walked into, and he cleared his throat, saying, "Just calm down. I'm here. Everything will be all right." To his driver, he nodded. "Sasha."

Sasha reached into his sports coat, lifted out a gun, a large black thing that he aimed at Pavel.

Pavel's eyes widened in horror and he shouted, "What? This is preposterous! What are you doing?"

"We have it under control now, Tanichka," smoothly said Viktor. "Don't worry. You can put away your gun now. I'll take care of everything."

Still aiming the gas gun at Pavel, Tanya blurted, "I was supposed to be killed but Sveta was stabbed instead."

"That's terrible. Awful."

"She's in the hospital."

"Don't worry, Tanichka my dear. We'll punish him."

From the stairs, Pavel screamed, "What?"

Viktor went on, urging, "Why don't you and your friend just leave now. This is a serious matter. Please, let us take care of this filth."

I moved forward, reached out, touching Tanya on the arm and saying, "Can I have the gun?" I grasped her hand in mine, gently pulled at her fingers, loosened her grip. "That's it, just give it to me. Let's just go, Tanya."

I couldn't imagine what Viktor was going to do. How he was going to handle this. And I didn't want to know either. I didn't want to be here, to witness any of it. So I kept working on Tanya's hand until her grip loosened. And then I took the gas gun, holding it in my right hand, aiming it at the ground.

"Come on," I quietly said, hoping we could just slip past Viktor, praying we could just make it out to the street.

"Very good," called Viktor. "Don't worry, I'll take care of Pavel."

A voice out of nowhere said, "No, he won't."

I spun around, stared down the dark hallway where we'd hidden. I heard more rustling. And then a short woman emerged. It was her. The waitress. The one who'd attacked Pavel at the restaurant. She'd been hiding back there as well. And now she was emerging, a long knife in hand.

She spoke in a halting manner. "He won't do any . . . anything."

"Isn't this interesting," interjected Viktor from the lobby. "She has a knife. Perhaps she's the one who went after your Sveta."

The waitress laughed, said to Tanya, "Pavel sells his secrets."

I eyed her, fearful of what she might be suggesting.

"Alex," pleaded Pavel from the stairs, "don't pay any attention to her. She came to me because of her extreme shyness. But she's crazy. She really is. And she's very dangerous."

The young woman's face flushed with fury, she raised the knife, screamed, "I went to him for help and he betrayed me! He hypnotized me and I told him my secret, that my husband was not the father of my baby, that the father was someone else. And then he blackmailed me!"

"What?" gasped Tanya.

Viktor calmly asked, "Alex, would you and Tanya please step back." And then he nodded to his driver, saying simply, "Sasha."

"He blackmailed me!" she screamed. "And when I couldn't pay him he told my husband, who then left me!"

What was all this about? What was going on? I wasn't sure if we could trust this young woman, yet it was too wretched an accusation to fabricate. On the heels of that, a worse thought slammed me. Could Pavel have done the same thing, could he have sold something he'd learned from Tanya's trance?

Viktor snapped: "Move!"

Sasha was raising his gun, aiming it at the waitress. Automatically, I shoved Tanya back against the wall. I stared at Sasha, the driver, big and burly and balding. He aimed the gun right at her, had it trained on her head. What was he going to do, blast her to hell? Holy shit. I watched as his hand tightened, his fingers squeezed . . .

I saw it then. His birth date on his right hand. The numbers were tattooed on his knuckles, starting on the forefinger. He was born in the forties: 1940 to be exact. But of course I couldn't see the first number because his forefinger was wrapped around the trigger. I could only see the last three numbers of his birth year. Three blazen digits: 940.

It was just an automatic reaction. I barely lifted my arm. Just raised the barrel of the gas gun I held. Then fired. The explosion was awful, as loud as from a regular gun, and a huge spray of gas spewed at Sasha, covering him in a cloud of noxious fumes. Taken completely by surprise and pain, Sasha stumbled back, cried out, clutching his chest one instant, the next grabbing his eyes. He fell, waving the gun, wanting to fire, to shoot, but unable to see. I fired again, aiming this second shot at Viktor, who shouted in pain and confusion. Suddenly the waitress started screaming and charging forward. I heaved Tanya back, pushed her out of the way. But it was such a small space. The gas was overcoming us all. Hitting our eyes, scratching with pain. I gasped, felt a hot fog burning the inside of my nose and scorching my lungs. I dropped to the stone floor, struggling for air, clawing my stinging eyes.

I heard Pavel shout something, and I looked up the staircase. He was holding a gun, a small thing, and aiming it at one of us. And now he was readying to fire. But before he could, a shot burst out to my right. A loud explosion that cracked the panic, shattered my fear. I looked toward the lobby, saw a figure standing there in the hazy gas.

A man holding a gun. It was Viktor, one hand over his mouth as he tried to seal out the gas. The other hand pointing the gun up the stairs at Pavel. And without hesitation, he fired a second time.

Pavel cried out. Through my watery, sizzling vision I saw him stumble in disbelief, for the first bullet hit him in the stomach, the second in the neck. But it was useless. There was a third shot and then Pavel took an awkward, fatal step, tumbling forward, his body rolling and bouncing down the stairs, landing only a few short feet from us.

It happened that quickly. Viktor started shouting at Sasha, and then the two of them scrambled out the door and to the car. Behind me, the waitress cowered in a corner, while Tanya sat in a heap, sobbing. I stared at the base of the staircase, saw the body of Pavel, the rich red blood swirling and twisting. It was over.

Or was it? Was this only the beginning of the end?

I peered down that hallway again and saw yet another person. It was her, the spy, the one who'd been tailing me. Wiping my eyes, I stumbled to my feet and away from that scene. Desperate to understand, I clambered forward, for I couldn't let this retelling of the story end without discovering who that was, what this was all about.

# Chapter 29

I left all of them behind, Tanya, the waitress, the dead Pavel. I stepped out of all that and moved into the mystical events, my imaginal fears, the ones that had been plaguing me throughout all this.

Wiping the gas from my eyes, I started running down the hallway. At once the spy took off, darting through one of the doors, disappearing into the dark. I came to the doorway, saw a set of steep old steps leading down into the cellar. I hesitated only but a moment, found a switch and flicked it on. In the dim light I descended into the depths of the building, determined that I would corner her and catch her, this person who'd been lurking in the shadows of the story.

I clambered downward, and when I reached the bottom I saw the last of her darting to the right. I rushed on, through a narrow passage, down another. The walls were thick and heavy, the ceiling low. Magically a series of light bulbs came on, and I turned from side to side. I couldn't see her in this maze, but I heard her steps, darting on, rushing away.

I took off to the left, running through an inch or so of water, the likes of which lingered in so many buildings of this swampy city and provided a year-round breeding ground for mosquitoes. And then I stopped. Except for my heavy breathing, all was silent. Where had she gone? Disappeared, vanished into nothing as before?

No. I heard steps darting through another puddle of water. I turned to the left, saw nothing, spun around. Yes. That way. And I was charging on, jumping over a pile of coal, dashing around rusty equipment. A rat scurried before me. I turned a corner, entered a long straight corridor, the ceiling quite low. And there she was, the woman shrouded in black, racing away. Crouching, I hurried along, pushing myself as fast as I could down the long passage.

Suddenly I was at the edge of a large dark room, and I stopped. The air was cool and moist. Yet she was in here. I was sure of it.

Something moved in the blackness, and I said, "I hear you."

She was breathing hard, finally admitted, "Yes, I'm afraid you've cornered me."

Good, I thought. My hand felt the wall. Was there a switch here, any kind of light that would illuminate the truth?

"Why have you been following me?" I demanded. "Are you with the KGB or . . . or the CIA?"

She laughed. "Don't be silly."

I detected movement. "Stay right where you are. You're not going to get away again."

"Do you mind if I just walk a bit? I won't leave, I promise. My legs are just a little cramped."

"Okay," I replied hesitantly, groping for the hoped-for light-switch. "Who are you?"

"Haven't you guessed?"

It was then that I found it, a thick old box with a switch on it. Immediately I flicked it and immediately a bare bulb hanging in the middle of the room burst on. The spy stood with her back to me. I couldn't believe it. Yes, now that I was this close I recognized her. I knew her very well, indeed. Tall and slender, long neck, short brown hair. How could this be?

"Turn . . . turn around," I gasped. "I have to see you."

She started to move, then stopped. "Are you sure? May I look at you, too?"

"Absolutely."

My God. As if she were a genie who'd finally and at last escaped from a magic lantern, this person had stepped out of her prisonly reality and into my trance. She gazed in shock at her own hands, looked up at me in disbelief, no, shock. Tears came to my eyes. Standing there in that dreadful, wet cellar, I held out my trembling hands, and she started moving, walking toward me on her own.

And finally we embraced, and I clutched her and held her and whispered into her ear as if to make totally real this impossible thing, calling her name, whispering, "Maddy."

# Chapter 30

I woke as if from a nightmare, my eyes bursting open with fright, my body sitting up, struggling to find some sort of reality.

"Shit," I muttered. "That was weird."

Still trembling, I looked over at my sister, who lay there, undoubtedly in a trance of her own making. Yet I'd just seen her in my trance, seen her walking, even looking about in that basement in St. Petersburg. What kind of cruel magic was this?

Shuddering, still trying to push myself to the surface of this world, I got up, went to the French doors. It had been all so real. So absolutely real. I touched my eyes, which stung as if there were gas still swirling around me, mixing this world with all that violence and death. But, no, that wasn't the case. As much as it felt as if I were still there—and I guess a real part of me would always be back there in Russia—I was home. Home. Back here on Maddy's island. I stared out at the blue water. That wasn't the flat, gray Bay of Finland. That was Lake Michigan.

In response to the rustling behind me, I turned around. My sister had woken and was now struggling to pull herself from her black recliner and into her wheelchair. I watched in pitiful silence as she did so, her thin arms flexing sinewy strong as she dragged her torso to the chair.

I couldn't help it, couldn't stop myself from saying, "I wish you were that way. How I saw you in the trance, I mean. Sighted and mobile."

Maddy bent over and strapped her legs down, sealing them in place with Velcro strips. Sitting up, she pushed her large sunglasses up her nose. And sniffled. Sure. She reached up beneath her sunglasses, pressed each eye with her finger, tried to keep the tears in her eyes. So it had gotten to her as well. But of course she was the all-powerful Maddy, never one to show her weaknesses or her pain, and she cruised right on.

"Rather amazing, isn't it?" she said, struggling not to show her true emotions. "I felt like I was there, like I was seeing it all." She placed a hand on her chest, took a deep, composing breath. "I understand why you wanted to go back. If everything hadn't gone so horribly I'm sure you would have had a lovely trip."

"But it couldn't have gone much worse."

She sighed. "All that business about Pavel and his videos. It makes me sick. I've never been used like that."

My sightless sister wheeled herself around the end of the recliner, came alongside me, reached out. With great care, she felt for my hand, found it, and pressed it against her lips.

"I'm glad you're home, little brother."

"Maddy, it . . . it was so strange to see you there. I mean I was chasing you. You were running . . . and you could see."

"The mind is very powerful, isn't it?" She kissed my hand again. "Don't worry, everything's okay."

I gazed out at the lake. The wind was up, whipping the waves. On the island I saw yellowing maples bend and swirl as if dancing right through the change of seasons.

Her head pointed ahead as if she were gazing out in contemplative thought, Maddy asked, "There are just a few things I don't understand."

"Maddy, do we have to talk about this now?"

"Yes, we do. Just trust me, I want to be done with it as much as you." After a moment, she pressed, "So tell me, who are the police prosecuting?"

"Both Viktor and Sasha—Viktor for the shooting of Pavel, Sasha for the death of Lev as well as the attack on Sveta."

"Oh." She paused in thought, then said, "But was Tanya sure about that? Could she really identify Sasha? And who can identify Sveta's attacker?"

"Sveta," I replied with a sigh, for I couldn't stand any more interrogation. "It turns out she saw enough to know it was Sasha who stabbed her. As far as Tanya, once she saw his hand with the numbers tattooed on it, she was positive. Hypnosis-induced memory isn't always admissible here in the States, but I think they'll accept it over there."

"But what about—"

"Maddy," I said, cutting her off, "are you going to grill me like the Russian police? Didn't I just tell you enough and then some?"

"I'm just trying to understand. It doesn't all fit together."

Good grief, I thought, when was I going to be done with this? I really didn't want to talk about it anymore. I just wanted to forget. I knew only too well, however, that my dear, wonderful sister wasn't one to let go of anything until it was all neat and logical, until everything fit into its own little box.

"You see," I explained, "Pavel knew Viktor pretty well. He knew that Viktor was big in the mafia there in St. Petersburg. And when Tanya described the car and then recalled those numbers on Sasha's hand, Pavel guessed who it might be, assuming that it had been Viktor and Sasha who had cornered Lev back in that courtyard. Actually, I'd say that was a pretty good guess on Pavel's part."

"Well, Pavel was very smart. And very intuitive." Maddy turned away, wheeled herself into the middle of the vast room with its soaring ceiling. "But actually that wasn't the case."

"What?"

"Pavel saw Viktor and Sasha at the airport."

I turned away from the window, stared after her, wondering, even fearing at what she might be getting at. This wasn't supposed to happen. This was my story. I was the one who was there.

"Maddy, what in the hell are you talking about?"

"When you arrived, Pavel was there. And he saw them."

"How in the hell do you know that?"

"Pavel told me."

"What?"

Maddy stopped right in the middle of the room, just to the right of the dome over the staircase, spun around so that she was facing me, and said, "Pavel knew I was anxious about your trip, so he went to the airport to make sure you arrived safely. He was worried that your friends might not show up. So he went there, and when he was looking for you at the terminal, he ran into Viktor."

"Are you shitting me?"

"No, and apparently he told Viktor he was looking for an American, just to make sure he'd arrived safely. When Pavel mentioned your name, Viktor said not to worry. He was on top of it."

I closed my eyes, cursed my meddling sister. "Let me guess, Pavel came right home and reported this to you via E-mail."

"Exactly. Pavel didn't know why Viktor was watching you and Tanya and Lev, but it didn't make any difference. He trusted Viktor. Pavel knew you'd be all right, and he just wanted to let me know so I wouldn't worry."

"How thoughtful of him," I snidely said. "Maybe I'd be all right, but not Lev." I clenched my fists, wanted to kick the wall. "Holy shit, Maddy, I can't believe you knew that and I didn't."

"Well, I knew that and then some." Rather flip, she added, "Plus I've figured out a lot more."

I didn't want to hear this. Didn't want my sister's rendition of what had been such a horrible experience. Still, I had to know all that she knew.

"Such as?" I nervously asked.

"It's quite obvious that Viktor and Sasha followed you from the airport. I mean, you took note of their car. And when Lev went to change money, it's quite clear that Viktor and Sasha entered the courtyard from the other side. Evidently Viktor pressured Lev not to sell part of the store to you, but Lev must have refused. And that's when the fight broke out."

Glumly, I stared away. "I'm sure Lev wanted to be in business with me, not Viktor. I'm sure just my being there gave him the strength to try to deny Viktor."

"So then there was the fight, and Sasha shot Lev. And that, actually, solved Viktor's problem, because then Tanya went with him."

I moved across the room. Looked at the dome, that huge mosque-like thing that hovered over the open staircase. And then I stared up through the glass panes above the dome and out at the blue sky above. On the one hand it was so complicated. On the other it was surprisingly simple.

I asked, "So let me guess, Pavel told you about protection, too?"

"Actually, he did. A couple of months ago I read an article in *The New York Times* about the Russian mafia, and I was worried about him. I knew about his show, what he was trying to do. I figured he'd be a target because of course he'd gotten famous, so I asked him about it. And he replied, yes, he had protection. It was a fact of life, he told me. He had to be under someone's *kreesha* not only because of his popularity but because he had to handle a lot of money for his show. But not to worry, he told me. He was under his cousin's roof and his cousin was one of the best."

Why was I surprised that my sister knew so much? That she actually did, though, was quite unsettling. The Russian police were nerve-racking. The several conversations with the KGB even worse. But I was an American. They were not eager to have it all blown up, not at a time when the mere thought of the Russian mafia seemed to be frightening off so much Western investment. So the police and the KGB asked me what I knew, I told them, and they didn't press that hard, really.

But not Maddy.

Hell, no. My dear sister was as shrewd as she was relentless. And there were certain things that I didn't want anyone to know. Particularly Maddy.

Trying to eke out exactly how much she knew, I said, "You really know a lot about this, don't you?"

"Oh, sure. I've pieced it all together."

"Really?"

"There's only one thing I don't quite get."

I tensed, tried to keep that tension out of my voice. "Which is?"

"Why would Viktor shoot Pavel?"

My voice shaking a bit, I asked, "You know what, Maddy? Now I understand why I felt like I was being spied on. Now I know why you appeared in the trance the way you did."

"Why's that, Alex?"

"Because you're always poking at things, trying to uncover what others don't want you to find. And that's how I imagined you there: as a spy."

"Now, this is getting interesting." She laughed, twirled herself in a small circle. "Spies exist for only one reason. One reason alone. Do you know what that is?"

"Maddy, this is stupid."

"Spies hunt for the truth, of course. That's their sole function. When the truth is so awful, so secret that it can't be told, spies go about their duties covertly and secretly to try to discover things." Calculating her next move, she paused, then said, "And isn't that what you were afraid of in that trance? Isn't that why your imaginal unconscious chose to portray me as a spy, because you were terrified I was hunting for something you didn't want known?"

"Stop it, Maddy."

"In that trance you saw me as a spy obviously because you're hiding something. Something you're afraid I'll find out. Isn't that right? Aren't you afraid of what I'll find?"

I stared at her. "What in the hell are you saying?"

"Alex, I'm saying you're lying now. And I'm saying you lied to the Russian police about what happened."

I coughed, struggled to remain calm. "What?"

"Viktor didn't shoot Pavel, did he?"

I quickly said, "Of course he did. Why in the hell would you think he didn't?"

"For one simple reason, they were related."

"What?"

"Oh, dear Lord, Alex. Think, would you? E-mail. Pavel told me all about Viktor."

I looked at her stunned, unable to say anything. Unable to believe she was able to turn up not only what I'd learned from Tanya after the shooting, but a fact that even the Russian police had overlooked.

"Alex, Viktor was Pavel's cousin."

"Pavel said that?"

"Right in the very first E-mail message, the one I received after you arrived at the airport." She waited. "Pavel was under his cousin's *kreesha*. His cousin was Viktor. So there's no way Viktor would have shot Pavel, is there? Not the way Pavel described their relationship. He said they'd been raised by their babushka and were really more like brothers than cousins." And then, "So who are you protecting, Tanya or the waitress?"

I couldn't believe it. Couldn't believe my own sister had caught me.

"Maddy, you've got to understand. Even though Sasha was the one that killed Lev, Viktor was there, right there. In fact, he probably ordered it. And he definitely ordered Sasha to go after Sveta. So Viktor had to be punished. He might not have physically harmed anyone himself, but he was ordering it done. Telling the Russian police that I saw him shoot Pavel was the only way to get him locked up." Desperately, I said, "You've got to understand, Maddy. Please, you've got to."

"Don't misunderstand me, Alex. I do. In fact, I think you did the right thing. You're right, Viktor was too dangerous to be out and about in the city. If it had been me, I hope I would have done exactly like you."

I was shaking. Couldn't help it.

"So who shot Pavel?"

"He had a gun. Pavel, I mean. He was going to shoot Tanya. He had it aimed right at her. It was self-defense."

"Certainly." Maddy asked, "So tell me, was it Tanya or the

waitress who ran over and grabbed Sasha's gun?'' And then after a long, horrible moment, she asked, ''Or was it you, Alex? Is that the truth you've been hiding from your spying sister?''

I looked at her. ''Please, Maddy. I did all the right things. All the right people are being punished. Can't you just leave this one alone?''

She was both silent and still, judgmentally cornering me, staring right at me with her sightless eyes. It was unbearable. I'd never known how to deny my sister anything, least of all the truth, and if she persisted, I knew she'd get it out of me. Maybe not now. But sometime, for she was and always would be the ever-determined spy, seeking both to know and understand everything.

''Oh, Alex, I do know what happened. And I understand,'' she finally said, raising a caring hand toward me. ''Come here. You're under my roof now. There's nothing to worry about.''

And I hurried over, took her hand, kissed it. Then dropped to my knees and embraced Maddy, hugging her tightly, and thankful because, of course, this was a very grand *kreesha,* indeed.